"The killer's trying to tell us something with those letters."

"What?"

"Maybe how to ca

"Like 'Stop me be

"Or maybe it's an e   a clue thinking we're too dumb   ure it out."

"What about the eyelid? Why'd he do that?"

"To make the crime special. Sort of a signature. And I don't think there's any point looking for it. Most likely, he took it as a trophy, something he can look at to relive the moment."

"You're describing one sick SOB."

—————————— ★ ——————————

"Andy and Kit are a match made in mystery heaven." — Jackson *Clarion-Ledger*

D. J. DONALDSON

New Orleans Requiem

WORLDWIDE®

TORONTO • NEW YORK • LONDON
AMSTERDAM • PARIS • SYDNEY • HAMBURG
STOCKHOLM • ATHENS • TOKYO • MILAN
MADRID • WARSAW • BUDAPEST • AUCKLAND

NEW ORLEANS REQUIEM

A Worldwide Mystery/January 1996

First published by St. Martin's Press, Incorporated.

ISBN 0-373-26188-8

ACKNOWLEDGMENTS

I can't express strongly enough my appreciation to
Dr. O. C. Smith, Assistant Medical Examiner for
Shelby County, Tennessee, who invariably points
me in productive directions and keeps me on track.
I've also benefited greatly from the counsel of
Dr. Jerry Francisco, Medical Examiner for Shelby
County, and Drs. Hugh Berryman and Steve Symes,
anthropologists with the Shelby County Regional
Forensic Center. Much of my knowledge about hair was
obtained during a pleasant chat with Dr. Walter Birkby,
anthropologist at the University of Arizona Human
Identification Laboratory, as we sat in the New Orleans
Hyatt Regency's Mint Julep Lounge during a recent
forensic sciences meeting. The kindness shown me by
the Memphis Police Department's homicide division
made the writing of this story considerably easier than it
might otherwise have been. I'm particularly grateful to
Sgt. Jack Ruby for allowing me to accompany him to a
prospective homicide scene one morning well before
dawn, and to Sgt. Paul Sheffield, whose enthusiasm,
encyclopedic knowledge and knack for giving me
exactly what I need are a writer's dream. Thanks
also to Dr. Frank Minyard, Orleans Parish Coroner,
and his secretary, Ann Black; Capt. James Rondell,
New Orleans Harbor Police; Dr. Jim Mahan;
Dr. Randy Nelson; Dr. Jack Enter; Dr. William Battle;
Dr. Bob Burns; Mary Lindsey, Ellen Karle; Les Seago;
Lori Krueger; Evelyn Brown; Sal Balsamo; and
Nancy Burris. Any mistakes are mine.

We should profane the service of the dead
To sing a requiem and such rest to her
As to peace-parted souls.

Hamlet, act V, scene 1

PROLOGUE

CISSY SPANGLER woke with a terrible ache slightly off center in the back of her head. She threw off the sheet covering her and slowly sat up, an act that sent the pain in her head to new heights. Elbows on her knees, she lowered her head and held it in her hands, the new position easing the hurt only slightly. She'd heard once that the brain can't feel pain. Whoever said that should be fired, for hers felt like someone was digging chunks out of it with their thumbs.

Gradually, through the pain, she became aware that she was fighting the mattress, which seemed to be pulling her back into bed. Wincing, she turned and saw a broad back she didn't recognize. She shot to her feet, a fresh stab of pain radiating down her neck. Without bothering to cover her naked body, she crossed to her dresser and grabbed for her purse. Hands shaking, she flipped the catch and poured the contents onto the dresser, trying to count the foil packets even as they came out mixed with all the crap she carried.

Two, three, four...

Thank God. Yesterday, there had been five of them in her purse and now there were only four. She was not going to die. Thus reprieved, her headache rolled back, only to be displaced again by another fear.

She dressed quickly, cursing good-looking men and the way they made you drink too much. With effort, she remembered a little now of what had happened.

She'd decided to call it a day around 5:30 and had packed her umbrella, her canvases, easels, and paints in her locker. She was sure of that much. Then this charming man had come by and struck up a conversation. He had suggested they go for a drink and she'd wandered off without securing her locker.

Damn. Men and alcohol. She was going to have to watch herself better in the future.... Hell, if she hadn't locked up, she might not *have* a future.

She hurried from her tiny apartment and rushed down the stairs, each step a mule kicking the back of her head. It was mid-February. In Chicago, where she'd attended the Chicago Art Institute, February was always cold and miserable. But here in New Orleans, it was generally mild. This year had been about like April in other years. And that had meant lots of foot traffic around the square and lots of business. With Mardi Gras barely a week off, the crowds were only going to get bigger. She'd believed that by the end of the month she'd probably have her back rent all paid off. Now this.

Damn.

She began to sprint toward Jackson Square, dodging the spray from one of the hoses that businesses in the French Quarter bring out each morning to wash the previous night's broom-elusive debris and body fluids from the flagstone sidewalks. The square was right around the corner and she was there in less than a minute. From Decatur, she couldn't tell if her locker was secured or not. But as she jogged toward it, her day was ruined, for the lock lay on the ground.

She approached the locker slowly, her second prayer of the day looping through her brain: Please let everything be there.... Please let everything ... She opened the lid reluctantly, her heart fluttering. When she saw the body inside, one eye staring blankly up at her, her scream sent a hundred pigeons into the air.

ONE

ANDY BROUSSARD, chief medical examiner for Orleans Parish, had already been up for several hours, his sleep disturbed by thoughts of the impending annual meeting of the American Academy of Forensic Sciences, which this year his office was hosting. As he sat at the kitchen table sipping his third cup of freshly roasted Kenyan Meru, he mentally went over one more time the long list of preparations he'd made for the meeting, concerned that there might be something he'd overlooked. If this had been simply a regional meeting of medical examiners, he might still be asleep. But it was *the* national gathering of all the forensic disciplines. Criminalistics, Engineering Sciences, Jurisprudence, Odontology, Physical Anthropology, Pathology-Biology, Psychiatry-Behavioral Science, Questioned Documents, and Toxicology—they'd all be there. And its success would largely depend on his efforts.

Perhaps it was the early hour or maybe it was just a sixth sense he'd developed after so many years as ME, but the moment the phone began to ring, he knew that someone was dead.

Thirty minutes later, Broussard pulled his head out of a deep coffinlike artist's locker near the iron fence around Jackson Square and put his penlight back in his shirt pocket. With him out of the way, Kit Franklyn, psychologist with the ME's office, could now see in.

Kit was not religious in the usual sense of the word. She wasn't even sure there was such a thing as a soul, except that when she looked at a man or woman dead only a few hours, she could find in their faces not the faintest imprint of the decades they'd lived. All traces of who they'd been were already gone—vanished so completely, it seemed that more was missing than could be accounted for in physical terms. Broussard had once advised her to forget the old cases, but she couldn't, and the victims' faces remained in her mind, accumulating at a worrisome pace.

Today, the body was that of a slightly built man who had perhaps been in his late thirties. He lay with the back of his head touching the wooden floor of the locker, his knees bent toward his chest. He was wearing poorly ironed cotton slacks, an unzipped poplin windbreaker, and a white crewneck T-shirt whose just-bought freshness was marred by a small slit in the center of a scant sunburst of blood just below his sternum. One eye was almost completely closed, dull cornea showing through the small slit between the upper and lower lids. The other was wide open.

"He's relatively fresh," Broussard announced. "Rigor's barely started."

"I'd guess it happened sometime after midnight last night," Lt. Phil Gatlin, senior homicide detective in the NOPD, said. "Before that, there'd have been too many people around."

Broussard and Gatlin were nearly the same age but had arrived there by different routes. Where Gatlin's heavily lined face made him look older than he was, Broussard's made him look younger, most of this effect deriving from the absence of crow's-feet or other signs of wear around Broussard's eyes, the rest of his face being largely hidden behind a short beard shot with gray. Gatlin weighed around 230 but didn't look particularly overweight because he was six foot four. Even if he'd been Gatlin's height, instead of five ten, Broussard's 270 would have seemed excessive.

"Could that little bit of blood have come from a lethal wound?" Gatlin asked.

"It's possible," Broussard replied. He shifted the lemon ball in his mouth to the other cheek. "Have to get him to the morgue before I know for sure."

"Knife?"

"Single-edged."

"I didn't see any defensive wounds. You?"

Broussard shook his head.

"What's with the eye?" Gatlin said. "Never saw anything like that before. Why's one open?"

"No upper lid," Broussard replied.

Gatlin's heavy eyebrows jigged toward the bridge of his big nose. "How come?"

"It's been removed."

"When?" he asked warily.

"Right after he was killed."

"Jesus. Why didn't I see that?" Gatlin stepped over to the locker and leaned down for another look, playing his flashlight onto the cadaver's face.

"He's got deep-set eyes and more fat in his orbit than most folks," Broussard explained. "Makes it hard to tell if the lid is there or not. And since it was removed postmortem, there wasn't any bleedin'."

Gatlin played his flashlight all around the body, then stood up. "Don't see it in there." He shifted his attention to the pavement and searched the area where they were standing.

Kit had been wondering why she'd been summoned to the scene. She worked for Broussard doing psychological autopsies in suicide cases and was occasionally brought in by the NOPD as a psychology profiler in unusual cases. A corpse with a missing eyelid certainly fit that criterion, but since Gatlin hadn't realized it was missing when she was called, there had to be something he hadn't revealed.

"Why did you want *me* here?" she asked.

"I'll show you," Gatlin said.

Half a dozen cops were spaced evenly along a perimeter that had been marked off by yellow crime-scene tape strung from the fence around Jackson Square to the columns on the Pontalba Apartments across St. Peter Street, which from Chartres to Decatur was usually closed to vehicles. Despite the early hour, quite a crowd had gathered. Most of them were on the sidewalk, but some had come out of their apartments over the shops, onto the balcony overlooking the square, where from that elevation, they likely could see directly into the locker.

Gatlin went to his car, which was inside the tape enclosure, and opened the front door on the passenger side. He came back wearing cotton gloves and holding a few pages of folded newspaper as a butler might carry a tray of drinks. "We found this on his chest." He held the newspaper out so Kit and Broussard could see what was on it.

"Scrabble letters?" Kit said.

Broussard leaned close and tilted his head so he could look at the letters through the bifocal part of his glasses. "KOJE—held together with transparent tape," he observed. He looked at Gatlin. "They were just sittin' on his chest?"

"Un-uh. They were on the newspaper."

"I don't like this," Kit said.

"We should start a club," Gatlin replied.

"Obviously, this was no spur-of-the-moment act," Kit said. "Is the victim carrying money?"

"Twenty bucks and two credit cards."

Kit glanced at the locker. "You know what this looks like?"

"Tell me."

"Act One, more to follow."

Gatlin's face twisted into a scowl of disbelief or of anger at what it would mean if she was right—she wasn't sure which.

"The killer's trying to tell us something with those letters," she said.

"What?"

"Maybe how to catch him."

"Like 'Stop me before I kill again...'?"

"Or maybe it's an ego trip.... He leaves a clue thinking we're too dumb to figure it out."

"What about the eyelid?" Gatlin asked. "Why'd he do that?"

"To make the crime special. Sort of a signature. And I don't think there's any point looking for it. Most likely, he took it as a trophy, something he can look at to relive the moment."

As she spoke, Kit found herself glancing at Broussard, trying to gauge his reaction to her comments. It was a part of herself she hated, this seeking of approval. If she'd been rejected by her father, it might make sense, but they'd always been close. So where did this come from? She found little consolation in the fact that she didn't act like this with all authority figures, only Broussard. As usual, the old pathologist listened attentively, his face unreadable behind his beard.

"Doc, you're describing one sick SOB," Gatlin said.

"No argument there," she replied.

"Anything else?"

"Since he brought his own weapon, chances are he came from another part of town and drove here."

Gatlin's weary expression clouded. "I don't see the connection."

"There's not actually anything to see. They're behavioral relationships discovered by analyzing large numbers of cases with similar features."

"Similar how?"

"Ritualistic... items left at the scene, arranged in a particular way."

"You've been saying 'he' did this or that...."

"The odds are overwhelmingly in favor of it being an intelligent white male in his late twenties or early thirties." She paused.

"Go on."

"It'd help to know for sure if that single wound was the deathblow."

"Let's say it is."

"Then he got in close, which means he's confident and skilled at interpersonal relations, the kind of guy who'll look you right in the eye when you talk to him. The absence of defensive wounds indicates that he didn't look threatening. He might have used some ploy to get close...asking for a light, directions, that sort of thing."

"Or the victim knew him," Gatlin suggested.

"Unlikely," Kit replied. "In these kinds of cases, the killer and the victim have rarely met previously."

"So why'd he pick this guy?"

"Probably because of the way he's dressed—tight T-shirt, open jacket, ideal for a single well-placed knife thrust."

Gatlin nodded and made a rolling motion with one hand.

"There's a chance the killer's in that crowd over there," Kit said. "Or he may come back here later, or he might even attend the funeral...they like to reminisce." She could see by Gatlin's drifting attention that she was now covering ground already familiar to him.

"And?" he said, his eyes wandering over the scene.

"He'll likely have poor credit."

That got him back with satisfying speed, but if he was expecting a new string of insightful comments, he was destined to be disappointed, for without further data, Kit had nothing more to say except, "End of analysis."

"What about this locker?" Broussard said. "Was it abandoned?"

"No," Gatlin replied. "Its owner discovered the body."

"Why was it out here? Most of the artists roll 'em into a frame shop or somethin' at night."

"Apparently, the good spots are first come, first served. If you leave your cart out, you can keep a good one. Anyway, that's what she said. But I had the feeling she just couldn't afford to rent storage space. Said she forgot to lock it when she went home."

"So somebody also stole her equipment," Broussard observed.

"Looks that way." Gatlin glanced at Kit.

"It wasn't the killer."

"I agree," Gatlin said. "Andy, how long before you can give me the skinny on the victim."

"Couple hours."

"How about we all meet again in your office at, say, ten o'clock to hash this over. Sorry about it being Saturday."

"You'll just owe us a big favor," Broussard said.

"How about I write you into my will."

"I sorta hoped we'd collect in this lifetime."

Watching the two old friends banter this way, Kit felt a twinge of envy. Broussard did it with her at times, but never as much as with Gatlin.

As the old detective turned to go, Broussard said, "Mind if I take those letters to my office?"

Gatlin turned, wearing a puzzled expression. "Why?"

"Look again."

Gatlin held the newspaper up to his face and stared at the letters, then looked back at Broussard. "What?"

"There's a hair caught in the tape holdin' the letters together."

Gatlin looked again and tilted the letters a little. "Damned if there isn't. I'll bag 'em for you."

Broussard liked nothing better than getting one up on Gatlin, who was no slouch himself. Today, he'd gone two up. Seeing the glitter of delight in Broussard's eyes, Gatlin added, "And you're outta the will." He glanced at Kit. "Not that I think you're wrong," he said, "but I'm gonna keep looking for that eyelid."

With nothing further to contribute, Kit ducked under the crime-scene tape and headed for her car, which she'd parked as close to the action as the scene tape allowed, the puzzle of the Scrabble letters occupying her thoughts. KOJE... What was the killer's purpose in leaving those letters? What was he trying to tell them?

She began rearranging the letters in her mind, trying to make them spell something recognizable. As she unlocked her car, she felt a touch on her arm.

"Dr. Franklyn..."

She turned and looked into clear eyes the color of the chalky green water in the quarry she used to swim in as a kid. The association of those eyes with a fond childhood memory was irritating, for she did not like Nick Lawson—not his eyes, not that stupid ponytail he wore, not what he did for a living. It was actually not so much what he did for a living that she resented but how he did it. From the paper's viewpoint, he was probably considered an excellent reporter. He certainly knew how to write. But he couldn't tell when to draw the line between the public's right to know and the damage public disclosure could do to an ongoing homicide investigation. When leaks occurred, Nick Lawson, it seemed, was always there with a bucket.

"What's in the box?" Lawson said, jerking his thumb toward the crime scene. "Or maybe I should say, Who's in it?"

"Talk to Gatlin."

"We aren't getting along."

"I wonder why. How'd you get here?"

"Same as you, internal-combustion engine."

"Such wit, and so early in the morning. What I meant was, how'd you know something was up?"

"Heard it on my scanner."

Kit doubted that. Cops don't like having to deal with reporters at murder scenes. And usually, at a typical generic murder, there aren't any to worry about, the event being so commonplace that daily perusal of publicly available police reports suffice. The cops know this and likewise understand that the more unusual the crime, the more likely radio chatter is to bring out a reporter. They therefore try to keep radio talk about unusual cases pared to the basics, giving the details only over the telephone.

"You think you're pretty clever, don't you?" Kit said.

Lawson's hands came up in a pleading gesture. "Just doing my job, like everybody else."

Kit became aware that he was making a faint whirring sound. "You need a new tape recorder," she said. "Your old one makes noise. I could probably have you arrested for that."

Grinning, Lawson took a small recorder out of his back pocket and pressed a button. The whirring stopped. The recorder was connected to a wire that ran under his shirt, probably the cord to the mike. "Look, I'm gonna get it all eventually," he said. "So why not make it easy on everybody."

"Because you're irresponsible."

"Since when has telling the truth ever made someone irresponsible?"

"When it prevents a murderer's slip of the tongue from being used as evidence against him because you had already made privileged information public."

"So, that newspaper Gatlin got from his car was like that . . . or something that was on the paper?"

Kit felt her face redden. She yanked the car door open and got in, so anxious to leave that she nearly backed into an old man in a beret who was crossing behind her on his way to see the reason for such a crowd.

She inched the car down St. Peter and backed onto De-catur, thankful that the carriages and horses that usually blocked the view of oncoming traffic on Decatur had not yet appeared. She took Decatur to Canal, crossed over, and headed uptown on Magazine, replaying practically every word she'd said at the murder scene, finding most of her performance acceptable. But that fiasco with Lawson... He had worked her like *he* was the one with the Ph.D. in psych.

Finally, as she turned onto St. Charles with its venerable live oaks that formed a canopy overhead, she began to put things in perspective. She hadn't really told Lawson a thing. Anybody standing outside the tape could have seen Gatlin get that newspaper from his car and could have concluded that it was something significant by the way he carried it and how she and Broussard had gawked at it.

She looked at her watch. Teddy LaBiche always left Bayou Coteau at 5:00 A.M., which meant he'd be at her house in just a few minutes.

Teddy... She pictured him at the door—most likely in a pale blue shirt of brushed oxford cloth, jeans that showed his slim athletic build, alligator boots and belt, his trade-mark stylish straw hat shading delicate but firm features that spoke of his aristocratic French lineage. And smelling so good, you'd never know he made his living as the owner of an alligator farm.

What with the Forensic meetings starting Monday in the Hyatt and her responsibilities there, she'd briefly consid-ered canceling out on Teddy, thinking that last-minute de-tails might cause her to be too occupied to give him much attention. Lord knows, she didn't want to cancel. They had precious little time together as it was—four weekends a month... certainly not the best basis for a relationship.

But then things had fallen together and she had *not* can-celed. Now with this murder and a meeting scheduled for ten... Well, they'd just have to do the best they could. Teddy would understand.

Kit lived a few streets upriver from the Garden District, in what is known as the Uptown Section. Where only the very rich could live in the wonderful old mansions that lined St. Charles, people with modest means and a significant amount of patience and luck could occasionally find a bargain among the smaller old homes a few blocks off St. Charles. Kit was one of those people. She had been in her house less than a year now and still experienced a rush of pleasure every time she stepped into the large entry with the massive oak columns and Victorian scrollwork. Today that pleasure was short-lived because something was wrong.

Even if her little dog, Lucky, was in the backyard when she drove up, he would dash through the kitchen doggy door Teddy had installed for him and meet her in the entry. But today there was no Lucky. Puzzled, she walked toward the kitchen, calling his name. "Lucky... Where are you, boy? Lucky..."

He did not appear to be in the house. Thinking that perhaps he'd lost his collar and, with it, the transmitter that allowed his door to open, she went into the backyard and scanned it. "Lucky... Here, boy...." She toured the yard, peeking between the azaleas that were large enough to provide a hiding place. No Lucky.

She hurried back into the house and began a room-by-room search. In her bedroom, she was alarmed to find that the footstool to her comfortable reading chair was soiled with vomit. And on the floor beyond the footstool, there was a small furry body.

With nausea thick in her own throat, she swiftly crossed the room to Lucky's still form. She reached under him and put her hand on his small chest, detecting a heartbeat so feeble, she was afraid that each tenuous contraction would be the last.

The doorbell . . . Teddy.

She dashed into the hall and threw the front door open. "It's Lucky," she said, her lips trembling. "He's dying."

Kit led Teddy to the bedroom, where he gently picked the dog up. "He needs help fast."

"My vet . . ." Kit said. "They open at seven."

Teddy shook his head. "He may need special equipment. An animal hospital'd be better."

"There's one about two miles from here."

"You take Lucky. I'll drive."

Teddy transferred the dog to Kit's arms and they ran to Teddy's shiny red pickup with the logo of the Bayou Coteau alligator farm on both doors. Because it was Saturday and traffic was light, they got to the South Carrollton Animal Hospital in under ten minutes.

Though Kit thought that the vet on duty appeared far too young and had large, clumsy-looking hands, she let Lucky go into his care. Then she and Teddy sat on one of the waiting room's molded plastic sofas to wait, murder and Scrabble letters forgotten.

Teddy focused his attention on his straw hat, which lay in his lap. But Kit's eyes roamed to the plastic seats, the tile walls, the linoleum floor. . . . She shivered. Such a cold, uncompromising place. Her gaze drifted to the bulletin board on the opposite wall.

MIXED-BREED PUPPIES, FREE TO A GOOD HOME. NEW LITTER: AKC-REGISTERED SHELTIES. CALL . . .

Puppies. Replacement puppies. Nothing lives forever, the flyers were saying. Move on . . . adjust . . . replace. . . . *Replace.*

No. Kit silently shouted. No. Rejecting the message the board was sending, she tore her eyes from it and concentrated on a tuft of brown hair that lay against the chrome leg of the sofa under the bulletin board. As she watched it, she saw the hair pulse against the chrome like a furry heart beating in time to the ceiling fan lazily turning overhead. She was so tense that when Teddy slipped his hand into hers, her flesh quickened in exaggerated surprise.

Finally, the door where the vet had disappeared opened. He came out wearing a serious expression.

"He's been poisoned," the vet said. "Warfarin, I think."

"Is he..."

"No, he's doing okay and he's going to be fine. But he'll have to stay here for a few days. Did he vomit?"

"Yes."

"That probably saved him."

"Poisoned?" Kit said. "I don't see how that's possible. What's warfarin?"

"The main ingredient in rat poison."

"I don't have any rat poison in the house."

"Well, he got into it somehow. You might want to consider the possibility that..." he paused.

"What?"

"That one of your neighbors did it."

Kit's jaw dropped. "Why would someone do that?"

"Does he bark a lot?"

"Only when strangers try to come in the yard."

The vet shrugged. "That could be it. Maybe you've got a neighbor who's tired of the noise."

"That's despicable."

"When you get right down to it," the vet said, "most people are no damn good."

TWO

BROUSSARD LEFT THE MORGUE about half past nine, having had no time for breakfast. The half dozen lemon balls he'd consumed since getting up had not prevented a hollow from growing inside him all through the autopsy and it now threatened to engulf his mind. When there was time for a real meal, he chose his food carefully, which is not to say he counted calories or considered its fat or fiber content; he was swayed solely by taste and texture. He was both gourmet and gourmand—when there was time. When there was not, it was the snack machines by the elevator in the basement that sustained him, today providing him with a pack of chocolate cookies and a log roll.

Thus fortified, he returned to his office, entering by the hall door, and set to work on the hair he'd found. As a first step, he placed a drop of Protex onto a clean microscope slide, which he put into a large tissue-culture dish. It was not likely that someone who had arranged such an elaborate crime scene would have left prints on the letters, but at this point, they needed to be handled as though he had. With this in mind, Broussard took the joined letters from their evidence bag with a long pair of forceps and placed them in the dish with the microscope slide. He put the dish on the stage of his dissecting microscope and removed his glasses, letting them dangle against his chest by the lanyard attached to the temples.

The letters were held together by a strip of tape on the front and one on the back. The hair was caught in the front strip angling across all four letters. Using a blunt pair of forceps to keep the letters from moving, he picked at the right edge of the tape with his best pair of watchmaker's forceps until he could get a decent grip. Carefully, he peeled the tape back. When the hair was fully exposed, he plucked it from the tape and put it in the drop of Protex. Since the tape was now almost free of the letters, he removed it completely and tacked it lightly onto the bottom of the dish. After marking the dish so the lab could tell what the tape's orientation had been in relation to the letters, he put a coverslip on the slide bearing the hair and put the slide on the stage of his compound microscope.

With the prize safely ready for study, he paused, relishing once again the way he'd found it right under Gatlin's nose. The only thing that kept this from being an entirely satisfactory moment was the fact that it came with a body, now cooling in the morgue frig. From the body, Broussard had learned much about the killer and hopefully he would soon know more.

He centered the hair in the light path of the scope and looked through the eyepieces. The first feature he saw was the pear-shaped root indicating that this was not a forcibly extracted hair but a shed one, as it should have been had it fallen onto the tape from the killer's head as he lined up the letters before taping them together. Then... Oh, yes, this was definitely going to hurt him.

WHEN HE WOULD LEAVE to go home early Monday morning, Teddy would depart without breakfast, planning to stop at a café he liked an hour out of New Orleans. Coming in, he always waited so he and Kit could have breakfast together, usually at a little place on St. Charles that made omelets lighter than seemed possible. After leaving the vet, they went to the restaurant as usual, but neither had much of an appetite. They then returned to Kit's home and tried to figure out which one of the neighbors might have poisoned Lucky.

Based on proximity, the three most likely choices seemed to be the neighbors on each side or the one directly in back. Any of them would have found it an easy matter to lob a piece of doctored meat over the fence. Of the three, Kit suspected old Mrs. Bergeron, the tight-lipped widow on her left, who, according to the man across the street, once kept a football a local kid had kicked into her yard, later giving it to her grandson for his birthday. Bergeron, of course, said she knew nothing about the poisoning. Kit found her expression of sympathy forced and unconvincing.

They then tried to clean the footstool Lucky had soiled, deciding after many attempts that it would have to be recovered. This led to a search for fabric and delivery of the stool to the upholsterer. But it was a traffic-halting fender bender between a new Mercedes and an ancient truck full of galvanized fencing at the Tulane-Loyola intersection that made Kit late to her meeting. When she arrived, she found Broussard behind his desk and Gatlin pacing the floor.

She muttered an apology and quickly sat on Broussard's green vinyl sofa next to a pile of medical journals that threatened to topple onto her.

Gatlin jerked his chin at Broussard. "You first."

Broussard leaned back in his chair and folded his small hands over his belly. "We're dealin' with a pro. The victim had a minor bruise on the back of his head that was inflicted very near the time of death. But he was killed by a solitary knife thrust that went under the sternum, through the diaphragm, and amputated the tip of the right ventricle. This is *not* an easy maneuver. Done correctly, there's very little external bleedin'. It mostly ends up in the pericardium—the sac around the heart."

"How long for someone to die with a wound like that?" Gatlin asked.

"Couple of seconds for blood pressure to drop to zero, another seven for him to gray out and go down."

"Long enough to yell," Gatlin said. "Or grab at the killer."

"*If* he realized what was happenin'. Most likely, he didn't—'specially if he never saw the knife, which could have been hidden under a newspaper or a map."

"So he just stood there?"

Broussard nodded.

"How's this for a scenario?" Gatlin said, beginning to pace again. "Somebody makes off with the contents of the locker and leaves the lid open; victim comes by, sees the open lid, and goes over for a look; killer approaches, says something to make the victim face him; the knife goes in, killer steps back, and the victim begins to sag; killer pushes him backward and he falls into the locker, making that bruise you found on his head; killer adjusts the body so all of it fits in the locker, performs his little eyelid operation, then puts the newspaper and letters on the victim's chest."

"Sounds all right," Broussard said.

"But it'd be dark in the locker and he'd need light to cut. Think he had help?"

Broussard shook his head. "There are ways one man could do that and illuminate his field at the same time."

Kit wanted Gatlin to ask Broussard for an example, but instead, he said, "You learn anything from that hair?"

"A little. It came from a straight-haired Caucasian who's either prematurely gray or over forty. He uses a black dye to hide the gray and had a razor cut between one and two weeks ago."

"You get his phone number?"

"Only the first three digits."

"You said, 'he.' That come from the hair or we still guessing about that?"

Kit bristled at the word *guess*. It wasn't a guess. It was practically a certainty.

"Still guessin'," Broussard said.

"Can't we do better?"

"Cells associated with the hair are too dried out to look for Barr bodies."

"DNA profiling?"

"Sex probes for such a small amount of material are just bein' developed, and those labs don't do criminal cases yet."

"Jesus, you aren't much help."

Gatlin made some notes in his little black book, then returned it to the inside pocket of his jacket.

"You run the scene details through the FBI Violent Criminal Apprehension Program?" Broussard asked.

"Yeah. Got zilch...no match nowhere. He's new and fresh and totally our problem. Let's talk about those letters." He went to the small blackboard next to the door and wrote KOJE on it with red chalk. "Anybody got any ideas?"

He looked at Kit, who had not given the letters a moment's thought since she'd arrived home. Thankfully, Gatlin's eyes left her and moved to Broussard. "Andy..."

"If you rearrange 'em, they spell *joke*."

Gatlin looked at the letters to see if he was right. "You saying they don't mean anything? It's a hoax?"

Broussard shrugged. "Too soon to tell."

Gatlin proceeded to list the four letters in all possible combinations.

OKJE	KOJE	JOKE	EOKJ
OKEJ	KOEJ	JOEK	EOJK
OJKE	KJOE	JKOE	EKOJ
OJEK	KJEO	JKEO	EKJO
OEKJ	KEOJ	JEOK	EJOK
OEJK	KEJO	JEKO	EJKO

He stepped back and surveyed what he'd done. "Well, *joke* is the only word *I* recognize. Maybe you're right and this *is* a waste of time."

While Gatlin had been writing, Broussard had unlaced his fingers and folded his arms over his chest, the index finger of his left hand stroking the bristly hairs on the end of his nose, a posture that usually preceded a perceptive comment. "I don't think he wants the letters rearranged," he said abruptly. "That's why they were taped together and not given to us loose."

This was such an obviously correct analysis that Kit was upset at herself for missing it. But, of course, she had Lucky on her mind.

"Maybe he taped them together just to make sure we found all of them," Gatlin suggested.

Broussard shook his head.

"Okay," Gatlin said. "Then what do they mean?"

"There's only so much a man can do without breakfast."

"Well, if you get any bright ideas after you've eaten, be sure and call me. Can I have the letters for the lab?"

Broussard handed two small plastic bags across the desk, one containing the letters, the other, the dish with the tape he'd removed and a note explaining what he'd done.

"And his clothes?"

"Over there." Broussard gestured to a large brown paper bag on some file cabinets.

While Gatlin signed a chain-of-evidence form, Broussard said, "You're not gonna leave without tellin' us more about what you been doin', are you?"

"The usual," Gatlin replied. "Talking to the deaf, the dumb, and the blind. Can you believe that with all those apartments facing the square not one person saw or heard anything?"

"It *was* probably pretty early in the mornin' when it happened," Broussard said.

"Which reminds me, we got a reasonably good fix on the time of death. It was sometime after one A.M."

"How'd you come up with that?"

"We caught the guy who stole the stuff from the locker. Walked right into a pawnshop and tried to sell it in front of two uniforms who'd just asked the owner to get the name of anybody trying to unload art stuff."

"I guess he didn't use black hair dye," Broussard said.

"It was Danny Delgado. You can tell it's spring or close to it when Danny hits town. He's sorta like a human version of the Capistrano swallows...with a bad liver. And as for hair, I don't think he even has eyebrows. He said he took the stuff around one-fifteen and there was no body in there then."

"Did the victim have a family?" Kit asked.

Gatlin sparked to her question with unusual interest. "No kids, no wife, but he did have a male roomie, if you know what I mean. They had a little shop in the Jax building where they sold jewelry made of polished stones and fossils. Last night, they had an argument about some guy the victim was getting too chummy with and the victim took a walk. That suggest anything to you?"

"You don't think the roomie did it?"

"No defensive wounds...could have been someone he knew."

"What about the letters?"

"Who knows? Something that has significance only to the victim and his lover. They don't spell anything except *joke* and Andy doesn't think we should rearrange them to spell that. And the guy has no alibi."

"Homosexual jealousy murders usually involve over-kill," Kit said. "This was done dispassionately."

"You said, 'usually'...that leaves me some room, Doc. And if you want to talk probability, how about the fact that two-thirds of all homicides are committed by acquaintances of the victim. Husband's murdered, look at the wife;

wife's killed, check out hubby; boyfriend, girlfriend, gay
lover, that's fertile ground, Doc.''

"What color's his roommate's hair?" Kit asked.

Gatlin tilted his head and looked down his nose at her.
"Black."

"Coincidence," Kit said. "Get some samples. I'll bet they
don't match."

Kit left the meeting shaking her head. Gatlin's idea that
it was the victim's lover was *so* wrong. Why couldn't he see
it? Well, he'd see it soon enough, for there were going to be
more...unless they could figure out what those letters
meant.

On the way home, she stopped at Gambini's deli and had
Mr. Gambini make up two box lunches of fried chicken.
After checking with the vet at the animal hospital and
learning that Lucky was doing fine, she and Teddy took
their lunches to the park across from Tulane and Loyola and
spread a blanket on the ground near the mansions that lined
the sidewalk connecting St. Charles and Magazine. Apart
from the Frisbees that students occasionally flicked their
way and a dog that tried to snatch a drumstick out of Teddy's hand, lunch was uneventful. It was also short on conversation, Kit's mind being heavily occupied with thoughts
of Lucky and the murder that morning. Knowing nothing
of the murder, Teddy assumed the silence was all because of
Lucky.

After lunch, while they were on their way to Old River
Road for a drive, Kit suddenly pointed at the entrance to a
small shopping center. "I want to go in there."

Accustomed to moving quickly to avoid being snagged by
one of his alligators, Teddy yanked the steering wheel to the
right, barely missing a gray BMW leaving the parking lot.

"Why'd you do that?" he asked.

"Over there." Kit pointed to some shops on the right and
Teddy cruised that way.

"Park beside that van."

Knowing that she'd tell him what was up only when she was ready, Teddy followed instructions.

"Be right back."

She slipped from the truck and Teddy watched her cross the asphalt, enjoying the way she moved, appreciating the fact that she could have any man she wanted. He had been waiting all week to see those liquid brown eyes and he wished now that he could think of a way to ease the worry in them. He longed to see the skin crinkle across the light spray of freckles on the bridge of her nose when she smiled. Puzzled, he saw her go into a toy store. She reappeared a few minutes later with a package under her arm.

Unable to wait any longer for an explanation, he said, "What's that?" as she got in.

"The key to a murder that took place early this morning in the Quarter."

Teddy gave her a lingering look of surprise.

"Just before you arrived this morning, I got back from a murder scene. The police found a body in an artist's locker on Jackson Square. The corpse had four Scrabble letters on its chest, KOJE, held together with transparent tape. We think it's some kind of message, but we don't know what. I thought if we played the game, it might help me figure it out? Do you mind?"

"Sounds like we *have* to play." He pulled from the lot, made a left turn at the first intersection, and headed for home.

Fifteen minutes later, they were sitting at Kit's kitchen table with the Scrabble board open in front of them, KOJE arranged horizontally in the center four squares for inspiration. From across the table, Kit saw Teddy give himself thirty points.

"What's that for?"

"KOJE," Teddy said. "Fifteen points, plus double for the pink square. It was my idea to put it out there, so I should get the points."

"What difference does it make?"

"It makes a lot of difference, because this is strip Scrabble."

"I never heard of that."

"Oh, it's a Cajun tradition. First game on a new board has to be strip Scrabble."

"And just how is this played?"

"Whenever one player accumulates fifty points, the other one has to take something off."

"So that's why you were so agreeable when I asked you to play."

"No," Teddy said earnestly. "I hate the idea, but what can I do? I'm Cajun and it *is* a tradition. My relatives ever hear I played straight Scrabble on a new board, I'll never hear the end of it."

Not wishing to ruin Teddy's weekend, Kit tried to ignore her somber mood and play along. "Well . . . since it's a tradition. . ." She began lining letters up vertically under the *J:* O-N-Q-U-I-L-S, ending on a red triple-word square. "That'll be one hundred and twenty-five points and your shirt and pants," she said brightly.

"How do you figure that?" Teddy complained. "Twenty-four times three is only seventy-two."

"My *U* is on a double-word square and I get fifty points for using all seven tiles."

"You're supposed to start with my shoes."

"I don't believe in conventional warfare."

Teddy's hands went to the buttons on his shirt. "Franklyn, you're ruthless."

Later, with Teddy spelling words like *gator* (six points), *snap* (six points), and *flies* (eight points), and Kit spelling things like *quixotic* (double word, fifty-two points and another fifty for using all her tiles again), Teddy was soon sitting there wearing not much more than a little-boy look of expectation. To even things out, Kit began to hold back. The game ended as they knew it would—in Kit's bed, where despite her good intentions, she was not herself.

Afterward, as she lay contemplating the ceiling, Teddy bunched his pillow under his head and watched her without speaking. Eventually, he said, "If I could, I'd help."

She turned toward him and stroked his hair lightly above his ear. "You are helping. It's just that... All the excitement with Lucky... and that murder. I feel like I should be doing something to catch the killer."

"You may have done more than you think. The Scrabble game we played has reminded you of the fine points. Give it time to settle in. You might be surprised at what pops out when you're not dwelling on it."

"Thanks." She leaned over and kissed him on the cheek.

THAT NIGHT, planning to stay only in well-lighted areas and let no stranger approach them, Kit and Teddy went to the French Quarter, intending to have dinner at Tortorici's. But they were both disappointed and surprised—disappointed at finding the restaurant closed for repairs, surprised at someone calling Kit's name.

At first, their view was blocked by the milling crowd on Royal. Then the throng parted briefly and they saw Broussard standing on the opposite street corner with another man. The two came toward them.

"Looks like we all had the same idea," Broussard said.

"What's that?" Kit replied.

"Italian food. Hello, Teddy. How're the gators?"

"Haven't had one complain in years."

Broussard chuckled. "You two, this is Leo Fleming. Leo heads up the human identification laboratory in Raleigh and teaches forensic anthropology at Duke. No relation to Doyle Fleming in the crime lab.''

Leo Fleming was a big, raw-boned man with a loopy smile and a chapped outdoorsy look about him that made Kit think he'd willingly trade his ill-fitting gray suit for a checkered wool shirt and Lands' End twills.

"Leo's helpin' with a workshop at the Forensic meetin' and he came down a little early so we could go over some things on a book chapter we're doin' together. He'll also be givin' a paper on his specialty later in the week. Leo, Kit Franklyn, my suicide investigator and profiler for the NOPD. This fine fellow with her is Teddy LaBiche. Teddy owns an alligator farm 'bout a hundred miles west of here.''

There was a round of handshaking and Fleming said, "Never met an alligator farmer before. Is it dangerous?''

"Only if you're careless.''

"That'll get you in trouble in most any line of work.''

"Since we can't get in Tortorici's, how about we go to Felix's?'' Broussard said. "Since this is Leo's first trip to New Orleans, that's probably a better choice, anyway.''

The five-minute walk to Felix's stretched to ten when Fleming wanted to listen to a guy with an accordion play *"Malaguena."* Actually, Fleming was more interested in the guy's dog, which would take a dollar gently from your fingers and put it in the guy's hat on the ground. By the time they left, Fleming was out five bucks.

A block later, they lost him again when he paused at the entrance to a strip joint where a girl wearing a denim halter, skimpy denim shorts, and cowboy boots invited him in by bending over with her back to him and slapping her thighs.

"We should have the meeting here every year,'' he said, rejoining them.

They made good time for about three minutes, until Fleming wandered across the street to join a crowd around a guy standing on a small box. The object of all the attention was wearing a tux, white gloves, and sneakers. His face was mime white and his hair was dressed in dreadlocks wrapped with gold braid that ended in a cluster of little wooden balls that jiggled with the slightest movement, except they weren't moving at all—this, of course, being his talent. He stood with his arms raised and bent at the elbows, fingers spread in a flagrant display of bodily control. After a few minutes, he mechanically shifted his arms to a new position and rotated his torso, once again becoming the Amazing Living Statue.

Broussard's stomach suddenly rumbled like thunder and Fleming looked back at him. "You tryin' to steal the show?"

"Tryin' to get somethin' to eat," Broussard growled. Fleming tossed a buck into the living statue's open satchel and recrossed the street.

At Felix's, they were shown to seats in the open, unpretentious main room. As Fleming studied the menu, Broussard said, "Leo, you should have the crawfish."

A waiter went by with an order of the bright red crustaceans nicely arranged on a big white plate. Fleming watched them pass and wrinkled his nose. "Where I come from, that's fish bait."

"That's because you never tasted one," Broussard said. "Now we're gonna educate you."

So it was crawfish all around and, in Broussard's case, a dozen raw oysters on the half shell for an appetizer.

Watching Broussard fork the slippery bivalves into his mouth, Fleming's lips curled in disgust. "That's the whole animal, right?"

Broussard nodded.

"Digestive tracts, gonads, everything?"

Broussard nodded again and reached for another. Fleming looked away, shaking his head. But when the crawfish came, he was soon shucking them like a native, though he found Teddy's suggestion that he suck the juices out of the head barbaric.

Between crawfish, Teddy said, "Leo, what's the subject of the paper you're giving?"

Kit had been around Broussard long enough to know that you do not ask a forensic pathologist or anthropologist such things while eating. Fleming's answer taught Teddy the same lesson. "Saw dismemberment of human bones: characteristics indicative of saw class and type."

Looking a lot like Fleming had when he was watching Broussard eat oysters, Teddy said, "Ah...interesting topic."

Broussard turned to Kit. "You come up with any ideas on those letters?"

"To be honest, I've been having a little trouble concentrating on them. When I got home this morning, I found Lucky nearly dead. The vet said he'd gotten into some rat poison. I don't have anything like that around, so we think it was one of the neighbors, angry at his barking."

"The penalty for killin' a dog ought to be the same as for a human," Fleming said, his jaw clenched, his eyes hard.

"The vet thinks he'll recover, but he has to stay there a while."

Fleming cleaned his fingers on his napkin and reached over and patted the back of Kit's hand with his own calloused mitt. "I'm sure he's gonna come out of this good as new. And your concern for him does you credit. I always believed that St. Peter gives double coupons for kindness to animals."

Almost as soon as she'd begun talking about Lucky, Kit had regretted bringing it up, thinking that it was only going to sound like an excuse for not having anything to contribute on the Scrabble problem. Now, Fleming's well-intentioned compliment made her feel that even more keenly. She was relieved, therefore, when Fleming turned to Broussard and said, "You mentioned some letters...."

Glancing toward the two couples at the next table, Broussard lowered his voice and told Fleming about the body in the locker and the hair they'd found. At first, Kit was a little surprised that he would talk so openly about it, but then she saw that, Fleming being a forensic colleague, it was like a consult. Moreover, it gave her a chance to ask Broussard the question that had been on her mind since she and Teddy had run into him.

"Did Gatlin get hair samples from the victim's lover?"

"He did."

"Well?"

"Not a match."

"I knew it. So we're all agreed now?"

"Not completely. Phillip's checkin' the possibility that the roommate might have hired it done."

Kit's eyes rounded in surprise. "*Hired* it done? The man's in denial."

"He's thinkin' a hired assassin might account for the lack of overkill. He wouldn't be a very good detective if he ignored that possibility."

"I have to agree with Kit," Fleming said. "I think there's gonna be more."

Remembering that Teddy had been left out of the conversation, Kit patted him on the leg. "Sorry for all the shoptalk."

"Yeah," Teddy said. "It's been really boring."

Back on Bourbon Street after dinner, Kit asked Broussard, "Where are you parked?"

"We walked from the Hyatt. Leo's there, and since I'm local chairman of arrangements, I took a room myself. Figured I'd just stay there durin' the meetin'. Anything goes wrong, I'll be easy to get hold of."

"That's a pretty long way and there *is* that killer to think about," Kit said. "We'll give you a ride back."

"Appreciate the offer," Broussard said. "But we'll just catch the hotel shuttle."

"I'll see you both Monday then, at the meeting."

"You all set with the hospitality table?"

"Unless something unforeseen happens."

"And people to man the doors outside each room?"

"Actually, they're all women. Every man I asked had something more important to do."

"We're an uncooperative lot all right," Broussard said. "But it's not our fault. It's that blasted testosterone."

Eyes dancing, Kit said, "I know a cure for that."

THREE

MONDAY MORNING, Kit saw Teddy off for the drive back to Bayou Coteau at 6:00 A.M. By 6:45, she was at the Hyatt for her appointment with the two dozen volunteers she'd rounded up to help keep the Forensic meeting's attendees well informed and happy.

The meeting was officially to begin at eight o'clock. That gave her plenty of time to pass out hotel maps and take her group on a tour of the pertinent areas, which were laid out much like one of the rat mazes in the Tulane behavioral psych lab. The group finished the circuit in about twenty minutes, at which time Kit handed out the assignment sheets she'd prepared. She then took everyone around to the Courtyard restaurant for breakfast, the tab for this and all the volunteers' other meals to be picked up by the national office.

Kit sat at a table with Edna Gervais, secretary of the rose society they both belonged to, and Edna's daughter, Bebe LaCour, a large woman with fine skin who wore earrings so heavy that she'd already stretched the holes in her earlobes to an alarming size. In her youth, Edna had been a stage actress in New York. Now, well beyond youth and acting, she could still project. Because of Edna's commanding voice and her willingness to stay all day, Kit had made her second in command of the volunteers. Edna and Bebe were also to serve at the hospitality table, where Bebe's size could be put to good use each morning, carrying the various brochures from the room where they were stored to the table in the Regency Foyer.

Everything was going so smoothly that Kit should not have been surprised to suddenly find Susannah Lester at her side. Susannah was the liaison between the local committee and national headquarters. "National needs a favor," she said, wearing an apologetic expression.

"What kind of favor?"

"Some of their people didn't make it. So they're short for the registration desk."

"And they want some of mine?"

Susannah winced. "Yeah."

"For how long?"

"The whole meeting."

"My schedule's all made out."

"Dr. Broussard said to tell you that anybody can lead when things are going according to plan, but that the true mark of character is how well you behave in a crisis."

"Is he down here?"

"I dunno. When I talked to him on the phone, he was in his room."

"How many people do they need?"

"Three."

"Okay, I'll work it out. I'll have them over there at eight."

"Fabulous."

Kit excused herself to Edna and Bebe and went to an empty table where she spent the next thirty minutes rescheduling her troops. At ten to eight, she stood up. "Okay everybody, time to get to our posts." She held up the revised schedule. "I've had to rework your assignments a little, so be sure and get a look at this. I'll leave it on the hospitality table. Some of you had to be reassigned to the registration desk. Just report there and they'll tell you what to do. I hope this doesn't create problems for any of you. If it does, Edna will handle it." She looked hopefully at Edna, who nodded her head reassuringly.

They all then followed Kit to the Regency Foyer. While the others looked at the revised assignments, Kit and Bebe went to the room where all the tourist brochures were stashed and began ferrying them to the table.

By eight o'clock, the table was ready and all the volunteers were at their posts. As Kit took her first relaxed breath of the morning, she saw Broussard coming toward her.

"Susannah find you?" he said.

"All taken care of. Thanks for the philosophy."

He looked her up and down. "Unless I'm mistaken, you've grown an inch or two." He shifted his attention past her, introduced himself to Edna and Bebe, and offered each of them his hand. "Good of you to help us out. We'd be in real trouble without folks like you."

When he turned back to Kit, she said, "Did you see Lawson's article in the Sunday paper?"

Broussard motioned to the side with his head and they moved away from the table.

"I don't think he hurt us too badly," he said, waving at two men by the message board. "He didn't say what the four letters were, and he didn't mention the hair."

"But he knew about the eyelid and everything about the wound and how it suggested the killer was an expert with a knife."

"Interestin' point. He could have learned about the wound from seein' the original or a copy of the autopsy report. But I didn't draw any conclusions in there about the killer. I only said that to Phillip."

"Maybe he got a look at Gatlin's report, too."

"I suspect Lawson is pretty persuasive with the ladies. If I had to pinpoint the leak, I'd look for a female clerk in Homicide."

"Hard to believe that a woman would risk her job for a guy with a ponytail."

"You just don't like him. It was good, though, that he warned folks about walkin' alone on deserted streets."

"I was so afraid there was going to be another one Saturday night, I woke up at five o'clock Sunday morning and just lay there waiting for the phone to ring."

"Maybe it won't happen."

"I'd like to believe that. Think we should issue a warning to our attendees about walking about alone at night?"

"Already got one in their packets."

"That was fast."

"Put it in the plans months ago to remind 'em this can be a dangerous place."

Broussard reached in his pants pocket, fished out a lemon ball, and slipped it into his mouth. From the other pocket, he produced two identical candies wrapped in cellophane, which he offered to Kit, who had often imagined that he bought both kinds in fifty-five-gallon drums. For the first few months after he'd hired her, she'd been offered only the naked ones, which she'd always refused, the offer frequently including small bits of lint from his pocket. Then the wrapped ones had appeared. Since he never unwrapped one for himself, it was obvious he'd begun carrying them just for her. Under the circumstances, she now found the offer impossible to refuse. The ritual transfer was made and Kit put them in her purse with the half dozen others she'd collected the week before. She wouldn't eat them, but she couldn't bring herself to throw them away, either. So on it went, the candies slowly filling a plastic garbage pail in her pantry.

"You gonna be around the hotel today?" he asked.

"There's nothing of interest here for me until tomorrow. I only came over to get my volunteers organized and off to a good start. If there's no line in the restaurant, I'm going to have something to eat, then I'm going to the office. You?"

"Thought I'd stop in at the radiology workshop."

While Kit went around to the restaurant, Broussard checked his program to refresh his memory on the location of the workshop. On the way there, he paused to watch a fellow at the registration booths get his packet and Forensic Academy tote bag, thinking that there was something familiar about... My God, it *was*. He headed that way.

"Brookie?"

The man turned, and Broussard was jarred by his appearance. Crandall Brooks, the Albany, New York, ME had been a faithful jogger, running five miles a day every day for the twenty-odd years Broussard had known him, a practice that, in Broussard's opinion, had always made him appear undernourished. Now, he'd gained at least thirty pounds. And his hair, which he still wore in a military crew cut, looked decidedly grayer.

"Hello, Andy."

Broussard took Brookie's hand warmly in his own. "When'd you get in?"

"Few minutes ago."

"Brookie, I am so sorry about Susan's death."

"Thanks. I really appreciated the flowers."

"I'm just sorry I couldn't have been there, but we had a major crisis here and..."

"No apologies necessary, I know you would have come if you could."

"I'm kind of surprised to see you. Considerin' the circumstances, thought you'd probably skip this one... to... well, you know, kind of regroup."

"I needed a change of scenery. And I did think about going off somewhere to be alone but figured if I did, I'd probably just sit around feeling sorry for myself. This is better. I'll be near old friends and I'll have something to keep my mind occupied. In fact, I signed up for the aircraft-accident workshop, which I believe is going to start in a few minutes. Can we have lunch?''

"Absolutely, I'll meet you right here at noon."

Broussard had been in forensic work for so long that he rarely saw his job as anything out of the ordinary. But now, as he watched this man who was hoping to get his mind off the death of his wife by listening to descriptions of aircraft mayhem, he saw that theirs was indeed a peculiar profession. He then reflected on the lie he'd just told. It hadn't been a crisis that had prevented him from attending Susan Brooks's funeral. It had been his wish to remember her as she had been, lively, quick-witted, warm. The three of them had spent many happy hours together over the years and he doubted he would ever be able to look at Brookie again without thinking of Susan.

"We've got a problem."

Broussard turned at the voice beside him and saw Corinne Samuels, senior toxicologist with the crime lab, looking very worried. This didn't particularly set him on edge, because she was always worried, sometimes with reason, often without. "What's wrong?"

"A barge hit the *Creole Queen* early this morning. She'll be out of commission for at least three weeks."

So this time she had reason. "Can they get a substitute?"

"They say no. I'm afraid the paddle-wheel panorama is a wash."

"How many signed up?"

"A hundred and twenty."

Broussard lapsed into thought. His hand strayed to his nose and began to rub the stiff hairs that grew on its tip. "It's too late to do anything but arrange for refunds," he said abruptly. "Also, have some big signs made announcin' the cancellation and place 'em on easels around the hotel . . ." The beeper on his belt went off. "Include somethin' like 'Refunds may be obtained from the registration cashier.'"

While Corinne went off to follow his instructions, Broussard walked down to the lobby telephones and dialed his office.

"Margaret, it's me. What have you got?"

"Lieutenant Gatlin called. You're supposed to go to Madison Street in the Quarter. He said they found another one."

Broussard hurried to the Courtyard restaurant. He spotted Kit sitting alone under a small green-roofed gazebo. When he reached her table, she took one look at his face and got up with only a single word. "Where?"

"The Quarter," he replied, already heading for the escalator, "near where we found the first one."

Kit stopped at the cashier's station, scribbled her name on the running Forensic Academy tab, and walked briskly after Broussard, who was just disappearing from view.

Broussard loved each of his six '57 T-birds equally and generally drove a different one each day. But since he was confined to the hotel for the next few days, he had access only to the yellow one he'd checked in with. It was brought around to the entrance without much delay and they were soon out on Poydras, heading toward the river, the steering wheel pressing firmly into his belly.

They took Poydras to Tchoupitoulas, crossed Canal on a yellow light, followed North Peters to Decatur, and turned the wrong way onto Madison, a short street just past Jackson Square. Halfway down, the street was blocked by two patrol cars. So far, it was a replay of the scene Saturday morning—a crowd around the crime-scene tape, people gawking from their balconies—except this time it was late enough that she saw no bathrobes, but she did see two detectives she knew mingling with the crowd.

Broussard parked in the middle of the street and somehow got out of the little car. Seeing them approaching, one
of the cops holding the perimeter lifted the tape so they
could duck under it. On the far side, Kit saw Nick Lawson
talking to a female cop.

There was no body to be seen, so it could only have been
on the other side of the partially open sliding wooden door
Kit saw in the stuccoed courtyard wall facing the street. She
followed Broussard inside and was surprised to find it was
not a courtyard at all but a small parking lot paved with
narrow strips of asphalt roofing. There were two cars
snugged against the right wall and two against the left,
leaving barely a car's width access to the old doorless brick
garage in the rear, where Kit could dimly see two more cars.
Gatlin was standing in the middle of the lot, talking to a tall
young woman with puffy red eyes who was wringing her
hands as she spoke. Seeing them, he broke off his conversation with the woman and pointed to the garage with his
pen. "Back there."

"You take pictures yet?" Broussard asked.

"Been here and gone. Ray's getting to be a real jackrab-
bit."

Though she would have preferred to stay with Gatlin, Kit
followed Broussard into the musty garage, where there was
a blue Lincoln and a cherry red Cadillac parked side by side,
front bumpers practically against the back wall. The body
was in a sitting position between the two cars, its back
against the Cadillac's open front door. He was a clean-cut
young man neatly dressed in blue slacks and a yellow pullover with a logo above the left pocket that read CHARTRES
HOUSE. The shirt had an inch-long tear in it just below his
sternum and the fabric there had absorbed a modest amount
of blood. His head was tilted to the side. One eye was fully
closed; the other was wide open. Having seen enough, Kit
turned away.

Broussard put his bag down, slipped on a pair of rubber gloves, and brought out his padded kneeling block. He got down on one knee and inspected the staring eye with the aid of his penlight. He manipulated the fingers of the corpse's hand, lifted the arm, then returned to his forensic kit and got two paper bags, which he secured over the victim's hands with rubber bands. Returning to the open area, they found the woman gone and Gatlin making notes.

"I'd guess he's been dead six hours at most," Broussard said. "Eyelid's gone, of course. We get letters again?"

With his pen, Gatlin pointed at the hood of a white Ford behind Broussard. "Over there."

He followed Kit and Broussard to the Ford, where, on a folded section of newspaper, there were more Scrabble letters. But instead of four, like last time, there were only three, KOJ, held together with tape as before.

Broussard turned to Gatlin. "You found the letters on the paper?"

"Yeah, sitting in the victim's lap." Gatlin tilted his head slightly upward and looked at Broussard from the bottoms of his eyes. "And there's another hair, too."

"I noticed. How'd it all happen?"

Kit bent down for another look at the letters, trying to see the hair.

"The victim was the night clerk at the Chartres House, a small hotel around the corner," Gatlin said. "This is where they keep the guests' cars. If somebody needs their car in the morning, the night man comes over when he has time and moves it close to the entrance. Then, shortly before it's needed, he brings it around and parks it in front of the hotel. Last night, the hotel was full and so was the lot—there were even two cars in the center here. You can see what a mess this is to get a car out. The victim was after the Cadillac. Apparently, he was killed after he'd moved the cars blocking the Cadillac out onto the street somewhere. We're checking to make sure the killer didn't take one of them."

"I wouldn't think he did," Kit said.

"Me, neither, but we need to know."

"He the only one on duty at night?" Broussard asked.

"Yeah. Which is why he wasn't missed until this morning. That girl I was talking to when you arrived is the day clerk. When she came on duty, the guy who wanted the Cadillac was hopping mad cause his car wasn't out front and he couldn't find anyone to help him. She came for his car and found the body."

"The killer must have been out trolling and followed him inside," Kit said. "Anybody in the neighborhood see anything?"

"We're checking that, too," Gatlin replied. "Guess you were right, Doc."

"This is one time I wouldn't have minded being wrong."

"The day clerk swears the victim's heterosexual. I got the idea she knows from personal experience. I'll dig some more, but right now, it looks like there's no gay thread connecting the victims."

"Opportunity and the way they were dressed," Kit said, "those are the connections."

"And both male," Gatlin said.

"So far...."

"Random victims," Gatlin said, shaking his head. "Toughest damn thing in the world for a cop to deal with. But he left only three letters this time. You think he's telling us there're only going to be two more... that he's winding down?"

"They don't wind down," Kit said. "So he may be telling us he's building to something."

"What happens, then? He just goes away? Moves to another town and starts over?"

"A small percentage do."

"I'd love to get my hands on him," Gatlin said. "But if I can't, I'd settle for him moving on."

"Wagon on the way?" Broussard asked.

"I put in a call right after Ray left. Should be here soon."

"I better go back to the office and get ready."

"You want to examine the new hair?"

"Sure."

"I'll bag the letters for you. And I don't think you need to worry about fouling up any fingerprints. The last set was clean."

The first thing Broussard did after reaching his office was to call down to the morgue to see if the body had arrived. It hadn't. While waiting for it, he decided to examine the new hair.

He prepared it the same way he had the first one they'd found and put the slide under the microscope, feeling no anticipation whatever, for this was old ground, his examination this time merely a perfunctory ritual.

As he dropped his glasses to his chest and leaned toward the microscope eyepieces, the image of Susan Brooks suddenly popped into his head.

Susan...dead...in the cold ground somewhere in Albany...her body...

He sat back and massaged his eyes through closed lids. This was no good. To dwell on events that couldn't be changed accomplished nothing. And if indulged, they could destroy a man's peace of mind and interfere with his work.

He put his eyes against the microscope eyepieces and twirled the fine focus, bringing the image out of its optical fog.

Like most professionals who have spent many years honing their skills and accumulating experience, Broussard was seldom surprised by a case that came under his scrutiny. Of course, they all had their unique fine points, but in the main, they were merely modest variations on themes he knew as well as he knew when étouffé had been made with west Louisiana crawfish rather than those from eastern bayous.

He also knew which restaurants in the city had the best chefs and what their best dishes were. He knew the used bookstores where he would most likely find a Louis L'Amour novel he'd not yet added to his collection and he knew where to get the mesh shoes that kept his feet from sweating. He knew how to catch speckled trout and the best bait for Sac-a-lait. He knew when it was going to rain and when clouds would pass by. He could recite the routes of every parade in Mardi Gras and tell you which roses could withstand the city's terrible summer humidity.

Knowledge of how to live in the city, knowledge of how one died there, knowledge that led to order...personally and professionally. Autopsies produced physical evidence that told you what caused death. Facts...one upon the other, leading in an orderly way to a conclusion that would stand up to minute dissection in a courtroom. In such a life, there was no room for error, no place for renegade facts like the hair under his microscope.

FOUR

WITH HIS AUTOPSY on the second victim completed, Broussard returned to his office. Pausing now by his desk to make sure he wasn't going to charge off to the Hyatt and forget something he needed, his eye fell on the brochure a salesman had left for chain-metal autopsy gloves. He sniffed in disdain at the thought of what the profession was coming to. Across the country, the autopsy attire adopted by the younger examiners consisted of surgical hood, plastic eye protector, plastic apron over a surgical gown, waterproof sleeve protectors, disposable plastic boots tied closed with twist-'ems and two pairs of disposable latex gloves. Some had even bought the salesman's metal gloves to keep from cutting themselves.

Metal gloves.

If you exercised proper care and had a modicum of co-ordination, you wouldn't *be* cutting yourself. And all that other paraphernalia just encouraged sloppiness. If you knew what you were doing, a plastic apron and two pairs of rubber gloves were enough. He allowed himself these thoughts to give his mind a break from thinking about that blasted hair.

He glanced at his watch—ten to noon, just enough time to make it to the Hyatt. He put a half dozen lemon balls from the bowl on his desk into his pants pocket and rang his secretary.

"Margaret, I'm going to the hotel and from there to Gramma O's for lunch. After that, I'll be back at the hotel. Anything new comes in, give it to Charlie. If Phil Gatlin calls, beep me on my pager."

Usually, he looked forward to his conversations with Gatlin because they consisted largely of Gatlin listening attentively while Broussard dispensed enlightenment. But this time would be different.

At the Hyatt, he found Crandall Brooks standing by the message board.

"How was the workshop?" Broussard asked.

"A little on the elementary side. But I enjoyed it."

Broussard scanned the small groups conversing in the foyer.

"Who you looking for?" Brooks asked.

"Leo Fleming."

"He left with Jason Harvey a few minutes ago."

"Guess I'll have to catch him later," Broussard said, sorry to have missed Fleming but happy to have avoided Harvey. "Let me just leave him a note." He scribbled a few lines on a piece of paper provided for messages, folded it, wrote Fleming's name on the front, and stuck it on the board. "If you don't mind a little walk, I thought we'd have lunch at Gramma O's."

"Sounds good. How is she? Still as crusty as ever?"

"That's a given in a changing world."

Brooks took off his meeting ID badge, which had been on a cord around his neck, and put it in his Forensic Academy tote bag. Broussard's ID was still in his shirt pocket, where he'd put it before the autopsy.

They left the hotel and set out on foot down Poydras, toward the river. Except for an observation or two from each of them about the weather and Brooks's comment about Mardi Gras being almost here when he saw some grandstands going up on an intersecting street, they talked very little.

Grandma O's was where Broussard ate lunch so regularly, she always held the largest table open for him even if the place was jammed, which it usually was. Today, Broussard saw a number of tables with Forensic Academy tote bags on the floor by the occupants. Grandma O came steaming toward them like an icebreaker, her black taffeta dress rustling like locusts in a wheat field, a broad grin showing the gold star inlay in her front tooth.

"City Boy, Ah see you brought me somebody Ah don' get to feed too often." Her smile faded and her eyes grew sad. "Dr. Brooks, Ah was real sorry to hear 'bout...what happened."

"Well," Brooks said, "it's a fact of life we all have to deal with sometime."

"Dat's sure true...but it don't make it any easier.... Come on back."

She led them to Broussard's table and stood with the Cajun shack-on-stilts menus against her large bosom while they got seated. "City Boy, Ah know you don' need a menu. How 'bout you, Dr. Brooks?"

"Do you still have alligator chili?"

"Everyday."

"I'll have a bowl of that, a catfish poor boy, and iced tea."

"Same for me," Broussard said.

Grandma O went off to the kitchen, leaving the two men to sit in awkward silence, Susan Brooks's death hovering over the table.

"Guess you noticed I've gained a little weight," Brooks said finally.

"It looks good."

"After Susan died, I lost interest in running.... I don't eat any more than I ever did, but the pounds keep piling on. Guess my metabolism is different now."

"Brookie...how are you doing?"

Brooks looked at Broussard for a moment without answering. In the depths of his eyes, Broussard saw a wistful longing that twisted at his own heart. Finally, Brooks said,

"Sometimes I think I've got it licked, that it's all behind me." He shook his head slowly. "But it's not gone. It's just hiding under a thin skin waiting for a weak moment...then for a few minutes it's like the first days again...." He sighed, making a faint sound like a far-off wind blowing across a desolate plain. "But it's not happening now as often...."

Searching Brooks's eyes, Broussard saw behind the longing and the pain a glimmer of something else—a spark of the old Brookie, intense, goal-oriented.... Thus, when Brooks said, "So I'm getting there," Broussard believed him.

But the conversation lapsed again and Brooks picked up his bread knife and began running it in and out of the tines on his fork, his attention wandering in directions Broussard thought it shouldn't. Fortunately, the food came and he seemed to rally, to where after he'd made serious inroads into his meal, he even initiated a new topic of conversation. "How's Kit been doing?"

"Okay until Saturday."

Brooks worried his brow and started to ask what had happened, but Broussard was ahead of him.

"She came home and found that someone had poisoned her dog."

"That's terrible. I didn't know she had a dog."

"Took him in as a stray some time ago."

"I know she's going to miss him," Brooks said, the hollow look in his eyes returning.

Broussard felt like an idiot for bringing up such a subject and he saw that it was going to be tough to keep his comments around Brookie properly edited. "They think he'll make it," he said quickly, happy to end the topic on an upbeat note. "But they're keeping him at the vet's for a few days."

"That's great. I'm glad. And professionally...how's she doing there?"

"Quite well, although she sometimes doesn't think so. When she gets a hold of a problem, she's like a bull alligator, won't let go until she's worked it through. And she's fearless, which sometimes gets her in over her head. One time she—"

"You like her a lot, don't you?"

Above his beard, Broussard's skin reddened. "I like all my people."

"But she's special."

Broussard thought about this a bit and finally said, "If things had been different and I hadn't..." Realizing that this, too, was taking the conversation into a touchy area, Broussard made his point without preamble. "She's the kind of woman any man would be proud to have as a daughter." But this didn't work, either, and Brooks seemed to wilt, probably thinking about the fact that he and Susan had never had children.

For the next few minutes, they ate in silence so awkward that Broussard considered knocking his tea over just to break its grip. In life, Susan Brooks had loved people and the situations that brought them together. Over the years, Broussard had attended numerous dinner parties at the Brooks's home in Albany. Where some hostesses might strive for common interests in their guests, at Susan's you might meet an opera star, a farmer, and a manufacturer of disposable diapers all in the same night. And Susan was the spark that made it work, adding the right word here, a question there. So it was ironic that in death she should have made conversation between Broussard and Brookie so difficult.

Still groping for something to say, Broussard noticed a serious-looking fellow with straight brown hair and a heavy five o'clock shadow heading their way.

"Andy," he said, "I'm glad I ran into you. I wonder if you'd do me a favor."

It was Zin Fanelli, ordinarily someone he'd go out of his way to avoid. But under the circumstances, he'd have welcomed anyone.

"Zin, my boy. Have a seat."

Broussard's effusive greeting took Fanelli by surprise and he took a small step backward, acting like one of Broussard's cats when he'd try to get close enough to grab them for a bath.

"Thanks, but I'm with some people," Fanelli said warily.

"Brookie, this is Zin Fanelli. He trained with me a few years ago. Zin . . . Crandall Brooks, ME in Albany."

They exchanged a handshake and Fanelli turned back to Broussard. "Hate to bother you while you're eating, but sometimes you can go for days at these meetings and never see people you're looking for."

Broussard doubted that Fanelli had any misgivings whatever about disturbing his meal. "What can I do for you?"

"Jason Harvey's looking for an assistant and I've applied for the job. Would you write me a letter of reference and send it to him?"

Fanelli's request was a surprise. Considering the many arguments they'd had over Fanelli's irresponsibility when he was in training, he had to know that Broussard didn't think much of him. The fact that he'd managed to get his present position without a letter showed he *did* know. So why was he asking for help now?

Then his reasoning became clear. Fanelli had to know about the Vanzant trial—Broussard testifying for the prosecution, Harvey flown in for the defense. It had been necessary to destroy Harvey's analysis from the witness stand and Harvey'd taken it hard. So that now, about the only way Harvey would hire a Broussard trainee was if Broussard had a low opinion of him, all of which would make this an easy letter to write. "Be glad to," Broussard said pleasantly, thinking that Harvey and Fanelli deserved each other.

Brooks started to say something but was interrupted by Broussard's pager.

"Hold that thought, Brookie. Zin, I'll be right back."

Broussard checked the number displayed on the pager and headed for the cash register, where Grandma O was making change for a couple of well-scrubbed guys in three-piece suits. Without being asked, she brought the phone up from under the register and plopped it on the counter.

He punched in the number he'd been given and reached Gatlin in the middle of the first ring. "Phillip...Andy."

"Anything useful develop on that night clerk?" Gatlin asked, his voice barely audible over the restaurant noise.

"You gonna be free around one-thirty?"

"I could be."

"Come on by my office and we'll discuss it."

Returning to the table, Broussard found only Brooks.

"Fanelli had to leave. He said to give you his thanks. No crisis, I hope."

"No more than usual. I do need to get back, though."

"No problem. I'm finished."

Seeing that Grandma O was being kept busy at the register, they didn't wait for the check but went to her instead.

"You two tryin' to get out before Ah see if you ate everything?" she asked, her dark eyes hooded. Not finishing your food at Grandma O's was a sin worse than any Moses brought down from the mount.

"Our plates are so clean, you might not even have to wash 'em," Broussard said, getting out his wallet.

Grandma O fished in her apron for the checks. "City Boy, you owe me seven dollars an' fifty cents." Looking kindly at Brooks, she added, "Dr. Brooks, Ah don' seem to have one for you."

Upon reaching the hotel, Brooks said, "Think I'll go to my room and look over the program and read some abstracts. You made any plans for dinner?"

"I've agreed to go with Leo Fleming. But you're welcome to come along. In fact, I wish you would."

Despite the uncomfortable lunch they'd had, Broussard was not about to start ignoring his old friend. Besides, with Leo present, there'd be no long silences.

"Okay, sure, why not."

"We're gonna meet here at six."

"Right . . . see you then." Brooks took a few steps toward the elevators, then stopped abruptly and came back, his hand going to his inside jacket pocket. "Almost forgot. I brought this for you."

He handed Broussard a textured white folder. In it was a picture of a younger Crandall Brooks in a tux and, beside him, Susan Brooks, wearing a low-cut black dress, her blond hair softly framing her face. Behind them were some friends, glasses raised in a toast.

"Considering that you knew Susan even before I did, I thought you might like to have this to remember her. It was taken at a party celebrating our twentieth anniversary. I thought she looked particularly beautiful that night."

Broussard stared at a Susan Brooks that looked so healthy and so vital, it was hard to believe that wayward cells could ever get a foothold in her. Swallowing hard, he said, "It was good of you to think of me. I do want it."

He watched until Brooks disappeared into the elevator alcove. He then opened the folder and looked again at Susan Brooks's picture. Though he dealt with death every day, he was no more equipped to accept it in relatives and friends than anyone else and he began to tick off a list in his head: Aubry and Miriam, his parents; Estelle Broussard, the grandmother who had raised him after his parents were killed; Alston Bennet, his forensic pathology mentor; Dick Rails, his gross-anatomy partner in med school; Brad Dunbar, the best radiologist he ever knew and the one who had sponsored his membership in the Greater New Orleans Gourmet Society; Claude and Olivia Duhon; Kurt Halliday; Arthur Jordan . . . and now Susan Brooks. The list was growing steadily longer . . . growing too long . . . growing too fast. With each of these deaths, he'd lost a part of himself. How much could a man lose and still have enough left to keep getting out of bed in the morning?

Suddenly, he felt hemmed in . . . by the hotel, by his life, by events he couldn't control. Finding the atmosphere in the lobby stale and oppressive, he made for one of the front doors and moved out into the fresh air, except under the huge portico, the air wasn't so fresh, but was tinged with taxi and limo exhaust fumes. He walked down to the edge of the portico and stepped out into the open, breathing deeply, tired of thinking, tired of responsibility, wanting just to *be*.

For a while, he watched some sparrows coming and going in the shrubs planted along the hotel, envying them their freedom and their small brains that surely did not bother them with old memories. Eventually, unable to ignore matters at hand, he reluctantly returned to the hotel, where, feeling very lonely, he went up the escalator to the Regency Foyer, hoping that Leo had found his note.

His spirits lifted when he saw Leo by the message board, talking to Hugh Greenwood, the ME from Indianapolis, who was also part of the faculty for the aircraft-accident workshop. Greenwood was clean-shaven, with a hairline rapidly going north. More notably, he had a lacework of fine scars over the lower half of his face that pulled the corners of his thin lips into a look of perpetual disapproval that often made people who didn't know him uncomfortable. It

was his personality that made people who did know him
uncomfortable.

"Hello, Andrew," Greenwood said. "I see from the paper you had an interesting day Saturday."

"You mean that murder?"

"Scrabble letters, the article said. That's a new twist."

"And we had another one this mornin'."

"Same guy?" Fleming asked.

"Looks like it. He left us some more letters."

"Now you see, it's just like I was telling Leo before you
walked up. You're a lucky guy."

"How so?"

"Your jurisdiction is one of the most interesting cities in
the country and now you've got the rarest of criminals...a
serial killer with a genuine sense of theater."

"Why don't I feel lucky?"

"Because you're caught up in the moment. If you could
step back and view it, you'd appreciate the drama...the
human spectacle."

Broussard did not answer right away, but spent a moment trying to figure out if Greenwood was pulling his leg.
With him, you could never be sure. Unable to decide, he
simply said, "You still gonna be here Wednesday?"

"Sure, why?"

"That's when the psychiatry and behavioral science
folks'll be havin' their business meetin' and I was thinkin'
I'd get 'em to examine you before they got started."

Greenwood grinned, his scars making it look more like
he'd pinched his finger in a car door.

Broussard looked at Fleming. "Leo, I wonder if you'd
have time to come over to my office and give me your opinion on somethin' related to the case?"

"Now?"

"If you're free."

"Am I gonna have to come back and testify when it comes to trial?"

"Way too soon to know. I'll try to keep you out of it, but if the defense wants to challenge your conclusion—whatever that's gonna be—I . . ."

"No, no. I want to come back. I *like* this town."

"I'll do what I can."

"You have things to discuss, so I'll leave you to it," Greenwood said.

Fearing that Greenwood might feel as though he'd been brushed off, Broussard said, "Hugh, if you don't have plans, come to dinner with us tonight."

"I'd like to, but an old college chum of mine lives here and he and his wife are taking me out."

"Tomorrow, then."

"All right. I'm sure I'll see you around. We'll fill in the details later."

Broussard and Fleming started for the escalator. Greenwood headed for a telephone. As he passed a potted bamboo a few steps from where they'd all been talking, someone without an ID badge stepped out and said, "Excuse me, who was that with Broussard?"

"Leo Fleming," Greenwood said.

"What does he do?"

"He's a forensic anthropologist."

"Thanks."

Watching him walk away, Greenwood shook his head. A ponytail . . . on a grown man.

FIVE

AFTER LEAVING THE SCENE of the second murder, Kit went back to her office and called the vet to check on Lucky. She then spent the morning trying to write up a suicide case she'd investigated the previous week, a dentist who had killed himself by shoving a dental drill into his brain through a skull defect he'd had since birth. It was truly incredible some of the ways people chose to do away with themselves. This case would most certainly go into her book. It had taken far longer to write this report than usual because her pen often strayed to the margin of the paper, as it was doing now.

KOJE...

What the devil did it mean? And why was the killer leaving fewer letters? Suppose it was all some demented trick, meaningless events intended to drive them as mad as he was. She could picture the killer, hunched over his beer in the dark corner of a sleazy bar, a self-satisfied smile on his ugly kisser.

Except that wasn't what the evidence suggested. He probably wasn't ugly. More likely, he was pleasant looking, or at least respectable in appearance. And that wasn't surprising. The Ted Bundys were more common than the Henry Lee Lucases. "He was a nice man who never bothered anybody"...if you don't count those sixteen mutilated corpses.

KOJE the first time...KOJ the second.

Hmmmm.

The more she thought about it, the more she liked the idea suggested by Gatlin at the second murder scene—that the killer was leaving fewer letters to indicate he was going to strike two more times. Did that mean KOJE meant nothing? Could he have used any four letters? No... Broussard was right: They were taped together to keep them in order, which meant that KOJE was a separate message.

She was so deep in thought the sound of the telephone made her start. "Kit Franklyn."

"Hi, it's me."

"Teddy. I wasn't expecting to hear from you. Is something wrong?"

"Why would something have to be wrong for me to call you?"

"It wouldn't, but we just saw each other a few hours ago."

"Maybe I missed you."

"Sure you did. C'mon, LaBiche, what's this all about?"

"Did you talk to the animal hospital this morning?"

"Yeah, he's still doing well."

"I'm glad."

"But we found another body, and some more letters...KOJ this time."

"That's awful. So you were right when you predicted it'd happen again. Actually, what's why I called. I had a thought about those letters."

"Great. I could use a new slant. It's a puzzle that's about to drive me nuts. What have you got?"

"Maybe you're concentrating on the wrong thing."

"How so?"

"Those wooden blocks have more than letters on them. They also have the little numbers you use to keep score."

Kit was surprised that she hadn't thought of the numbers herself or that it hadn't occurred to either Gatlin or Broussard. But of course, for the most part, they hadn't been looking at the actual tiles. Saturday, Gatlin had written the letters on a chalkboard, and she'd been looking at them on her legal pad. She felt a brief rush of excitement, then saw that four numbers were as puzzling as four letters that didn't spell anything. Unless . . .

"Is there more?"

"Hey, I'm surprised I came up with *that*."

"I don't suppose you know what the values are for KOJE."

"Vowels are one each, but I don't remember the others."

"I think the *J* is worth eight. Why is there never a Scrabble set around when you need one?"

"I have to get back to work. Hope I helped."

"At least you've given me a new way to look at the problem. If you come up with anything else, call me."

"I wouldn't hang around the phone waiting. One idea a week is about my limit."

"Don't let 'em get behind you."

"I won't. You be careful, too."

Kit hung up and looked at her legal pad.

KOJE

?181

If she was home, it'd be easy to get the value of *K* and verify that the *J* was an eight. Maybe she should just *do* that—go home and look. Lot of trouble, though, for something that might not even be a real lead. She put her elbow on the desk, rested her cheek on her hand, and stared at the paper. Probably she'd just wait until tonight, get out the Scrabble set, and look.

Her finger began to twirl a lock of her hair until she caught herself at it and quit. It was hard enough to get her hair to lie right without that.

Her fingers began to drum on the desk. Tonight was hours away. . . .

Drum . . . drum . . . drum.

She could guess at the value for K and see what the entire number looked like. . . . Bad idea. Why waste time thinking about the wrong number?

Drum . . . drum . . . drum.

She stopped drumming, got out the Yellow Pages, and looked up the number of the store where she'd bought the Scrabble set on Saturday, which according to their ad in the phone book, shipped anywhere.

Someone with the voice of a child picked up and said, "Hello" without reciting the store's name. Kit figured that she either had the wrong number or some customer's kid had gotten to the phone. "Is this Happy Pastimes?"

"Uh-huh."

"Is there an adult there?"

"Like, how old a person did you want?"

"Are you a clerk?"

"Uh-huh."

Kit briefly wondered what the applicant pool was like when this guy got hired. "I wonder if you'd do me a favor. I need to know how many points the K and the J are worth in Scrabble."

"Gee lady, I don't have any idea."

"I didn't think you'd know without looking. Could you check?"

"Like in some big book?"

"One of the Scrabble sets in stock might be a more direct approach."

"They're all sealed up."

"Could you open one?"

"I'm not supposed to do that. Plastic gets torn, that thing'll sit on the shelf like it's diseased. Won't nobody buy it."

"Suppose I buy it."

"Then you can do anything you want with it."

"Can I make the purchase over the phone?"

"If you got a MasterCard, Visa, or American Express."

"MasterCard."

"You want the deluxe model or the regular?"

"Regular, or anything cheaper."

After the kid took her card number, he said, "Where do you want this sent?"

"I don't. I just want you to open it and tell me what the point values are for the *K* and *J*." There was a silence on the other end. "Hello...you there? Hello..."

"You gonna pick it up?" the kid asked.

"No. I really don't want it."

"If you're not gonna come in, I have to ship it."

"You keep it. You don't want it, give it to a friend."

"Lady, it's gotta go either in 'Will call' or 'To be shipped.' You don't come in, I can't *not* send it. We got forms we gotta fill out. I don't follow procedure and fill out all my forms, I could get canned. I don't send it anywhere, I got nothin' to put on one of my forms."

To get over this impasse, Kit gave the kid her address. "Now will you open it and answer my question?"

"Okay."

For a minute or two, there was no sound, then she heard the crinkle of plastic wrap, the sound of the lid coming off, then some noise she couldn't identify. Finally, the kid's voice came back on.

"The *J* is worth eight points and the *F* is worth four."

"I didn't want the *F,* I wanted the *K.*"

In the background, Kit heard a voice say, "Young man, are you going to be on that phone all day?"

"No ma'am," the kid said. "I'm finished right now."

Kit was afraid he was going to hang up, but he came back with the news that the *K* was worth six points. Before she could say thanks, he was gone. What an ordeal. But she had what she wanted.

KOJE

6181

Now what? She stared at the four letters and four numbers, waiting for a thunderclap of insight.

Automobile license plates.

Except in license plates, the maximum combination of letters and numbers was seven, with the standard pattern, at least for cars, being three numbers, a letter, and three more numbers, an arrangement that didn't speak to her needs at all.

Vanity plates—they could have any combination of letters and numbers up to seven places.

She reached for the phone and called a friend in motor-vehicle registration who checked the computer and found that there were no Louisiana plates with the sequence KOJE or 6181.

She went back to staring at her legal pad and drumming on the desk. Getting nothing out of the numbers, she went back to thinking about the letters. KOJE—that sort of sounded Japanese, like a town maybe. She got up and went down the hall to see Margaret, the senior forensic secretary.

The forensic office had two secretaries, Margaret Thibi-deaux and Jolanda Sizemore. Margaret had been there even before Broussard. And when Kit had first arrived and be-gun working around her, Phil Gatlin, and Broussard, with their long history together, she'd imagined herself associ-ating with the human equivalent of old-growth redwoods. Margaret, in fact, fostered this impression by never calling Jolanda, a ten-year veteran of the forensic office, by name, always referring to her instead as "the new girl."

Even before entering the office, Kit knew what each woman would be wearing. Very heavy and shaped like a salmon croquette, Jolanda would be in a circular piece of fabric with a hole in the center for her head. Proud of being slim and perhaps wanting to flaunt that in front of Jolanda, Margaret would be cinched at the waist with a wide belt and would most likely have accessorized with a crystal pin depicting some kind of insect.

Kit's prediction for Jolanda went unchallenged, for her desk was empty. Margaret, though, was working at her word processor. She'd come to see Margaret because of her interest in travel. A reformed smoker, Margaret no longer headed for a cigarette on her breaks, but stayed at her desk and planned future trips by studying a large world atlas she kept close by, often picking obscure destinations purely by the sound of the name.

"Margaret, can I bother you for a minute?"

She typed a few more words, then looked up, a smile of pleasant indifference on her lips.

"What can I do for you, Dr. Franklyn?" Today, her pin was a large crystal bee.

"Is there a town in Japan called Koje . . . K-o-j-e?"

She thought for a few seconds and said, "There's a Kobe. I don't know about the other." She reached down and came up with her atlas, which she held out in both hands. "But you're welcome to look for yourself."

Kit thanked her and took the tome back to her own office, where she thumped it onto the desk and sat down. After checking the table of contents, she turned to the picture of Japan, which spread across facing pages like a large green amoeba. Even before beginning her search, she saw something promising. The picture was divided by a series of widely spaced horizontal lines—latitudes or longitudes, she guessed. Along the left margin, each line was identified by a two-digit number. This led to the hope that 6181 was a map coordinate. But 61 was not among the numbers on the margin. And when she checked the top of the map, the vertical lines were identified by three-digit numbers.

Unwilling to let go of this idea, she began at the lower-left corner and worked her way across Japan town by town, giving no thought to what it would mean if she *did* find a Koje but feeling good to be doing something.

Japan had no shortage of towns, and that meant lots of tiny names to read, so that when she ran out of land at the upper-right corner, without having seen a Koje, she found a kernel of pleasure in simply being finished.

She closed the book and let her hands rest on its slick green jacket. So Japan was not the way to the killer. Her exercise with the atlas got her to thinking about great distances and how one traversed them. This sent her again to the Yellow Pages, where she looked up airlines and began calling each one, asking if they had a flight 6181, thinking that the killer might be a crewman on such a flight. But no airline used that number.

This was impossible. To solve the riddle, she would have to be able to read the killer's mind, and she'd never taken a course where they teach you to do that. She should just pack it in. No one could blame her for giving up on such a hopeless thing as this—no one except herself and probably Broussard.

She went to the window and pulled the blinds. Looking out over the city, she thought about her attempts so far to solve the riddle, soon seeing that they had not come from any logical analysis but had been desperate leaps into the wind.

So, analyze....

Teddy's call had shown her that she needed to keep in mind the total picture, not just zero in on one aspect, divorced from the whole. That's how she'd forgotten there were numbers as well as letters on the Scrabble tiles.

What was there in the big picture that had become lost in her thinking? Put that way, the answer was obvious. In both murders, the tiles were sitting on a section of the *Times-*

Picayune. Was that significant or was the paper merely something convenient to put the tiles on so that they'd be easily seen?

To assume they meant so little would bring that line of thought to an end. She therefore decided to take the other position and assume that the paper was important.

At the second scene, she'd noticed that the Scrabble tiles were on the front page from the previous Friday's paper. Making a call to the police property room, she learned that the pages left at the first scene were from Friday's Sports section. Papers came out every day. Why did he use Friday's paper both times? Was it simply because the paper was already in his car from the first murder? No. That trivialized the paper, and she'd decided it wasn't trivial. So it was important that the same day's paper was used in both murders.

Friday...

She went to her desk and flipped her calendar back to Friday—February 14, Valentine's Day. And he kills by amputating a part of the *heart*. Her own heart began to beat faster, for this seemed like progress. Hearts... Hearts... Love... The killer's wife had left him for another man. He's killing other men for revenge. Wrong. He wouldn't kill *other* men; he'd kill the one who'd crossed him, and maybe his wife, too. And the killer isn't striking out in anger. He's calculating.

Loves to kill? Could be it. Doesn't help find him, though.

Sensing for the first time an empty feeling in her belly, she looked at her watch and found that it was *way* past lunch.

BROUSSARD BRIEFED Leo Fleming on the salient features of the two murders as they walked from the Hyatt to Charity Hospital, finishing up as they entered Broussard's office.

"How can I help?" Fleming asked.

"On the first victim, the knife went through only soft tissue," Broussard said, closing the door. "But on the second, it severed one of the rib cartilages. I was hopin' you'd take a look at the cut surfaces and see if you can tell us anything about the weapon. They're over here."

Fleming followed Broussard to the dissecting microscope on the long table against the right wall, where Broussard helped himself to a pair of disposable gloves from a box near the scope and gestured for Fleming to do the same. He sat down at the scope and opened a wide-mouth screw-top jar sitting nearby. With a long pair of forceps, he fished a pinkish white nodule out of the liquid in the jar and put it in the culture dish sitting on the microscope stage. He returned to the jar for the second nodule and placed it beside the first.

"See you're still usin' the same filin' system," Fleming said, looking at the piles of papers and journals stacked about the room.

Broussard was so absorbed in what he was doing, he didn't answer. Dropping his glasses to his chest, he leaned into the eyepieces and fiddled with the nodules until he was satisfied with their placement. Then he got out of the chair and stepped away from it, gesturing for Fleming to take over.

"All yours. I've got 'em arranged so the two surfaces produced by the knife are facin' up."

While Fleming examined the nodules, Broussard paced the room.

Seeing Broussard's shadow pass by the frosted glass pane on his office door and wondering if he'd found anything of significance in the autopsy of the second victim, Kit knocked and leaned inside.

"Kit, come on in," Broussard said. "You should be here for this. On the second victim, the killer wasn't as precise as before. This time, he cut a rib cartilage. Leo's checkin' the cut surfaces for tool marks.''

Fleming's eyes were pressed against the microscope eyepieces, his attention totally on one of the cartilage nodules, which he held suspended between the index finger and thumb of both hands. Dissatisfied with the angle of illumination, he reached over and twisted the limber gooseneck on the light and began to tilt the nodule back and forth in the altered beam. He did the same with the second nodule then leaned back and stripped off his gloves. "They're pretty faint," he said, "but I can see rills.''

"Knicks in the blade or serrations?" Broussard asked.

"Serrations.''

"Any way to tell how many teeth per inch?''

"If it was a saw, I could. But the curve on the tip of a knife makes that impossible.''

Kit had no idea why that would be, but it seemed to make sense to Broussard.

"What's going on?" Phil Gatlin said from the doorway. "Or am I being too nosy?''

Broussard introduced Gatlin and Fleming to each other and told Gatlin why he'd brought Fleming in and what Fleming had found.

"Always helps to know what we're looking for in a murder weapon," Gatlin said. "Appreciate the help." He looked at Broussard. "Same internal injuries on this one?''

Broussard nodded.

There was a pause where Kit could have mentioned the relationship she'd found between the newspaper and the way the victims had died. But on reflection, she realized that there was really nothing to tell.

Broussard would have been grateful for any discussion

that would have kept Gatlin from asking him the question he knew was coming, for he was struggling with a situation quite unfamiliar to him—confusion. And it was about to become evident to everyone there.

SIX

"THAT NEW HAIR give us anything we don't already know?" Gatlin asked.

Broussard took a deep breath. "I'll show you," he said, going to his desk. He picked up two Polaroid photographs and laid them side by side. "This is the first hair we found."

Everyone moved in closer. Broussard's chubby index finger went to the fat part of the hair. "This is the root, and this—" his finger slid along the length of the hair "—is the shaft. This darker central core in the shaft is the medulla. There are three significant features to this hair: It has a narrow spindle-shaped root, the shaft is naked, and there's no medulla just above the root. That makes this a restin'-stage hair, the kind that's shed naturally every day.

"This new hair—" his fingers moved to the other picture "—has a large club-shaped root. This clear material surroundin' the shaft is part of the follicle. And if you look close, you can see that the medulla extends all the way into the root."

Kit had no trouble seeing the first two features, but the third eluded her even when she bent down for a better look. The expression on Gatlin's face was one of tolerance rather than interest. He obviously would have preferred that Broussard give him the bottom line without all the buildup.

"This hair did not fall out naturally," Broussard said. "It was forcibly removed."

"Could be it's a hair that got tangled in his hairbrush," Gatlin said. "He cleaned the brush, the hair falls on his clothes, and later it drops onto the tape while he's working on the letters."

"Two things wrong with that idea," Broussard countered. "One, it's unlikely this hair is from the same person as the first one. The first hair is a gray hair that's been colored with a black dye. The second is a red hair with no dye in it. Generally, you can't determine from a single hair what color a head of hair is, because we all have several different colors of hair in our scalp, but someone who dyes their hair would most likely treat all of it to get a uniform color. If this red hair came from the same scalp as the first one, it should show some evidence of dye."

"Maybe one's a beard hair," Gatlin said.

Broussard shook his head. "Don't think so."

Gatlin seemed about to suggest another explanation but then appeared to reconsider. "You said there were two reasons I was wrong about the second hair coming from the killer's hairbrush...."

Broussard picked up the picture of the second hair and held it so Gatlin wouldn't miss his next point. "See this dark band across the shaft?" He pointed to a region a short distance above the root.

Gatlin nodded.

"It indicates a degenerative change in the poorly keratinized zone just below the skin surface."

"So?"

"That means the hair comes from a corpse."

There was a silence as they all grappled with this surprising revelation.

"How do you know the degeneration didn't take place *after* the hair was plucked?" Gatlin said finally.

"Any degeneration after plucking would go all the way to the root. Bein' in the scalp apparently protects the deeper region."

"How long after death before this band shows up?" Gatlin asked.

"Been seen as early as eight hours. Usually, it's typical of longer times."

"Not likely then that it could have come from the second victim."

"Or the first one, either," Broussard said. He did not mention that this hair had seemed so peculiar, he'd collected a number of hairs from both the first and second victims and compared them to the odd hair, even though he knew it couldn't possibly have come from them. But he'd done it all the same, finding, as well he should have, significant similarities.

"So what are you saying?" Gatlin asked. "There's a body we haven't discovered yet?"

"Certainly would fit the facts."

"A body he decided to move several hours or days after death?" Gatlin sucked his teeth in thought. Eventually, he said, "I don't get it. The other bodies were in places where they'd be found. And with him leaving those letters, he obviously *wanted* them found. What is there about this other one that makes it different?"

Broussard had no answer, a fact that irritated him as much as the supposition he'd accepted as fact earlier and that he must now confess. "I should point out," he said, "that if the second hair didn't come from the killer, it's possible the first one didn't either."

It was now clear to Kit and Gatlin that this had always been a possibility. Rather than blaming Broussard for the oversight, they each felt at least partially responsible for not seeing it themselves when the first hair was being discussed.

"On the way over here, I had the feeling we were gaining on this guy," Gatlin said. "Now, I'm not so sure. I hope the fiber evidence holds up. It's not much, but..."

Broussard's expression reminded Gatlin that they had not spoken of fibers previously. "Guess I didn't tell you. The lab found a few white fibers stuck to the first victim's shirt in the bloodstain. They said it was something called viscose. It's an absorbent material used in camper's towels. The way I figure it, the killer had to make sure he didn't get blood on him, so he wrapped his knife hand in a towel."

With nothing further to discuss, the meeting broke up and Kit headed to Grandma O's for a sandwich. Gatlin returned to Homicide to do some paperwork.

"You goin' back to the hotel?" Fleming asked Broussard after the others left.

"I need to do a few things here. You mind walkin' back alone?"

"Nope. Don't forget tonight."

"I'll be there. Thanks for the consult."

"Just make sure I have to testify."

Left alone, Broussard sat behind his desk, got two lemon balls from the glass bowl, and put one in each cheek. He reached across the desk and pulled the picture of the red hair around to where he could look at it.

A long moment later, he pushed it away and picked up the white folder Crandall Brooks had given him. Leaning back, he opened the folder and stared at Susan Brooks's picture.

So many friends and relatives gone now...lives whose time had passed. Was his time passing, as well? Is that why he felt so ill at ease and out of step with this case? Was that how it began—forgetting to be cautious, seeing only what you want to be there, spinning satisfying facts from smoke?

Feeling very much in need of some time off, he wedged the open white folder between his electric pencil sharpener and his beaker of pens and pencils. He then turned to a task he could delay no longer and that he had no real interest in—putting the final touches on his talk for the session tomorrow afternoon, where he would face hundreds of colleagues with an address entitled "New Orleans: Food, Fun, and Murder."

KIT STEPPED onto the street and cast her eyes skyward, where the odds of rain had gone from a long shot five hours earlier to a serious possibility. New Orleans is several feet below sea level, the highest terrain being Monkey Hill at the zoo, built so the children could see what a hill feels like. And it is surrounded by swamps. Like most New Orleanians, Kit rarely thought about any of this. But occasionally, like today, when the sky turned pewter and hugged the city, she could faintly catch the sweet vegetable odor of the wild environs and was reminded that were it not for the huge pumps scattered about the city, it might well be a swamp itself. Close behind this thought was the realization that she had no umbrella in her office.

She considered going somewhere close, but out of loyalty to Grandma O, she decided to risk the longer walk. In case she didn't make it, she stopped at a vending machine and bought a *USA Today* to use as a rain hat.

There was only a handful of customers in Grandma O's when Kit arrived. On the bar sat a stuffed pelican, its wings spread, mouth open. Bubba Oustellette, the proprietor's grandson, was up on a ladder behind the bar, affixing a small shelf to the wall above the long one holding Grandma O's collection of stuffed armadillos and nutrias. As usual, Bubba was dressed in blue coveralls and was wearing a green baseball cap. He was only about five four but made up for his lack of size by a good heart and boundless resourcefulness. He ran the police vehicle-impoundment station and kept Broussard's cars running. On occasion, he'd done Kit some very large favors and she liked him immensely.

"Didn't think Ah was gonna see you today," Grandma O said, coming her way with a big grin.

"I sort of lost track of time."

"Then you mus' be real hungry."

Kit gestured toward the bar. "Nice pelican."

"Foun' it in a shop over on Royal. Paid way too much, but when you see a stuffed pelican, you better grab it 'fore somebody else does."

Kit had the vague notion that it was illegal to possess a stuffed pelican but was too unsure of her facts to bring it up. In any event, it seemed like a real dust-catcher.

"C'mon back," Grandma O said, moving toward Broussard's table in the rear.

Kit detoured past the bar. "You make sure you get it straight now," she said, looking up at Bubba.

"Hey, Doc Franklyn. You didn't think Ah was gonna put it up crooked, did you?"

"You be careful, too. That's a long way to fall."

"Ah can't fall. Gramma O won't allow it."

Kit waved and went to her table, where Grandma O took her order before disappearing into the kitchen.

The restaurant was as empty as Kit had ever seen it. At a table in the center of the room was a prosperous-looking older couple—the man wearing a canvas hat bristling with travel pins; she in a sweatshirt advertising the Cunard cruise line.

Used to be you had to pay people to wear commercials, Kit mused. Now the wearer pays.

Her thoughts went back to the meeting in Broussard's office. A hair from a corpse—that was bizarre. But then the whole case was bizarre. Her gaze drifted to the right and for the first time she focused on the three people sitting near the wall—a man in his thirties and two gray-haired women. Not a particularly unusual combination, except that half the man's face was covered with a port-wine stain and the two women were identical twins both dressed in red-and-white polka-dot blouses and red slacks. Seeing this strange trio gave Kit the peculiar sensation that perhaps the two murders had not really happened at all, that she was actually asleep and the last few days had merely been a lifelike dream. Either that or there was a door open somewhere letting in the unusual.

From this unproductive little detour, she went back to thinking about Scrabble letters, numbers, and newspaper pages. She pulled a napkin from the dispenser on the table and got a pen from her purse.

KOJE

6181

For a few seconds, she stared at what she'd written. Then, elbow on the table, fist propped against her cheek, she began to doodle, first drawing a box around the cluster of letters and numbers, then making the inside corners into little triangles. She attached curly pigtails to each corner and began connecting the horizontal sides of her box with vertical lines.

"Never saw you do dat before," Grandma O said, interrupting with Kit's food. "You mus' have somethin' botherin' you."

Grandma O moved around and looked at Kit's scribbling right side up. Her face fell and her Grandma O demeanor wilted, an amazing conversion for a woman who could bend tenpenny nails with her fingers and eject abusive patrons by force.

"What's wrong?" Kit asked.

"Nineteen eighty-one . . . dat's when my Albert passed."

Looking at her scrawls on the napkin, Kit saw that her doodling had divided the 6181 into 6 1 81, June first, 1981. "I'm sorry I reminded you of something so sad," she said.

"Albert was a good man an' Ah know he went to a good place," Grandma O said bravely. "Person can't go back to what was. We gotta jus' move on. You have somethin' to eat an' you'll see your way through dat problem."

She put Kit's food down and headed for a sailor at the bar, who was fondling the pelican.

Kit went to work on her sandwich, her eyes returning to the napkin while she chewed.

6/1/81

She felt the stirring of an idea. Farfetched? Perhaps. Perhaps not. She certainly had nothing to lose in checking it out. And it could be done on the way back to the office.

She chewed faster now, wanting to be done with lunch and on her way. Had she been in any other restaurant, she wouldn't have bothered finishing her poor boy, which suddenly seemed enormous. But she was as intimidated by Grandma O as any of her other regulars were, so she stayed, chewed faster, and got it all down.

She was a block from the restaurant before she realized she'd left her rain hat behind. This caused her to pick up the pace.

The library was on Tulane Avenue, a few blocks from the hospital. She went directly to the Louisiana Room on the third floor, where the librarian directed her to some gray cabinets in the back, past the microfilm readers. In those cabinets were rows of small cardboard boxes containing microfilms of old copies of the *Times-Picayune*. She found the box containing the issue printed on 6/1/81 and took it to the readers.

She checked the instructions on the reader and threaded the film according to the diagram. Black pages flew by as she turned the crank. Finally, she got to the front page. As she scanned it intently, a small voice said, "Dear, can you read this?"

It was a birdlike old lady at the next machine. Kit leaned over and saw on the reader something that looked like the guest register for a hotel. She bent closer to the entry above the old lady's veined finger and squinted at the faded signature. "It looks like... Vorheis."

"Yes," the old lady said. "I see that now. Thank you so much."

Kit went back to her own search but, unlike the old lady, had no idea what she was looking for. Over the next few minutes, she encountered nothing but page after page of uninteresting old news and old ads, so that when the front page for June second rolled into view, she reversed direction, rewound the film, and put the spool back in its box. Her failure to solve the Scrabble riddle was not to be the only negative associated with her visit to the library, for when she reached down to get her purse, it was gone.

Heart thumping, she looked on the other side of the chair. Her purse was not there, either. With an inventory of her credit cards mentally rolling by like frames on the microfilm reader, she shoved her chair back and hurried to the gray cabinets, thinking she might have left it there when she was searching the drawers for the right box.

Nothing.

Concentrate.... When did she have it last? She'd definitely had it at Grandma O's, because she'd taken the pen out of it to write on the napkin... and she had it at the cabinets, because she remembered setting it right here... and she also had it at the microfilm reader, because she distinctly recalled putting it on the floor next to... the old lady.

She rushed to the elevators. Having been so intent on reviewing the film, she had no recollection of when the old lady had left. She could be blocks away by now.

The elevator took forever to get to the ground floor and when it finally did, she ran through the lobby to the exits, one of which opened toward city hall and the other toward the Tulane-Loyola intersection.

She dashed to the Tulane-Loyola exit and went out onto the steps. No sign of her. She continued onto the sidewalk and looked to her right, down Loyola. There she was, about forty yards away, carrying a shopping bag and walking fast.

Kit started after her in a dead run, giving out an ill-advised shout. "You with the shopping bag. Stop."

The old lady looked back and then began to run like a whippet, her long dress flipping around her thin legs as she flew over the pavement. She was fast, but Kit was faster, and the distance between them steadily closed.

The old lady ran to an occupied car waiting at the curb and began clawing at the door handle. She got it open just as Kit reached her. As the old lady dived inside, Kit grabbed at the grocery bag, which ripped in half as the car sped away, the door on the passenger side still partially open.

There was dried mud on the license plate, so there was no chance to get the number. But Kit did retrieve her purse, for it had fallen out of the bag and onto the street.

A quick survey of the contents showed that everything was there. Heart still thumping, she slipped the bag onto her shoulder and headed back toward Tulane Avenue as a misty rain began to fall.

SEVEN

KILLER CLAIMS SECOND VICTIM

Yesterday, police found the night clerk at the Chartres House hotel murdered in the hotel parking lot on Madison, where, based on the estimated time of death, he had gone around 2:00 A.M. Monday morning to move a guest's car. The victim, Danny Racine, 20, was killed by a single knife wound in the heart, exactly as another New Orleans man was killed early Saturday morning near Jackson Square. The presence of Scrabble letters on the bodies of both men have caused authorities to label the perpetrator the Scrabble Letter Killer. There were four letters on the first victim and three on the second, leading to speculation that there will be another two victims. Visitors and residents of the French Quarter are therefore urged to travel in groups or remain indoors after midnight. Though there are presently no firm leads to the killer's identity, useful information has been obtained from hairs left at both murder scenes. Dr. Leo Fleming, head of the human identification laboratory in Raleigh, NC, here for the American Academy of Forensic Sciences meeting, has been called in as a consultant. Authorities have not disclosed what they hope to learn from Dr. Fleming.

KIT THREW THE PAPER DOWN in disgust. The Scrabble Letter Killer... She hadn't heard *anyone* call him that. Nick Lawson was really playing this for all it was worth. At least he didn't know what Fleming had found—not yet, anyway. But by tomorrow, who knows?

She rinsed her coffee cup in the sink and put the Pop-Tarts back in the cupboard. She wiped the kitchen table and went to the pantry for Lucky's leash.

Ah Lucky... He wasn't there. He was still at the vet's. Surely he was well enough to come home today.

She went to the phone and called the animal hospital.

"Good morning, this is Kit Franklyn. You have my dog, Lucky. When can I pick him up?"

Instead of answering, the girl on the line asked her to hold for the vet. Kit's heart fell and she prepared for the worst. If Lucky had died... This was so terrible to consider that she pushed the thought from her mind and tried not to let it creep back in.

They kept her waiting a thoughtlessly long time, then she heard the vet's voice. "Dr. Franklyn, I'm afraid Lucky..."

Oh no... He *did* die. Her eyes blurred.

"...has had a small relapse. It's nothing to be concerned about; we just need to keep him a while longer."

"Of course. I understand," Kit said, her heart settling. "You'll call the minute he can come home, won't you? You have both my numbers?"

The vet turned her over to the girl, who correctly recited both Kit's home and office phone numbers and also expressed optimism over Lucky's recovery.

Reluctantly, Kit hung up and sat for a moment, pulling herself together. That little dog had certainly given her some bad moments over the last few days. Her thoughts were interrupted by the doorbell. When she opened the door, she saw a UPS driver heading back to his truck at the curb. On the porch was a package from Happy Pastimes. For a few seconds, she did not understand what this could be. Then she remembered—the Scrabble game she'd had to buy to find out the value of *K* and *J*.

Having no use for it now, she took the package inside and put it on the hall table. She looked at herself in the mirror over the table, reset one of the tortoiseshell combs that kept her long hair from her face, and inspected her lip gloss. Satisfied that she was presentable, she got her purse from the bedroom, along with the umbrella she planned to keep in the office, and left the house.

With her key still in the lock, she hesitated, the package inside reminding her that she'd never looked at actual tiles comprising the riddle sequence since Teddy had pointed out that they had numbers on them as well as letters. And the riddle had yet to be solved. This caused her to go back inside, where she picked up the package and carried it to the kitchen.

Even as a child, she'd always been neat, so the brown paper around the package went directly into the wastebasket. There was, of course, no plastic wrapper around the box, the clerk having already taken that off at her request.

She removed the lid and lifted out the game board. Under it were four plastic tile holders and a pouch of tiles, whose contents she poured onto the table. Since there were many O's and E's, she found these quickly. Because there was only one *J* and one *K,* they took longer.

She located the *J* and lined up what she had so far:

OJE

Just when she was beginning to think the clerk had lost the *K,* she found it and placed it in sequence.

KOJE

Her eyes widened. The *K* was worth *five* points, not *six,* as the idiot clerk had told her. She remembered now how a customer had been riding him for taking so long on the phone. He had apparently gotten flustered and told her the wrong number.

All the ideas she'd had about the riddle swam before her. With the mix-up in value for the *K,* none, except for the map of Japan, had been properly checked. License plates... airline flights... No. She had evolved beyond those theories. The newspapers...

May first, 1981. Not *June* first. She'd looked at the wrong microfilm.

But was it worth going back? She recalled how she'd felt looking at the film—at loose ends, not knowing what to concentrate on. But maybe that was because it was the *wrong* film. If it had been the right one, the answer might have been obvious. And if it was worth doing once, it was worth doing correctly. She hurried from the kitchen, leaving the Scrabble set littering the table and forgetting her umbrella.

Thirty minutes later, she was at the microfilm reader in the library. She had not seen the old lady this time and had reported her to the library staff so they could be on the lookout, but she still sat with her purse firmly between her feet.

Black pages... black pages... page one.

The first interesting fact she noticed was that May first, 1981, had been a Friday—just like the paper that had been left with the Scrabble tiles. But back in 1981, the paper was called the *Times-Picayune—The States Item.*

SOVIETS SCOFF AT U.S. PLEAS ON MIDEAST... Well, they won't be doing that anymore, at least not as Soviets, Kit thought, looking further.

HOUSE BEGINS DEBATE ON BUDGET... How unusual.

Schwegman's had sirloin for $1.85 a pound; an irate citizen had written the editor complaining about the litter at city hall; new asphalt walks were going to keep this year's jazz fest attendees dry; Winn Dixie was opening a new store in Algiers. DEAD JUDGE LAUDED FOR SERVICE . . . Real sensitive phrasing there.

She leaned back and gave her eyes a rest. This issue of the paper was as useless and dull as the other one she'd checked. It was tough going, but there couldn't be too many more pages. She pushed on.

The next page was the Vivant section, which was largely devoted to coverage of a lot of kids celebrating their sixteenth birthday. Whoopie.

She cranked along to the Lifestyle section and suddenly grew much more interested. A picture at the top of the page had a hand-drawn circle around it. Drawn on the original newspaper or on the film? To find out, she lowered the film gate and slid the film out of the reader. But tilting it and holding it up to the overhead lights, she could see that the circle was drawn on the shiny side of the film.

She reloaded the film and studied the picture, which was of a small dance band consisting of three men and a woman. One man was posed with a guitar, another with his hands on the keyboard of one of those abbreviated pianos, and the third was at a set of drums. The girl, a pretty blonde, also with a guitar, was standing in front singing into a microphone.

According to the accompanying article, they were a group called the Heartbeats. All four worked at the same hospital; the drummer as a cardiology resident, the piano player as a respiratory therapist, the male guitarist as a lab tech, and the girl as an EKG tech. The article went on to describe how they'd met and how they managed their double lives.

Was this what she was meant to find? Was one of the Heartbeats the killer? Then she saw the connection . . . hearts again.

This had to be it. The killer was one of the members of this band. Probably not the girl; most likely, one of the other three.

Shouldering her bag, she went to the copy machine and made three copies of the picture and the article, then returned the film to the cabinet where she'd found it.

The copies of the newspaper photograph were not very good. Therefore, when she reached the office, she pulled out the phone book and looked up the *Times-Picayune*.

There were many numbers listed but none for the paper's library, where Terry Yardley had been transferred a few months earlier from the news photo desk, so she dialed Terry's old number and got them to transfer the call.

"Terry, this is Kit Franklyn."

"Why, honey, I thought you married that alligator farmer and moved away, it's been so long since I've heard from you."

"I know. It's terrible how friends can live so close and still lose touch. Have I forfeited any chance of a favor?"

"You want me to take that man off your hands?"

"Actually, I was hoping you might be able to get me some prints of a photograph that appeared in an old issue of the paper."

"Pooh. I'd rather have the man, but I'll see what I can do about the other. What issue we talking about?"

"May first, 1981. It was a photograph of a small dance band that appeared in the Lifestyle section."

"It'll take a few minutes for me to see if we have the negative. Give me your number and I'll call you right back."

While waiting for Terry's call, Kit reread the article accompanying the picture, her finger twirling a lock of her hair. When the call came, she snatched up the receiver.

"I've got the negative," Terry said. "And Photography says they can have some prints by three o'clock."

"Terry, you're terrific."

"How many prints and what size?"

"Three, and—how big can I get them and still have everything be sharp and clear?"

"I don't think I'd go eight-by-ten. They might be a little grainy. Let's say five-by-seven. What's up?"

"It's kind of a long story."

"Oh good. Is there sex in it?"

"Not that I see at the moment."

"Gossip?"

"Not really."

"Gee, Kit, you used to be more fun. When you get here, come up to the newsroom on the third floor. I'm way in back."

Kit had barely hung up when the phone rang again. It was Edna Gervais, at the Forensic meeting, telling her that someone had misplaced the restaurant guides and the ones on hand were going fast. Therefore, she put all other plans on hold and left for the tourist commission to get more.

BROUSSARD CLICKED the projector control and a slide appeared, showing him in shorts, at the top of a ladder, getting a kitten out of an oak tree in his yard. A ripple of laughter spread through the audience.

Not only had he *not* put the slide in there; he'd never even seen it before. Then he remembered.... It was last spring, the day Charlie Franks, the deputy medical examiner, had come over to return the rice cooker he'd let Frank's wife try before she bought one. Franks must have had a camera with him.

"Believe me," Broussard said, embarrassed that his concern for a helpless animal should be displayed so publicly, "I wasn't the one who put this slide in. But since it *is* in, you should know that I wasn't gettin' the cat *down;* I was puttin' him up there."

It was exactly the right thing to say and the crowd warmed to him even more than they had before. Near the back of the room, Franks shook his head in admiration of Broussard's ability to improvise under pressure. Sitting next to him, Kit, too, was impressed. Considering how slow and dull-witted he'd felt all morning, Broussard had even amazed himself.

Usually, he was so well prepared and so suited to this sort of thing, he could shift into automatic and glide through even an hour talk without a hitch. But today, he felt seconds away from total disaster, his mind sending out warnings of imminent shutdown. When he left one slide and proceeded to the next, he was sorely afraid he might not remember what he intended to say.

All because of those hairs... Something there wasn't right. Or maybe *he* wasn't right. God knows, this talk was going rotten. Somehow, he got to the end, his brain so numb, he barely remembered the trip. Surprisingly, there was much applause. His talk was the last one before the afternoon break and he headed directly for the foyer, wanting to be out of the room.

"Great save, Andy," Franks said, following him into the foyer.

Broussard turned and wagged a finger in Franks's grinning mug. "Charlie, I'm gonna get you for this."

"Apparently, you're forgetting that letter inviting me to give the plenary lecture at the international Forensic congress in Rio last year."

"I stopped you before you ordered your plane ticket."

"Now we're even."

"I don't think so. That letter was just between you and me. You pulled your shenanigan in public. And I was already barely keepin' my head above water. You nearly sank me."

"Didn't see you in any trouble from where I sat," Franks said.

"Me, neither," Kit echoed. "It was a great talk."

"Unprincipled, if you ask me," a voice said from behind Broussard.

He turned to confront a hefty fellow in horn-rimmed glasses who had a narrow mustache that he wore low on his lip, except where it rose in a small central triangle to meet his nose. He was dressed in a dark blue suit and vest laced with pinstripes and having lapels so wide, he looked like a Mafia lawyer from the forties. Actually, it was someone far worse: Jason Harvey—accompanied by Zin Fanelli.

"Unprincipled," Broussard said coldly. "In what way?"

"Getting sympathy by using that kitten as a prop. Oh, you're clever, I'll give you that. Pretending you had nothing to do with the slide and then putting that reverse spin on it. Clever but, as I said, unprincipled."

Charlie Franks stepped forward. "For your information, I—"

He was interrupted by Broussard's raised hand. "Guess I should give that some thought," Broussard said, "comin' as it does from such an expert on lack of principles."

Harvey let him have that one and shifted to another front. "I hear you're not having much success catching that killer. How many is it now . . . two? Soon to be three, according to the paper. I hope when that third one occurs, you don't have any trouble sleeping at night. Maybe if you didn't spend so much time thinking about ways to ingratiate yourself with the membership, you'd have learned something from the bodies the police could use. Unless, of course, you're in over your head, which I suppose is the case, since you have to call in Fleming for help. Fanelli here says you never were very good with knife wounds."

Fanelli's eyes widened and he began to shake his head in disavowal of Harvey's remark, but he had to stop when Harvey looked at him.

"I'll be interested in your paper Thursday," Harvey said. "I hope it can stand close scrutiny."

Harvey turned and walked away, leaving Franks with his fists clenched. "Where does a forensic whore like that get off criticizing anybody?" Franks said.

Broussard put his hand on Franks's shoulder. "It's okay, Charlie. We'll just consider the source and forget it. Now I'm goin' back inside and hear the next talk. You two comin'?"

Franks nodded, but Kit said, "Can't. I've got an appointment at the newspaper."

"We're gettin' up a group for dinner," Broussard said. "You should come."

"Where and when?"

"Lobby, by the escalator, at ten to six. Better be on time, 'cause we're gonna take the hotel shuttle and it won't wait."

EIGHT

KIT HAD NEVER BEEN to the newspaper offices and she soon wished she had obtained directions from Terry, for the city's expressways had chopped up Howard Avenue so badly she could not follow it directly to her destination. When she finally saw the lighthouse-like clock tower with *TIMES-PICAYUNE* lettered across it, she felt a flood of relief.

Two things impressed her upon entering the light, airy lobby: the extremely tall escalators against the right and left walls and an unusual sweet smell that she concluded was likely printer's ink. Following Terry's instructions, she took the escalator to the third floor and found her way to the newsroom, a football-sized space divided into a hundred cubicles by partitions so low that you could see the entire operation from any position. It was not particularly noisy, but Kit still felt that she would have trouble concentrating without real walls around her, a longing for the safety of the womb, perhaps.

She gave her name to the woman at the reception desk, stated the reason for her visit, and was waved inside, where she followed the dirty blue-green carpet through the heart of the newsroom to the library. Happily, she did not run into Nick Lawson.

Terry Yardley was at her desk going over a pile of file folders with clippings in them. Even women who prefer slacks will occasionally wear a skirt, but to Kit's recollection, Terry Yardley never did, which led Kit to suspect that she was hiding something. But it would have taken a man a long time to catch on to that, so there must have been some other explanation for her perpetual lack of male companionship. A good possibility was her perfume, which was so strong that after a few minutes with her, you could taste it. Seeing Kit, she stood up and put her hands on her hips. "Girl, you look so good."

"So do you."

Terry patted her tucked hairdo, from which several pencils protruded. "I'm tryin' the honey blond look. Ash blond got me nothin'."

"How have you been?"

"I'll sum it up for you. I just about got enough saved for a boob job and now I'm gettin' afraid to have it done . . . all that stuff on TV."

"Can you even *get* implants anymore?"

"Some kinds, but I dunno. . . ."

"So take a trip with your money."

"When you come back from a trip, your money's gone and you still look crappy in a sweater. But I've been thinkin'. . .what do you suppose a boob job looks like when you get old, when you got this wrinkled little body and these big firm headlights? That could look real weird. I mean, I wouldn't want some mortician callin' all his friends over for a look." Her eyes went to Kit's chest.

"They're real," Kit said, reading Terry's mind.

"You're lucky." Suddenly, she clapped her hands together. "Enough about tits. You wanted some prints." She opened a drawer in her desk, took out three photographs, and handed them to Kit, who looked at each of them and said, "Terry, they couldn't be better. I really owe you."

"I like bein' owed."

"Good, then maybe I can add some to my account. What can you tell me about Nick Lawson?"

Terry's eyes widened with pleasure at the question. She motioned Kit into the chair beside her desk, leaned over, and said in a conspiratorial voice, "He's a good-lookin' guy, you know that, sittin' in his red two-seater, the top down, Fos-

ter Grants tilted onto his head, that 'go to hell' ponytail . . .
Heady stuff, for some women. Actually, I'm surprised he's
still alive.''

''Why's that?'' Kit said, Terry's perfume faintly bitter in
her mouth.

''I figured some female would have shot him or he'd have
killed himself with the crazy stuff he does.''

''Details, Yardley, details.''

''He's a real rake, usually stringin' two or three women
along at a time. There's a couple I could name here at the
paper who'd like to put his balls in a nutcracker.''

''Not you?''

''Much as I'm attracted to toxic men, that's one I've
managed to avoid.''

''What do you mean, 'crazy stuff he does'?''

''He's an adrenaline junkie. Always jumpin' out of air-
planes or white-water kayakin' or some other nutty activity. Last year, he was out for a month with an allergic
reaction to a shot they gave him when he got bit at a Texas
rattlesnake-baggin' contest. If that happened to any normal person, they'd have learned a lesson. . . . No, that's not
true, any normal person wouldn't have been baggin' snakes
in the first place.''

Kit had asked about Lawson out of mild curiosity, her
interest piqued by his recent articles on the killer she was
chasing and their run-in at the first murder. Now, with what
Terry had just said, a crazy idea entered Kit's head.

Terry punched at the side of her head with her finger.
''Somethin' very wrong up here with that guy, which I guess
explains why he stays in the cop shop.''

''Cop shop?''

''Police beat. He could make a lot more money coverin'
business or politics.'' Her eyes narrowed and she shifted to
a slightly mocking tone. ''Why all the interest in Lawson?

You wouldn't be after his bod would you... 'cause, like I said, he's—''

"Hardly. He's been putting a lot of privileged information in his articles about those murders and we'd like to know where he's getting it.''

Terry's brow wrinkled. "Can't help you there, 'cause I don't know. And I'm glad. 'Cause if I did, it'd put me in kind of a spot, since I work for the paper too, know what I mean?''

"Sure. I hope you don't feel I've tricked you or anything. That wasn't my intent. I should have explained the situation before quizzing you. I'm sorry.''

"That's okay. I didn't say anything that'd hurt the paper, did I?''

"Not at all. There's a Forensic convention in town, so I'm going to be pretty busy this week. But how about I take you to lunch next Tuesday... and no questions about the paper?''

"I'd like that.''

Walking to her car, Kit tried to talk herself out of the wild idea ricocheting through her brain. Lawson was an adrenaline junkie. Where most people hated the racing heart, the flushed face, and the wet palms that fear brought on, Lawson loved it. She knew the type. They aren't suicidal. They don't want to die. They just can't live without risk. Was it possible that he...

No.... It was ridiculous to think...

But was it ridiculous? Was it really so farfetched to believe that Nick Lawson might be the killer? That would explain his presence at both scenes and how he knew so much. Then, too, there were the Scrabble tiles. That clue had led directly to the place where he worked. Maybe he'd run out of dangerous stunts and could no longer get the rush he needed from things he'd already tried. This could be the ultimate risk, playing games with the police with his life at stake. And it wouldn't be over in a few minutes. Every day, there'd be the possibility he'd be caught. The risk wasn't confined to a few minutes; it would exist at some level every minute of every day, spiking each time he passed a cop.

Before leaving the building, Kit stopped at the reception desk in the lobby and spent a few minutes with a phone book. In her car, she pulled her city map from the glove compartment, studied it for several minutes, then drove away, leaving a tiny amount of rubber on the asphalt.

THE ADDRESS SHE'D FOUND for Nick Lawson turned out to be a small two-story apartment building in Harahan called the Kitura. Lawson's decision to remain in the cop shop, coupled with his taste for adventure, apparently left him without much housing money, for the Kitura was a drab and desolate place. There were ten apartments: five up and five down. The front doors of the upper five opened onto a covered walkway that functioned as the roof for a similar walk serving the lower apartments.

At each end of the building, there was a simple black metal staircase leading to the upper level. The building was clothed in a nice old brick with pleasing soft edges, but the trim and the doors were a hideous shade of turquoise. Landscaping was practically nonexistent—a dozen or so tiny boxwoods against the slab foundation and a foot-wide strip of brown grass between the walk in front of the building and its parking lot. Scattered over the grounds were bags and papers from a variety of fast-food joints.

There were two cars in the parking lot, neither of them red. She followed the drive around to the rear where there were a few more lined parking spaces and a blue Dumpster. Wherever Lawson was, he wasn't home.

Kit felt that she'd uncovered some tantalizing stuff and she longed to find Broussard and discuss it. At the same time, she was reluctant to do so, mostly because of the supposedly inspirational Babe Ruth anecdotes he dispensed when he thought you'd made an ass of yourself and needed bucking up. So far, she had been Ruthed twice and she did not want it to happen again. Then, too, she was not unaware that her desire to run to him with some half-developed ideas was that same old desire for a pat on the head. Ugggh.

"ARE WE ALL TOGETHER?" Kit said, astonished at the number of people gathered by the escalator.

"Leo invited some of his students and they invited some of *their* friends," Broussard explained.

"Hope you don't mind," Fleming said.

"Not at all. It'll be fun."

Charlie Franks was standing by two older men she didn't recognize. One of them was looking at her as though they knew each other.

"Hello, Kit," he said, extending his hand. "How are you liking that house of yours?"

Ah...of course. She took his hand. "Dr. Brooks. It's good to see you again."

"Forget that Dr. stuff. Call me Brookie."

"All right."

"I'm not convinced you can. Show me."

It was difficult to call someone she barely knew by such a familiar name, but he gave her no choice. "Brookie... As for the house, I love it." Broussard had told her about Brooks's recent loss and she considered saying something appropriate. But he seemed in such good spirits, she decided not to bring it up.

"I don't believe you know Hugh Greenwood," Broussard said. "Hugh, this is Kit Franklyn, my suicide investigator."

"A pleasure," Greenwood said, his faintly scarred face giving no indication of pleasure.

"That's it...everybody's here," Fleming announced. "There's already a full load out by the shuttle, so we'll have to walk."

The students did not wait for the senior members of the party to lead the way, but went for the door in a happy noisy rush. On Poydras, they turned toward the Quarter like lemmings.

The dozen or so students moved as a unit, hanging together so all could hear whatever was said. The others paired off: Charlie Franks with Hugh Greenwood; Kit and Broussard; Leo Fleming and Crandall Brooks bringing up the rear.

Kit had obtained three prints of the Heartbeats from Terry Yardley, one for herself, one for Broussard, and one for Gatlin. Despite having already decided that it would be wise to keep them to herself until she'd done some more legwork, she'd brought Broussard's along in her bag, putting it in an envelope with his copy of the newspaper article.

"You know what tonight is?" Broussard said.

"What?"

"The first murder occurred early Saturday morning and the second, early Monday, a two-day interval. And this is Tuesday...."

"You think we're due for number three?"

"He's a guy who likes patterns, so if there's gonna be a third one, I'd say it's worth considerin'."

Kit had been so occupied with the Scrabble puzzle, she hadn't given any thought to when the killer might strike again. Broussard's concern seemed reasonable.

"Gatlin taking any precautions?"

"He's got some men out in plainclothes and he's set up a quick-response plan to blanket any area where they think he's been."

Greenwood turned and began walking backward, his hands in his pockets. "The use of a knife is a real art," he said. "I once saw some Turkish knife fighters in training, and I swear they were poetry in motion. With guns, there's no real involvement in what happens. They require nothing of the operator. You can drop it and it'll go off. But it takes knowledge and skill to use a knife properly. In hand-to-hand combat, when you strike a lethal blow with a knife, it makes you want to throw your head back and howl like an animal. There's no greater feeling in the world—not sex, not a good bowel movement, nothing."

Greenwood faced forward and continued walking, leaving Kit and Charlie to exchange surprised looks. His remark had no effect on Broussard. Kit looked back to see if Fleming and Brooks had heard it, and Brooks said, "If I had to die at the hands of a killer, I'd rather it be by a bullet than a knife. There's something about being penetrated by a blade...I don't know...maybe it's the comparative size of the invading object, or maybe, like Hugh said, it's the idea that with a knife there's an intelligence guiding it all the way, making the whole thing more personal." He shivered. "Is that a typical reaction or just me? What does everyone else think?... Kit?"

"Great choices. But I agree, a knife is worse."

"Andy?"

"I don't like either one."

"The point is to choose," Brooks said.

"Wouldn't happen either way," Broussard said. "'Cause I'd take his weapon away from him and make him eat it."

"I think this man is hungry," Brooks said good-naturedly, patting Broussard on the back.

A couple of intersections later, the group crossed Poydras and headed for Canal Street. Three blocks shy of Canal, the students stopped to point and giggle at the displays in the window of a T-shirt shop. They seemed to particularly like a shirt titled THE HAPPY FISHERMAN, in which a submerged fish had hold of a certain part of a wading fisherman's erect anatomy.

Two of the students were female. One, a cool blonde with a perfect complexion, was wearing blue slacks and a short-sleeved blue-and-white-striped sweater that showed off a great figure. The other, a brown-haired girl-next-door, also with fine skin and a beautiful smile, was dressed in baggy jeans and a loose pullover. Of all those gathered around the window, she seemed to be getting the biggest kick out of the risqué T-shirts. She had an ingenuous bubbly energy that Kit liked very much, but it was strange indeed to think that before too long she would be an instrument by which sadistic killers got what they deserved.

The attraction of the T-shirt shop allowed some time to reconnoiter.

"Where we headed?" Fleming asked.

"How about Tortorici's?" Franks suggested.

Brooks shook his head. "Can't. It's closed."

"No it isn't," Greenwood said. "I had dinner there last night, so I'd rather try somewhere else."

"I wouldn't mind goin' back to Felix's for more crawfish," Fleming said. "That okay with everybody else?"

Getting no objection, Fleming looked at Broussard. "It's on Bourbon, right?"

Broussard nodded. "A block off Canal."

"Okay, Bourbon Street, everybody."

In Felix's, the six senior members of the party were shown to a large round table near the front door, while the students were put nearby at two square tables pulled together to accommodate their number. The arrangement struck Kit as similar to the Franklyn family Thanksgiving back in Speculator, New York—the adults at the main table, the kids off by themselves.

After they ordered and were brought their drinks, Crandall Brooks asked Kit if she knew Otto Schatz. She didn't.

"He was the prosecutor's psychiatrist at the Wilhoit trial," Brooks explained. "We had lunch together today and he told me that as a kid Wilhoit used to dissect road kills, which came as quite a shock, because I used to do the same thing."

"Yeah," Greenwood said, putting down his beer after a long sip, "but he was masturbating while *he* did it. That's the difference." He paused, then added, "There *was* a difference, wasn't there?"

"Hugh, you're a crude man," Brooks said.

"But I'm not infatuated with road kills." Hand cradling his beer, he looked at Broussard. "Now, Andy, let's talk about *your* serial killer. What's being done?"

"Everything that can be."

"So he hasn't made a big mistake yet?"

"Remains to be seen."

"I take that as a no, because if it had been a *big* mistake, I don't think you'd have to wait to find out. So it was a small mistake or *no* mistake, which means the hairs you found didn't help."

"Hugh, you're havin' a conversation with yourself," Fleming said.

Ignoring his remark, Greenwood turned to Kit. "Have you thought about going on TV with a sympathetic piece about the victims? If it's done well enough, it may make your killer commit suicide."

Brooks dismissed his comment with a wave of the hand. "That might work if he had remorse over the killings. I don't think he does."

"Neither do I," Kit said. "And beyond that, it would be immoral."

Greenwood's eyes widened. His scars made interpretation of any of his expressions unreliable, but Kit now thought he definitely looked amused. "Immoral?" he repeated. "It's immoral not to try everything and anything you can to stop him."

"I just have a problem with that approach," Kit said. "Besides, even in cases where it might work, it's unpredictable. Sometimes it backfires and sets him off."

"Apparently, he's going to go off at least twice more, anyway. Have you thought about what he's building up to? Maybe he's going to pop up at some mall and slash his way through the crowd."

Kit shook her head. "You're confusing two different psychological types."

Greenwood snorted derisively. "And if it happens, there'll simply be a new subtype in the psychology literature."

Kit was about to reply when the brown-haired female student approached Fleming with a package wrapped as a gift.

"Dr. Fleming...this is from all of us..." She gestured to the student table. "To you on your birthday."

Judging from the look of admiration in her eyes, Kit concluded that Fleming must be a fine mentor.

"I'm touched, Diane," Fleming said. He looked toward the student table. "So much so that I won't hold it against any of you for remindin' me I'm another damn year older."

That brought laughs from the students.

"Open it," Diane urged.

The package was about the right width and length for a tie. Fleming opened it fastidiously, carefully loosening and unfolding the paper as though it was a Dead Sea Scroll. He removed the lid and smiled.

"Show everybody," Diane said.

He reached in the box and took out a wicked-looking serrated knife, which he waved at the student table, prompting applause and whistles.

"I have a saw collection on my office wall," he explained to those seated at his table. "And a serrated knife is actually a type of saw." He looked back at the students. "Thank you all very much. It's a fine gift."

The other patrons in the room stared at the noisy group with great curiosity and Kit was struck by the fact that whatever theories they might have about who these people were, they wouldn't begin to guess the truth.

As Diane went back to her colleagues, Greenwood said, "So, Leo, how old are you?"

"Old enough that if my hair doesn't quit droppin' out, I'm gonna look like one of those damn carnival Kewpie dolls."

The waitress arrived with a large round tray loaded with crawfish and other Cajun dishes. When it was all distributed, conversation flagged while they ate. Kit had bypassed the crawfish, choosing instead a spicy jambalaya that, after a few bites, made her mouth feel as if it was harboring a smoldering grass fire.

This proved to be a mild harbinger of what was to come, for her lips were soon an open conflagration. In a place that served such food, there was no greater sin than to allow a guest to run out of liquid to quench the flames. Their waitress understood this and deftly kept the fires from consuming her tip.

After the meal, Broussard, Kit, and Franks decided to catch the shuttle back to the hotel. Everyone else wanted to stay in the Quarter a while. The shuttle pickup was near the Jax Building on Decatur, which meant the group remained intact for a few blocks down Bourbon. This time, Kit found herself paired with Crandall Brooks.

"Andy told me about your little dog," Brooks said. "Despicable thing for someone to do. How is he?"

"When I first took him in, the vet said he'd be fine, but this morning he had a relapse. Now I don't know what to think."

"I have a vet friend here. I wonder if he might be the one you're using."

"Dr. Samuels, at the South Carrollton Animal Hospital?"

Brooks shook his head. "Nope. Not him."

Brooks's interest in Lucky made Kit feel guilty that she'd not acknowledged his wife's death. "I was extremely sorry to hear about..."

"I know," he said. "When I first arrived, I thought that coming might have been a mistake. But it wasn't. It's been a big help. Being with all of you...seeing the life in those young people. I've drawn from that. And I'm stronger for being here. So don't you worry about me. I'll be fine."

Behind them, Kit heard Diane say to her companion, "So when they found her brother and x-rayed him, the whole side of *his* face was full of shotgun pellets, too. Isn't that totally *wild*?"

NINE

AT THE HOTEL, Kit said good night to Charlie Franks, then turned to Broussard. "You'll call me if anything happens?"

"Absolutely."

"Gatlin has your number?"

"All taken care of."

Realizing that Broussard and Gatlin had managed for a long time before she ever arrived on the scene, she said, "Sorry, I'm just really into this one."

"I know what you mean. Part of me hopes he *won't* go out tonight... that he'll just disappear and we'll be rid of him. But another part of me wants him to go again and give us one more crack at him, 'cause the more he works, the more likely he is to make the mistake that'll do him in. It won't even have to be a big mistake. It's not the big thing that sends you over the cliff, but the untied shoelace. I want him to make that mistake."

Kit was taken aback by the passion in Broussard's voice. Obviously, he, too, was into this one.

Heading for her car, Kit congratulated herself for resisting the temptation to give Broussard his copy of the article and picture of the Heartbeats. A scant second or two later, it struck her that she should *not* be going home. There was a potentially more productive place she should be.

On the way, she thought about what a long shot she was playing. If the killer *was* going out tonight to do number three, he likely would be nervous, jumpy, unable to sit still—which meant he wouldn't likely remain at home until the time came, but would be out somewhere already, walking or driving.

The sight of a red sports car in the parking lot of Nick Lawson's apartment building brought mixed feelings. If she was right about the murderer's mental state prior to a kill and Lawson was her man, he shouldn't be home. But all that was guesswork. Maybe he was cooler than she imagined. Then it occurred to her that the car might not even belong to Lawson; after all, she'd never seen him in it. This concern left her when she looked at the plate: NICK 1. There was also a light on in Lawson's apartment, the third from the left on the upper level.

Across the street from the apartment building, there was an auto-parts store with a tall sign made of a half dozen orange fifty-five-gallon drums welded in a zigzag pattern to a metal pole. Just the thing to spruce up a neighborhood. But its empty parking lot was an ideal place from which to keep an eye on Lawson's car.

She parked, checked the doors to make sure they were locked, then took her Mace canister off her key ring and put the keys back in the ignition. Then she waited, her finger on the button of the canister in case passersby got any ideas. She had been there only a few minutes when she felt the first small stirrings of her bladder. This was a problem without a good solution. She recalled seeing a Burger King about three blocks away but did not want to leave her post.

A few minutes later, a car pulled into the apartment parking lot and a woman in a white uniform got out and went to the trunk, where she removed two bags of groceries and struggled up the steps with them. At the apartment to the right of Lawson's, she rang the bell with her elbow and the door was opened by a little girl who hugged the woman's knees. Most likely, a single mother and her daughter just trying to get by.

Over the next hour, there was a steady procession of visitors to the apartment nearest the left stairs on the lower level. But no one was ever invited in. There was always a brief conversation at the door, what appeared to be a quick handshake, and that was it. They were so obviously drug transactions that Kit wondered how they got away with it, but then she realized there were probably far more dealers in the city than cops to catch them.

Surveillance was a huge bore, a fact that made her keenly aware of the increasingly urgent messages from her bladder. Burger King was only three blocks away. She could make a quick run and be back in ten minutes. It was a gamble, but at the moment it didn't seem—

A scream suddenly filled the car, a shriek from her own throat. In thinking about the Burger King, she'd turned to look in the direction it lay and saw something that almost made the trip unnecessary; a scant few inches away was a face pressed against the side window.

Recoiling as much as possible in a bucket seat, she screamed, "What do you want? Go away."

Amphibious eyes stared at her from a matt of greasy hair that parted around a pitted nose, permitting lips the color of spoiled meat to flatten against the glass. In the dark space between the lips, yellow chisels tried to gnaw through to her.

She flashed on a childhood incident when her father had bought her an aquarium and put one huge snail in with the goldfish. Her interest had lasted only until the snail had crept onto the front of the tank and she saw its rabbit teeth and rippling mouth. She had fled from it, screaming, and from that moment would not go near it. Now it had come to her.

She held up the Mace. "This is tear gas. I'll spray you if you don't leave. Go away!" She pounded on the glass with the palm of her hand, which made the face begin to move. It shifted up to the right corner of the window and slid horizontally across to the other side, lips stretching with the drag.

"Go away!" She pounded again on the glass, aiming her palm at the ugly nose. The face left the glass and she felt better, until it reappeared on the windshield when its owner climbed onto the hood.

She turned on the wipers and the one on the passenger side began to clack over the glass. The other hit the face a frail blow and jammed against it. God. Now he had his tongue pressed against the glass, the pressure flattening it into a grotesque pink spatula.

She shuddered and closed her eyes in disgust, but that was worse. With her eyes closed, there was no telling what he was doing.

She pulled the lever for the windshield washers and a small jet of fluid wet his beard, making him pull back and wipe the spot with his hand. Without waiting to see what he would do next, she started the engine, put it in reverse, and slowly backed up a few feet to let him know he better climb down, which he did, but not before putting his thumb against his nose and wiggling his fingers at her.

Free of him, she backed up quickly and stopped fifteen yards away, from where she watched him stagger off into the darkness. Shifting her eyes from the drunk to the parking lot across the street, she saw that Nick Lawson's car was gone.

BROUSSARD LAY IN BED, a lemon ball in each cheek, his head propped up with two pillows, a used copy of *The Sackett's* in front of him. When he finished this one, he'd only have thirty-nine more to go and he'd have read every novel Louis L'Amour ever wrote. Considering the day he'd had, it didn't seem excessive to expect to relax and read a little before going to sleep. But the ruckus next door was making that impossible. Reluctantly, he got up, slipped on his silk bathrobe and his slippers, and went into the hall.

Surprisingly, his knock was answered by Leo Fleming, with a beer in his hand. "Hey, Andy, c'mon in."

"Anybody else in there wearin' a bathrobe?" Broussard growled.

"Actually, I'm the only person *not* in one."

"You're probably gonna feel lousy tomorrow."

"It's my birthday."

"*Yesterday* was your birthday. It just turned tomorrow. How about pullin' the plug on this shindig?"

"Did I mention that this was the annual anthropology wingding?"

Broussard groaned. Every year, the anthropologists threw a loud party in one of their rooms, usually ignoring all requests to quiet down until they were on the verge of being ejected from the hotel. He had remembered to ask for a room no higher than the seventh floor, the highest a firehouse hook and ladder could reach, but he'd neglected to specify a room at least four away from any anthropologist. To expect them to quiet down simply because they were disturbing him was quite hopeless. "Well, just do what you can to keep the inmates from destroyin' the asylum," he said with a sigh, going back to his room.

The melee went on unabated another thirty minutes or so, then miraculously there was silence. Too tired to keep reading, Broussard put his book on the nightstand and clicked off the light.

IT WOULD BE another fifteen minutes before Mike Haskins, patrolman with the harbor police, joined him for his meal break, but Tim Bouchet was so hungry, he unscrewed the lid to his thermos and poured some chicken soup into it, wishing he'd not said those things to his wife, Maggie. But Christ, it was just askin' too much, both of them with full-time jobs and now her and that night course. He never saw her anymore and the house was *filthy*.

From his truck deep in the shadows, he could clearly see all of the *Natchez* and the *John James Audubon,* but his other responsibility, the *Cotton Blossom,* was anchored upriver about fifty yards, a viewing promontory of the Riverwalk and its railing blocking his view of all but her upper parts.

On most nights, a fair number of tourists wandered down to the *Natchez* for a look and occasionally a couple might do some making out before they noticed his truck, and that helped the time to pass. But tonight, things were really dead. There had been that gimpy old couple around ten and nobody else. He put the cup to his lips and sampled some soup.

English Lit, for Christ's sake. What is she ever gonna do with that? She don't even read anything written by Americans.

Seeing a figure come up the steps to the Riverwalk down by the gazebo, he put his soup on the dash and picked up his binoculars. Through them, he saw a man with a briefcase pause on the Riverwalk, look around, then stroll toward the gazebo. He watched until his view was hindered by the temporary toolshed the city had set up on the near side of the gazebo, then lowered the binoculars and reached for his soup. Some of that stuff she was readin' didn't even make sense. Like that crap by John Donne. Whoever heard of poetry that didn't rhyme?

He went back to the binoculars and watched the man who'd come up onto the Riverwalk go onto the promontory that blocked his view of the *Cotton Blossom.* The guy leaned on the rail with both hands and stared at the barges pushing their loads through the black water. Bouchet himself liked to do that when he first took the job, but now, except for sometimes when he'd shoot dock rats with a slingshot and ice cubes, he mostly stayed in his truck and listened to the radio.

Another guy, carrying a folded newspaper under his arm, came down the Riverwalk, opposite from the direction Bouchet was facing. He wasn't strolling, like the first guy, but was moving briskly.

Maybe he should just put his foot down, *demand* that she give it up. 'Course she don't take to that approach too good. He did that, she'd probably sign up for *two* courses next time. It was bad that the house was dirty, but even worse, she'd been actin' like she thought he was... dull. Dull for Christ's sake, as if he hadn't bowled 250 for the first time in his life last week. And she talked like it was nothin'. That simply ain't normal.

As his view of the fellow who had just passed became partially obscured by the supporting poles of the canopied staging area for the riverboats, Bouchet's CB radio crackled to life. "Hairless, this is Father Joe. They don't make a jock that small, so you'll have to play without one."

Grinning, Bouchet turned off his portable Sony and reached for the CB mike. "Father Joe, there's a guy here wants to talk to you about some altar boys in Cleveland. What should I tell him?"

"The truth, son, the truth...that Father Joe drowned last year in the baptismal pool. Will be there in ten minutes, so work fast."

No two ways about it, Bouchet thought, grinning as he hung up the mike, Haskins was plain *nuts*.

He turned on the Sony and fiddled with the dial, trying to get rid of the hiss it was making whenever a singer used a word with *s* in it. He didn't get it perfect, but it improved to where the sound didn't make him want to smash it on the cement. Probably, he should start thinking about rounding up a replacement.

He looked up and saw the fellow who had been walking fast now coming his way. This time, he wasn't carrying anything. But he was walking even faster than before. At the little building where they sell riverboat tickets during the day, he turned and headed down the riverfront extension of Toulouse Street, toward Decatur.

Bouchet raised his binoculars and looked toward the promontory. The fellow who was standing there earlier was no longer around. Shit. He should have been paying attention instead of fooling around with Haskins and the radio. And the city needed to get that damn toolshed out of the way. Very unlikely that the guy had gone onto the *Cotton Blossom,* but he ought to check.

He pulled his flashlight from under the seat, reached for his pistol in the glove compartment, and got out of the truck. Shoving the gun in his back pocket, he set out for the *Cotton Blossom.* When he reached the gazebo, he saw the fellow he was looking for, bent over, holding his stomach like he was having cramps.

"Hey, buddy, you okay?"

The fellow groaned and Bouchet stepped up and touched him lightly on the shoulder. "You need a doctor?"

He tried to raise himself but could get his eyes no higher than Bouchet's chest. "Maybe you should lie down so I can—"

Suddenly, the fellow was draped all over him. For a split second, Bouchet thought the guy had collapsed, but then he felt a blow to his midsection, like the guy had slugged him. He felt a peculiar stirring sensation deep inside.

The fellow stepped back and looked at Bouchet, a cool face with no emotion in it. Puzzled, Bouchet's eyes moved downward, to see why he felt so strange. At practically the same instant that he saw the blue towel wrapped around the fellow's hand and the knife, its blade a dull red in the dim light, the image began to fog over like a bathroom mirror when the shower's on. Though he was sinking to the ground, he felt as if a hand was pulling him upward. As his life poured into the sac around his heart, he said one word: "Maggie."

TEN

FROM ALL APPEARANCES, Mike Haskins was a good cop—trim physique, sharp creases in his uniform, well groomed, although Gatlin thought he'd do well to ease up on the shellac or whatever it was that held his hair so stiffly.

"I talked to him on his CB radio at two-twenty," Haskins said. "And I pulled up at his truck at exactly two-thirty, but he wasn't there. It couldn't have been more than another two or three minutes before I found him.... I checked his pulse, then I went to my car and called in.... Ten lousy minutes...how can something like this happen in just ten lousy minutes?"

It was a question that Gatlin had often asked himself over the years, but he, too, was still looking for the answer. "I know it doesn't help much," he said, "but your quick call-in could help nail the guy who did it."

Haskins looked up, his eyes swimming. "You're right. It doesn't help much."

From over Haskins's shoulder, Gatlin saw Broussard coming toward them. "Stick around, will you? I may have a few more questions."

Haskins nodded and slowly walked back to his patrol car down near the *Natchez*, head hanging.

"Two letters this time?" Broussard asked, out of breath.

"Take a look. Ray, hold up a minute, will you, so Andy can get in there."

Jamison, the police photographer, dropped his camera to his chest. "I'm finished anyway, unless you want something exotic. How you doing, Andy?"

"Gettin' by, Ray, gettin' by."

"You two enjoy yourself. I'm going home and play spoons with the wife."

Gatlin and Broussard exchanged a look of incomprehension at Jamison's remark and Gatlin stood aside so the old pathologist could see the body, which lay faceup on the bricks of the Riverwalk, one lidless eye examining the low-slung clouds overhead. On the victim's chest was a section of newspaper with two Scrabble tiles on it; a *K* and an *O* . . . and more. Also on the newspaper was a bloody knife.

"Why the gift?" Gatlin asked, echoing the question running through Broussard's mind.

"If this was the fourth victim," Broussard said, "I'd guess it was a going-away present. But now, I dunno. . . ."

Broussard put his bag down on the bricks, got out his padded wooden block, and knelt by the body. He felt for a pulse at the neck and said, "He's officially dead."

Gatlin looked at his watch and jotted in his little notebook. "We know almost exactly when it happened," he said. "Friend of his on the harbor police was in radio contact with him ten minutes before he found him like this. Died without ever getting to his gun."

"He's armed?"

"Had a pistol in his back pocket. Killer probably never even knew it."

Broussard played his penlight onto the Scrabble tiles and bent to look at them. What he saw erased the gnawing self-doubts he'd been having. "There's another hair," he said, looking up.

"I know," Gatlin replied. "One hair could be a chance occurrence, two . . . still could be chance, but three?"

"He's leavin' 'em on purpose," Broussard said, shamefully excited over this discovery. "That's why they haven't added up to anything."

"I don't like being toyed with," Gatlin said grimly.

Broussard got to his feet, breathing hard. "I do," he said, "and so should you. Every little thing he does like this is a product of who he is. The more he plays with us, the more he gives us to work with."

Broussard was no longer tired, but felt energized, for now he saw the killer more clearly. He glanced at the face of the body on the bricks, regretting that it had taken another life to bring him to this better understanding. And he vowed that there would not be a number four.

"Which brings us back to the knife," Gatlin said. "Why leave it if he's going to need it again?"

"Here's Kit," Broussard said. "Let's ask her."

"Ask me what?" Kit said, hurrying from the steps leading to the riverfront extension of St. Louis Street. Hesitantly, she looked past the two men, at the body, and her face paled. Another memory to store. "Who is he?"

"Riverboat security guard," Gatlin said. "We got a break this time. He was found by a harbor cop minutes after it happened. We got men all over the area interviewing and taking names of everybody on foot."

"Let's hope he didn't make it to his car," Kit said, feeling this death more keenly than either of the others, for had she not let Nick Lawson get away earlier, this might never have happened.

"Doc, you in there?"

Gatlin had said something to her that had been lost in her thoughts about Lawson. "Sorry. What did you say?"

"He left the knife. We were wondering why."

She looked again at the body and wished she hadn't. "Did you read Nick Lawson's article after the second murder?" she asked.

"Every word."

"Remember how he mentioned that Leo Fleming had been brought in as a consultant?"

Gatlin nodded, wondering where she was going with this.

"It's almost as if the killer knew what we learned from Fleming . . . that it was a serrated knife. Now, he's giving us the knife. . . . It *is* serrated?"

Gatlin nodded.

"He's given us the knife to show us it won't help."

"We got another hair, too."

"Another one . . . that seems like—"

"He's leaving them on purpose. Yeah, we noticed."

"Lieutenant."

They all turned at the voice.

"Andy, Kit, this is Mike Haskins," Gatlin said, "the patrolman who found the body. What is it, Mike?"

"I just remembered . . . when I was on Decatur on my way here, I saw a guy cross the street at St. Louis, coming from this direction. He was a little taller than average, with a black mustache and straight black hair. He was wearing a brown-checked sport coat and brown slacks and was carrying an oxblood briefcase. And he was clearly in a hurry."

Kit relaxed a little. If that had been the killer, she was wrong about Lawson.

"Mind if I take those letters back to my office?" Broussard said.

"Now?"

"No way I can get back to sleep. And I want to see that hair. I'll take the knife too, if you like and see what Leo makes of it. You can check it for prints later, though I doubt you'll find any."

"Do that."

Broussard put on a pair of rubber gloves, whose pungent odor mixed with the faint smell of creosote in the air. He put the Scrabble tiles and the knife in separate plastic bags from his forensic kit, then secured a paper bag over each of the victim's hands.

Wearing cotton gloves, Gatlin picked up the newspaper and carefully folded it.

"What paper is it?" Kit asked.

Gatlin held it up to the light filtering down from a pole overhead. "Friday's. Why?"

"No reason."

He looked at her curiously for a second, then indicated to the ambulance attendants lounging at the river guardrail that they could load the body.

"What say we get together and kick around whatever we got at ten o'clock?" Gatlin said.

Broussard shook his head. "Can't. I'm in court tomorrow mornin' and I'll need time to get Leo's opinion of the knife. One-thirty'd be better."

With some doubt cast over her idea about Lawson, Kit decided to keep it to herself a while longer. There being nothing further for her to do, she went back to her car. While still several yards from it, she saw through the rear window that someone was sitting in the front passenger seat. With a half dozen cops nearby protecting the crime scene, she approached her car more boldly than she would have had they not been there. Instead of going to the driver's side, she veered to the right to see who the devil it was that thought so little of private property.

She recognized him even before he turned to look at her: Nick Lawson. He rolled down the window.

"You really should lock your car when you leave it."

"What are you doing in there?"

"Waiting for you. Get in."

"No. You come out here."

He opened the door and Kit backed up further than was strictly necessary to get out of the way.

"Why are you so jumpy?" he asked, getting out and closing the door.

"I'm not. Now tell me what you want."

He looked back at the stretcher being loaded. "Is that number three?"

Kit did not respond.

"Of course it is," he said. "Why else would *you* be here?"

"I suppose *you* were just driving by and saw all the action."

"Believe it or not, that's exactly what happened this time. Not that I wasn't expecting something."

"I'm not going to tell you anything," Kit said. "So you might as well forget it."

Lawson gave her a big smile and raised the spiral pad and manila folder in his left hand. From the folder he removed a glossy picture and showed it to her. "What's this all about?"

Kit felt her jaw drop. It was a copy of the picture Terry Yardley had printed for her. "Where'd you get that?" She reached for it, but Lawson pulled it back, grinning broadly.

"You didn't think you could come into my territory and get away with something like this without me knowing about it, did you?"

"Actually, I don't think about you at all," Kit said, folding her arms in front of her.

"Not even a little?" Lawson coaxed.

"Not at all," she responded in measured tones.

The sly expression he always wore left his face and Kit was surprised to see that under it, he wasn't bad-looking. "I don't enjoy making enemies," he said, omitting the bantering tone he'd been using. "I'd much rather have friends, and I was hoping we could declare a truce ... maybe help each other. I've got a lot of contacts in the city and I sometimes hear things you might find useful. So I was thinking that we could sort of work together. I wouldn't expect you to tell me anything you considered sensitive. Just help me out with the other things. And to show you I'm willing to reciprocate, I'll tell you how I got the picture."

He waited briefly for Kit to answer, then forged ahead. "I was in the photo lab when Terry called down to inquire about it and ask for some prints. The lab is on speaker phone and she mentioned the ME's office in connection with the request. Then later, I saw you at Terry's desk. So I just put two and two together. Does it have anything to do with this case?"

Kit's mind sorted through the implications of what Lawson had said. If he was the killer, he was simply pumping her to find out how far she'd followed the clues he'd been leaving. If he wasn't the killer, he was merely being Nick Lawson. Either way, he wasn't going to get anything.

"You're a clever man. You figure it out," she said.

Lawson's sly look returned. "I'd hoped we could reach an understanding. But apparently that's not to be. So I guess I'll just have to be clever. See you in the trenches."

Kit watched him for a few seconds as he walked toward the cops guarding the Riverwalk. Then she got in the car and started the engine. Heading for home, she began to think about the Heartbeats and Lawson's interest in them. If he was the killer, or even if he wasn't, it seemed likely that they were the path to follow.

IN HIS OFFICE, with the city still sleeping, Broussard twisted the fine focus of his microscope, sharpening the image of the third hair. He moved along the shaft to the root, which had the configuration of an actively growing hair—another plucked specimen. He moved back up the shaft and studied it, varying the setting of the iris diaphragm, fiddling with the condenser. Finally, he leaned back in his chair, folded his arms over his belly, and lapsed into thought, his finger straying to the top of his nose, where he began to stroke the bristly hairs growing from the tip.

This specimen, brown in color, was from a straight-haired Caucasian, all obvious facts, all disappointing. Where was the clue that he was certain the killer had included in the selection of this particular hair? There had to be one, for the person behind this was extremely intelligent, of that he was certain. He was equally certain that the killer was following a plan that had been worked out to the smallest detail.

This analysis did not permit the existence of a third meaningless hair. Growling aloud, he applied his eyes again to the microscope and began a millimeter-by-millimeter appraisal of the new hair.

When he leaned back five minutes later, he knew no more than he had earlier. Frustrated and angry, he got up, paced briefly, then went to his desk and sat down. Getting a lemon ball from the glass bowl, he slipped it into his mouth, tilted his chair back, and laced his fingers over his belly. He closed his eyes, trying to just let his mind run free, concentrating on nothing, thinking of nothing.

His new insight into the killer had partially freed him from the crippling self-pity he'd been experiencing, but enough still remained to drag him down. Unable to think of nothing, he thought of the killer. This was war.... His enemy was still faceless, but that did not diminish the personal nature of the conflict between them. The Scrabble tiles, the hairs, the knife—every one was a slap in the face, a...

His eyes widened and he rocked forward in his chair. Quickly, he went to his microscope and removed the slide containing the hair. He cleaned away the Protex and stretched the hair flat on a fresh slide, fixing it in place with a strip of Magic Tape at each end. From a drawer near the microscope, he got out a Polaroid picture coater and removed the protective sleeve. He then spread the contents of the coater over the slide.

Now, a twenty-minute wait.

Remembering how Franks had sabotaged his talk the day before, he unlocked his file cabinet, took out the slides for his next talk, and loaded the carrier on his viewer. Rump against his desk, he checked the slides and mentally reviewed what he was going to say about each one. Satisfied that Franks had not meddled with this talk and that it would be okay, he clicked off the viewer, replaced the slides in the file cabinet, and locked it.

His review had lasted only fifteen minutes. The next few, he spent pacing. Finally, the coating was dry enough. Carefully, he freed the hair, placed it in a small plastic dish, and put a cover on it. He then put the coated slide under the microscope and began his examination of the hair's scale pattern, which had been left as an imprint when the Polaroid coating chemical ran under the hair and dried.

A quick look sent a chill down his spine. The hairs... the knife... the fibers in the bloodstains on the first victim's shirt... He knew now where to find the killer.

ELEVEN

KIT WOKE forty-five minutes later than usual, having no memory of turning off the alarm and going back to sleep. Today, the Forensic meetings would shift into high gear with a three-hour opening session on the Tawana Brawley case. She was particularly interested in the psychiatry portion of the presentation, which promised to provide some insights into the mind of pseudovictims. She would, of course, not be there, having more important things to do. But first, she needed to check on Lucky.

Her call to the animal hospital brought good news. Lucky could probably come home on Friday. She was so pleased, she gave the vet's bill barely a thought.

The clouds of the previous night had moved on without delivering rain. Though bright, the sun was so cool, it almost seemed a different celestial body than the one that would be cracking windshields of closed cars and baking the life out of the city in a few months.

Upon reaching her office, Kit skimmed the article on the Heartbeats, refreshing her memory about who was who in the picture. The drummer's name was Gene Ochs. He had dark deep-set eyes and hollow cheeks that made him look every bit like an overworked cardiology resident, which, except for the overworked part, the article said he was. Apparently, the life of a lab tech was easier, for Bill Pope, the guy on guitar, had clearly been expending fewer calories than he'd been taking in. The article identified the keyboardist as Kyle Ricks. Ricks looked older than the others, probably because his hair was gone on top. Like many men with his condition, Ricks wore his hair long on the sides and back, making an unfortunate turn of nature distinctly worse. By day, Phyllis Merryman, was an EKG technician. By night, she was the singer for the Heartbeats. In both jobs, she was blond and beautiful.

Where to begin? So much time had passed.

She took out the phone book and began a search for the four names. This yielded a number for only one of the four, which, if it actually belonged to the correct Kyle Ricks, would be more than she'd expected. She tried the number and got no answer.

Her obvious next move, a call to the personnel office of the hospital where the Heartbeats all had worked in 1981, produced the news that none of the four were current employees, nor did the hospital have any records of what had become of them. Thinking that former colleagues of the four who were still at the hospital might have information on them, she asked for likely names but was told it would take several days to generate such a list. Personnel suggested that they put a note in the hospital newsletter asking anyone with pertinent information to give her a call. This, of course, was worthless given the time constraints the killer had imposed. Nor could she wait for that list of names. A call to the departments where each of the Heartbeats worked turned out to be equally useless, which left her only one other avenue—to call the personnel offices of every general hospital in the city.

Heating... Hobby... Horses... Hospitals. A look at the list made her groan aloud, for the city had a great many hospitals. Since the only way to get through the list was to start, she punched in the number for Bayou Oaks.

Thirty-six calls later, her once-slender hopes had become paper-thin. Three dozen calls without results. But with the next call, her luck improved. Kyle Ricks, the keyboard player and the one name she'd found in the phone book, was working as a respiratory therapist at St. Francis. From

the shift supervisor of his department, she discovered that
Ricks was at that moment on the cardiac ICU ward but
could be freed to come to the phone if she wished. Since she
wanted to gauge Ricks's facial expressions while they spoke,
she declined this offer and arranged instead to interview him
in person.

St. Francis Hospital consisted of a central tower and two
large wings of almost equal height. It sat impressively at the
rear of a huge lawn that was now a uniform shade of brown
but which in summer was surely a perfect carpet of green.
As Kit walked past the drive to the emergency room, she
heard a noise above and to her right. Looking up, she saw
the silhouette of a helicopter. It descended with surprising
speed, swung over the lawn, and dropped neatly onto the
cement pad twenty yards from the hospital's main entrance, the wind from its blades blowing bits of dried grass
into her face and ravaging her hair.

Squinting, she moved quickly toward the entrance and
went inside, pausing a moment to watch the occupants of
the helicopter hand a prone figure to a pair of gurney jock-
eys that had come from the emergency room. A messed
hairdo and something in her eye seemed a fair price for the
good the helicopter was doing.

Putting her hair and her watering eye ahead of her need
to see Ricks, she passed by the information booth and went
down the hall until she found a ladies' room, where she
washed the grit from her cornea with tap water held in her
palm. Since she rarely used eye makeup and had no need for
foundation, this act did not require any cosmetic repairs.
She ran a brush through her hair a few times, reset the
combs that kept it from her face, and was then ready to get
on with the reason she'd come.

From the length of time it took the woman at the information island to locate Respiratory Therapy on her map, Kit
concluded that it was not a popular destination of hospital

visitors. The first leg of the trip took her past the gift shop and the coffee shop, the latter smelling strongly of buttered popcorn. Like the main hall that ran through the heart of the hospital, the tributary she was in was lined with green marble. It seemed a cheery place in which to be sick, as long as you had plenty of insurance.

The elevators at the end of the hall took her to quite a different world, one of freshly remodeled functional simplicity, which probably rarely saw anyone but hospital employees. There was no directory to guide her, so she simply wandered off to her left, looking for help.

At a door marked MEDIA SERVICES, she found a chubby young man sitting at a desk whose nameplate said he was Sandra Ferguson.

"Respiratory therapy?"

"Straight ahead, through the doors at the end of the corridor."

This took her deep into the hospital's netherworld; to ancient terrazzo floors and venerable yellow tiled walls, a place not unlike the floor in Charity Hospital where she and Broussard had their offices.

The area seemed quite deserted. On her left was a tiny room full of green oxygen bottles, resembling large Vienna sausages, stacked in shopping carts. To her right was a much larger room littered with electronic equipment fitted with ribbed blue hoses—and something with a head of blond hair. . . .

"That's Resusci Annie," a voice said.

She looked down the hall and saw a woman dressed in white coming toward her. She had a big body but thin little legs that looked like pipe cleaners stuck into her thick-soled shoes.

"Resusci Annie," she said again in response to Kit's puzzled expression. She pointed into the equipment room. "Our clinical simulator."

Now Kit saw what she meant. The blond hair was on the head of half a female torso that had a ribbed blue hose coming from its mouth.

"Better Annie than a real person for some of these green kids they send me," the woman said. "You ever been intubated?"

"It's something I try to avoid," Kit said.

The woman smiled. "Good one. I'll have to remember that . . . 'something I try to avoid.' Ha."

"I'm Kit Franklyn . . . here to see Kyle Ricks. Was it you I spoke to?"

"Yes. I'll get him for you and cover his floor while you talk. You can wait down here. . . ." She led Kit to a bleak room containing an old dinette table, a microwave, a midget frig, and a bank of cubbyholes with lockable wooden doors. Then she was gone.

Looking for something to occupy her mind while she waited, Kit went over to a sepia-tinted photograph hanging on the wall. It was of a long row of what appeared to be nurses, each standing slightly turned to the side. They were of varying heights, but their skirt hems were all exactly the same distance from the ground, forming a line so sharp and precise, they looked as though they might suddenly loop their hands behind one another and start doing high kicks.

From there, she wandered to the grimy window, where through the bars fixed on the outside, she watched two pigeons quarreling on the roof of the adjacent building. When a third pigeon chased the other two away, she moved on, picking up a worn magazine from one of the dinette chairs.

Red letters beside a downy-cheeked nymphet on the cover asked, "Is It Love? Ten Questions to Help You Know if He's Mr. Right." She opened the pages and checked the table of contents for the quiz.

Teddy did fine on questions one through five, but number six asked, "Does his view regarding the nature of your relationship five years down the road agree with yours?"

Five years? She hadn't been able to get Teddy to talk about this at all. She'd tried once and he'd gotten out of bed, thrown on his clothes, and driven back to Bayou Coteau in the middle of the night. Some discussion. She'd let it pass because she wasn't sure herself what she wanted to be when she grew up—forever single, married, a mother, childless—tough decisions. And she hadn't been—wasn't even now—ready to tackle them. But she could feel within her the ponderously slow turning of gears, the stirring of machinery that before too much longer would produce a decision. Soon, Teddy would have to choose. And so would she. Then she would find out what they had. Until then, it remained possible that theirs was what the article called "a relationship of convenience," in which she was deluding herself regarding her own depth of feeling to validate the fact that they were sleeping together.

"Do we know each other?" a voice said from the doorway.

Kit looked up and saw a man that did not seem to be the Kyle Ricks in her picture. Irritated at wasting so much time, she put down the magazine and started to apologize for also wasting his, then realized that this *was* the Ricks she wanted—his face fuller and with a complete head of hair. "Mr. Ricks, I'm—"

"It's Kyle. Mr. Ricks is my father."

"Kyle, I'm Kit Franklyn. I'm investigating a series of murders we've had in the city over the last week."

Ricks crossed the room and took the card she offered but didn't look at it.

"The killer has left certain clues that led us to this..." She reached into her bag and produced one of the prints she'd gotten from Terry Yardley. Ricks accepted it with significantly more interest than he had her card.

"Boy, this brings back memories," he said. "Most of 'em bad. Gene Ochs, M.D....minor deity. No, that's wrong. In Ochs's case, it's major deity. Doctors are not only a pain in the ass in the hospital but outside it, as well. Nobody ever had a decent idea but Ochs. And did he have the hots for Phyllis...." He held the picture so Kit could see. "That's Ochs and that's Phyllis...but she wasn't interested. Made for a lot of tension." He looked at the picture again and shook his head. "God, I hate this picture of me."

Kit marveled at Ricks's level of self-absorption. She'd told him people were being murdered and he was more interested in his appearance in an old photograph.

"Twenty-six years old and I look fifty. Don't know why I put up with it as long as I did. You ever look at old pictures of yourself and wonder what possessed you to buy that dress or those shoes? Of course back then, I don't think they had the technology they do now." He lowered the picture and bent his head. "Go ahead...feel it. You can't tell it from the real thing, so help me you can't. Go on...." Ricks grabbed Kit's hand and put it in his hair. "Didn't I tell you?"

She withdrew her hand, resisting the impulse to wipe it on her slacks. Ricks looked at her with a happy twinkle in his eyes. "Want to know how it's done?"

"Mr. Ricks...Kyle...it's very becoming, but I'm here to talk about those murders."

"Oh right. Sorry, sorry, sorry. What can I do to help?" Finally, her opening statement sank in. "You said some clues the killer left led you to this picture?"

"And the accompanying article in the paper. Do you have any idea what the connection might be?"

"None whatever."

"Do you know a man named Nick Lawson?"

Ricks shook his head.

Thinking that he might know Lawson by a different name, she added, "Well-built fellow, tanned, green eyes, blond hair he wears in a ponytail."

Ricks continued shaking his head.

"Would you mind telling me where you were this morning between two and three A.M.?"

Ricks shrugged. "Here at the hospital, in cardiac ICU, just where I was a few minutes ago." The implication of her question got through and he drew a sharp breath. "You don't think I'm..."

"Of course not," Kit said, "but I had to ask. I'd like to speak to the other people in the picture, but I'm having trouble finding them."

"Well, Ochs, thank God, moved away. I think he's in California, or Washington, or maybe Mount Olympus. Don't remember where. Phyllis had a drug problem and got sacked from the hospital. I don't know what happened to her after that. Bill Pope went into a real tailspin when the band broke up. Begged us to stay together... cried in front of us... funny guy."

"He still in town?"

"He's got a pet shop across the river in the Three Oaks shopping center. Calls it Paw and Fin."

"Kyle..." A slim redhead wearing a green dress that reminded Kit of theater curtains stood in the doorway. "Leona called from cardiac ICU. Easton wants a stat IPPB with a half cc of albuterol in two cc of saline for the patient in four-oh-two. You're to get blood gases in thirty minutes and call him."

Ricks looked at Kit. "Leona's real good about covering for you long as nobody needs anything. I gotta go. You think of any more questions, call me."

The redhead stepped aside to let Ricks pass. "Sorry about the interruption," she said to Kit.

Moving closer and lowering her voice so Ricks couldn't hear, Kit said, "Was Kyle on duty this morning between two and three A.M.?"

"He was scheduled."

"Could anyone have covered for him?"

"For a few minutes, like Leona's doing now."

"I mean like work part of his shift without telling you."

"No. If he got sick or something, the supervisor would cover for him until we could get someone else in. Everybody on each shift has distinct obligations, procedures that have to be performed. And we need to know who did them. We keep close track of our people."

THE ELEVATOR had been empty coming up. When the door opened to take Kit down, she encountered an old man and woman. He was in coveralls, a denim shirt, and a John Deere cap. She was in a loose flowered dress. They moved to one side to let her on, then the old man leaned out and looked up and down the hall, holding the door open with one weathered hand. Finally, he turned to Kit and said, "This here the floor where they clean out your plumbing?"

Kit showed the old couple the way to the information island, then went to her car, mulling over her interview with Ricks. The only part of the entire experience that had any relationship to the three murders was Ricks's pride in his new hair.

A hair left at each scene . . . Ricks has new hair. It was a weak connection indeed, and since Ricks had a firm alibi for the last murder, surely nothing but a coincidence.

TWELVE

THERE WERE KITTENS in the window of Paw and Fin, a half
dozen romping, fuzzy, lovable little creatures that made Kit
forget for a moment that she was on the trail of a killer.
One, a dusky mite so tiny that it would fit in Kit's hand,
came to the window and tried to touch her with its paw. She
wondered briefly how Lucky and the kitten would get along,
then forced herself to turn away, thinking that Ralph Na-
der or somebody ought to require that kitten displays have
warnings on them.

Inside the shop, it was the puppies that got to her—clear-
eyed, intelligent, full of pep, and in such tiny cages. . . . She
thought of Lucky and wondered if the vet was keeping him
like that. She should have asked to see him even though he
couldn't come home.

Thankfully, the birds were not as persuasive as the kittens and the puppies, except maybe for the peach-faced love-
birds, which sat wing-to-wing and took turns nibbling one
another's necks. The dimly lighted back room of the shop
was walled with fish tanks. Seeing no evidence of a clerk or
a storeroom where one might be hiding, she walked toward
the fish.

There she found a large back bent over a long glass tank
with no water in it. "Hi, I'm looking for Bill Pope."

The fellow turned and looked over his shoulder. "Be with
you in a minute. He's about to take it."

A brief glance was enough for Kit to see that she'd found
her man. Curious as to what he was doing, she moved to the
end of the tank and looked inside, where a large black snake
watched a ball of raw hamburger bounce past its nose. The

hamburger was being played like a puppet, a thin thread running from Pope's hand to a loop tied around the meat.

"The secret is to make it look like it's alive," Pope said, hopping the meat past the snake's nose, "and to make sure it's heated to mammalian body temperature."

Suddenly, the snake's head darted forward and it seized the meat in its mouth, its body looping forward in an attempt to throw coils around the catch. Pope reached toward the snake's mouth with a pair of scissors and snipped the thread. "He'll digest the thread along with the meat," he said, putting a wire top on the tank. "Won't hurt him."

Pope's forehead was sweating profusely and there were wet rings under his arms. "Used to feed them mice, but I never liked that, too cruel. Then I got this hamburger idea."

He mopped his forehead with a handkerchief and returned the cloth to his back pocket. He was no more overweight than Broussard, but Kit felt he was much bigger, possibly because she no longer saw a fat man when she looked at Broussard, but saw only a good friend. Not knowing Pope at all, his weight could not be overlooked. Then, too, Broussard's shirts fit and Pope's were too small, the fabric around each button stretched so tightly, he looked segmented, like an insect.

"Now, what can I do for you?" he said. "We've got a special on cordon bleu finches this week, or I could make you a good deal on one of those oscars." He gestured to a tank containing large flat fish with an orange circle on the tail. "No. You look like a dog person. I got a little malamute you're gonna love."

"I'm not a customer," Kit said, obviously disappointing him. She gave him her card and got the band's picture from her bag while he read it. "I want to talk to you about this...." She handed him the picture and his expression brightened.

"Son of a gun," he said. "Where'd you get it?"

"A friend at the *Times*."

"From that old article they did on the Heartbeats, right?"

"Yes."

"Son of a gun." Without taking his eyes from the picture, he said, "The year I was with the Heartbeats was the best time of my life." He looked up, his eyes watery. "When you're on a bandstand, it's like...you're somebody. Instead of bein' an anonymous schmuck, you're special.... People look at you and it really registers. They don't look through you. Gene, Kyle, Phyllis...it was magic. Back then, the amps were covered in a fabric called Tolex. After they'd been on a while, they gave off a sweet sweaty smell like girls who'd just come from a gym class. I really miss that."

He wiped his forehead with his handkerchief and Kit imagined him peeking through a hole drilled into the girl's locker room.

"Kyle Ricks said that Ochs had a divisive influence on the group and that Ochs was romantically interested in Phyllis," she said.

"We were all in love with Phyllis. Who wouldn't be? But I don't remember any problem with Gene. Like I said, it was magic. If I could, I'd turn the clock back to then and stay there forever. Why are you interested in the band?"

"There's been a series of murders in the city and the killer has left certain clues that have led us to that old article on the band in the *Times*. I was hoping you might be able to tell us why."

"Led you to us? The Heartbeats?" He wiped his brow. "That's freaky. Who was killed?"

"The owner of a small jewelry shop, a clerk at the Chartres House hotel, and a waterfront security guard. I'm surprised you haven't read about it in the paper or seen stories on the news."

"You work a place like this by yourself, cook your own meals, and try to keep from livin' like a pig, it doesn't leave time for readin' the paper or watchin' TV. The Heartbeats? The killer led you to the Heartbeats?''

"Does the name Nick Lawson mean anything to you?"

"No. Should it?"

"Not necessarily." She described Lawson, but Pope still didn't know him. "I'm sorry to ask you this, but where were you this morning between two and three?"

"Asleep, where else?"

"Alone?"

He turned his hands inward and gestured to himself. "You have to ask?"

"Would you know where I can find Phyllis?"

His faced reddened. "Not really."

He was lying. "I think you do. And I should remind you that there are legal penalties for obstructing a police investigation."

He considered this and wiped his forehead, which by now would have been better served by a sponge. "Okay, I *do* know where to find her. Two weeks ago, I didn't have any idea, but then I happened to be in Shirley's Place on Bourbon Street." His face grew redder still. "And she came on-stage...."

"As a singer?"

He shook his head. "A dancer. And she was really good, certainly the class of *that* field."

"Did you speak to her?"

His eyes went to the front of the store as though a customer had come in. "No. In fact, I...I left before she was finished."

"Why?"

"She has this thing she does...right down where the guys sit at the table that rings the stage. I didn't like seein' her all spread out and I didn't want her seein' me...to know I went to places like that. So I took off."

SINCE THERE WASN'T TIME to go to Grandma O's for lunch and still make her one-thirty meeting with Gatlin and Broussard, Kit went into a Chinese restaurant a few doors from the pet store. The place didn't have much decor—a few paper lanterns hanging from the ceiling, a couple of pearl-inlaid panels on the wall. But there were a lot of Asians eating there, a barometer usually as reliable as truckers at an expressway café.

She was shown to a booth by a tiny doll in red and gold. Another, even prettier, took her order, bowing timidly before withdrawing.

What to make of the Heartbeats? Pope was a maladjusted, unhappy man to be sure and there seemed to be a dark undercurrent to the relationships among the band members, juicy stuff—if it had been a band member who had been killed.

Her waitress returned bearing a white teapot decorated with a green dragon, from which she filled Kit's cup with deliciously fragrant jasmine tea. Kit thanked her by tapping twice on the table with two fingers, an act of respect she'd learned from Betty Woo, a friend in graduate school. In response to this simple act, the waitress smiled for the first time and bowed more deeply than before, leaving her then to enjoy her tea.

So far there wasn't a shred of a relationship between the Heartbeats and the murders. The problem lay mostly with the victims—particularly number two. He was only twenty. In 1981, he would have been just a kid. What could a kid do to cause his murder so many years later? Nor was there any connection with the band and Nick Lawson.

The waitress returned with a huge bowl of Hong Kong soup and one of those flat Chinese spoons that seems more like a table decoration than an eating utensil. After placing the soup in front of her, the girl put a small plate beside it.

"Something—how you say...on house," the girl said, gesturing to the plate. "Very good for taste. Try now."

Whatever was on the plate was quite pretty, strips of a material that looked like smoked glass with a lovely white curly strip in the center. She took the chopsticks the girl held out to her and unwrapped them. Expertly, she picked up a piece of the smoked glass and carried it to her lips. The taste was subtle and not readily identifiable with anything she'd previously eaten. Though not terribly impressed, she nodded and said, "Very good. Thank you. What is it?"

The girl's English was not up to the question, so Kit pointed with her chopsticks and repeated it. "What is this?"

Nodding rapidly, the girl replied, "Pig ear...very special."

STILL THINKING OF PIG EARS and how they were not so different from detached eyelids, Kit arrived at Broussard's office as he was opening the door. With him were Leo Fleming and Crandall Brooks. She exchanged greetings with the visitors, then said to Broussard, "How was court?"

"Jury seemed attentive. I think I got my points across."

They all followed him inside, where he went to his desk and picked up the plastic bag containing the knife left on the third victim. He held it out to Fleming. "Make us love you, Leo."

Everyone waited while Fleming examined the knife through the bag. In only a few seconds, he handed it back to Broussard. "Five bucks at any Wal-Mart."

"Not what we'd hoped for, Leo," Broussard said.

There was a knock at the door and Gatlin came in. He acknowledged Kit and Fleming with a wave of the hand and looked vacantly at Brooks. Broussard introduced them and said, "Brookie's agreed to sit in and give us his views."

Gatlin nodded, then put his hand to his chest and groaned. "Damn those chili dogs." He turned to Broussard. "Got any Rolaids?"

"Sorry."

"What have we got?"

"Leo said the knife is nothin' special. Real common."

"So we're right where we started."

"Not exactly."

"You gotta forgive me this impatient streak, but I'd sure like to know what the hell you're talking about."

"At first, I thought that last hair was from a straight-haired Caucasian," Broussard said. "But somethin' didn't seem quite right. Then when I looked at the scale pattern, I realized it was not a human hair."

"Dog . . . cat?" Gatlin asked.

"Bear."

There was a shocked silence in the room.

"A bear?" Gatlin said finally. "This is getting crazier by the minute."

"Not true," Broussard said. "For the first time, it's beginnin' to make sense. Most animal hairs have distinctly more medulla than cortex. In humans, it's the reverse. That makes it easy to tell animal from human. But bears have human-type medullas. You have to look at the scale patterns to tell they're animal."

"So the killer's not your average guy," Brooks said. "He knows hair."

"There's more," Broussard said, going to a drawer in the microscope table. He withdrew a piece of fabric and showed it to Gatlin. "This was cut from a morgue pad . . . paper on one side, plastic on the other, and in the middle—"

"Viscose fibers?" Gatlin guessed.

"Right. For the killer to use this material around his knife hand, he'd have to cut a piece from a bigger pad, which exposes the fiber center. I sent some samples over to the lab and they said the fibers on the first victim could have come from a similar pad."

"Am I followin' this?" Fleming said. "Are you suggestin' the killer is someone—"

"In town for the Forensic meetin'," Broussard said, not wanting Fleming to steal his summation.

"Hard to believe," Brooks said.

"And I'm not suggestin'," Broussard said. "I'm certain of it. Kit saw it before I did."

"When was that?" Kit exclaimed.

"When we asked your opinion of why the killer left the knife, you pointed out how Leo's name was in the paper and that it almost seemed as though the killer knew what we expected to learn from him. You also said he gave us the knife to show us it wouldn't help—and it didn't, at least not the way we thought it might."

Kit was flattered that Broussard had thrown some of the credit her way, but she also believed she didn't deserve it since she'd been thinking of Nick Lawson when she'd made that observation. Thankfully, she'd never mentioned those suspicions to anybody. If she had, right about now, she'd probably be hearing a Babe Ruth story.

"How many people at the meeting?" Gatlin asked, already shying from the answer.

"About eighteen hundred," Broussard replied.

Gatlin's hand went to his chest and he exhaled through ballooned cheeks. "Maybe I'll die in my sleep tonight and not have to deal with any of it. They all at the Hyatt?"

"Most, but we got 'em in the Holiday Inn, Le Pavillon, Comfort Inn, and the Clairmont, too," Broussard said.

"Eighteen hundred suspects," Gatlin moaned. "Gotta hand it to you, Andy, when you narrow it down, you really hone in."

"It's not as bad as it seems," Brooks suggested. "You're looking for someone familiar with anatomy and the physiology of knife wounds, someone who had access to morgue supplies, a person who knows the microscopic anatomy of hair and knows that Leo's specialty is tool marks. If it was me, I'd concentrate on just the anthropologists and the pathologists.''

This was exactly what Broussard was going to suggest, but he was just as happy to have it come from Brooks.

''How many would that be?'' Gatlin asked.

''Couple hundred,'' Brooks said.

''Still a lot,'' Gatlin said. ''But at least they're all in just a few hotels.'' He looked at Broussard. ''Can you get me the right names and where they're staying?''

''Sure.''

''What'll you do then?'' Kit asked.

''Interview every single one.... Find out when they got to town and where they were when each murder occurred.''

Remembering what Bill Pope had told her, Kit said, ''I expect a lot of them will say they were in bed, and if they have single rooms...''

''Thanks for the optimism,'' Gatlin said. ''But that's all I can do.''

''You're going to take their word for when they arrived in town?'' Kit asked.

''I'll also check the hotel records.''

''Suppose they arrived a few days early and registered at a different hotel under an assumed name?''

''I can't deal with that.''

''Sure you can. You could call the home office of every anthropologist and every pathologist here and ask when they left.''

''Let's take that a step further,'' Gatlin said. ''Suppose they didn't register at all. Suppose they're in town and have never shown up at the meeting.''

''What's your point?''

"All good detective work is based on the kiss principle—'Keep it simple, stupid.' I don't mean you, Doc. I mean me...us.... You let yourself get bogged down in minutiae and the big things'll get away from you. Andy, you got any ideas on the best way to set up the interviews?"

"After we get the names, I'd make up a schedule and leave a message for each person at their hotel, givin' the time and place for the interview and a phone number they could call if they need to change times."

Gatlin nodded. "Hope we got some detectives with nothing to do, 'cause I'm gonna need help."

"If you want to lighten your load, you could probably eliminate women," Kit said.

"I don't imagine that'll lighten it much," Gatlin replied.

"The interviews are certainly necessary," Broussard said. "But we'd help ourselves a lot if we could figure out what the Scrabble tiles mean. The hairs meant something, and so do the tiles. There's no doubt about it. Solve the riddle of the tiles and we'll find the killer's identity."

Since her meeting with Ricks and Pope had revealed nothing, Kit had considered not mentioning the Heartbeats. But seeing that no one else had any ideas about the riddle, she decided to risk a Babe Ruth anecdote and get the idea on the table.

"I may have something to contribute on the riddle," she said, going to the chalkboard. She picked up a stub of chalk and wrote:

KOJE

5181

"Scrabble tiles don't have just letters on them. They also have numbers indicating the point value of the letter. The number five-one-eight-one can be divided into a date, 5-1-81.''

Sensing that this was going to require a little time, the four men had taken up comfortable positions, Gatlin and Broussard with their rumps against the desk, Fleming sitting on the microscope table, Brooks sitting in the microscope chair, which he'd turned backward. She was heartened to see that all of them were listening receptively.

"It occurred to me that there might be a connection between this date and the fact that a different section of last Friday's paper was left on each body. So I went to the library and looked up the issue of the *Times* for 5-1-81. I found a picture and a story there about four local hospital workers who in their spare time performed together as a band called the Heartbeats.''

"And the victims were all killed by injury to the heart,'' Brooks said.

"That's interesting, but not what attracted me to the article. Someone had circled the picture with a grease pencil on the microfilm. I copied the article and also got some prints of the picture from a friend at the paper.'' She went to her bag, which lay on Broussard's vinyl sofa, took out a copy of the article, and unfolded it. "Should I read it aloud?''

Gatlin nodded, his lined face expressionless.

After reading the article, she produced one of the prints and handed it to Gatlin. "I've talked to the piano player and the guy on guitar...." To this point, she'd presented her story with an energy suggesting that she'd really stumbled onto something. Now having reached the end, she was reminded that her investment in this lead had yet to pay off. "But I didn't get much. The piano player is still working as a respiratory therapist and he has an excellent alibi for the time of the third murder. The guitar player owns a pet shop across the river. He's got the same alibi that most of the anthropologists and pathologists are going to have—he was in bed, alone. So far, that's it."

"What about the other two in the picture?" Broussard said.

"The drummer moved away years ago. I don't know where, West Coast maybe. The girl is still in town, but I haven't talked to her yet."

Gatlin shook his head. "Sounds like a wrong turn to me. Andy's got a convincing story that it's somebody at the Forensic meeting. What does this band—" he gestured at the picture, which by now had made it to Brooks "—have to do with the meeting?"

"I don't know. But, like I said, there are still two members I haven't spoken to. One I haven't located, but I know how to find the other. Possibly she'll tell me something."

Gatlin's heartburn bubbled again. When it subsided, he said, "Doesn't seem productive to me, but it's your time."

"Sounds like one of our colleagues is takin' you all on a real sleigh ride," Fleming said to Broussard.

"We don't have snow down here," Broussard said.

"From what I've heard, I'm not so sure about that," Fleming replied.

"Leo, I just thought of something," Broussard said. "*You* came in early."

"Arrived Saturday, if you'll remember, *after* you found the first body. Sorry."

"Too bad," Broussard said, looking disappointed.

THIRTEEN

GATLIN HAD BEEN so negative when Kit had told her story that she didn't offer him the article or the picture. Broussard had been kinder, or at least it seemed that way. So she left them with him. Returning to her office, she looked up the number of Shirley's Place. The phone rang a long time before a voice that sounded as though it ran on a battery answered.

"Shirley's. We ain't open."

The synthetic voice was so distorted that Kit couldn't tell if she was talking to a man or a woman. Suppressing a shudder incited by the thought of destroyed vocal cords, she said, "I'm trying to locate a woman named Phyllis Merryman and I've been told she works there as a dancer."

"Never heard of her. Try the FBI."

There was a click and the phone went dead. Apparently, she was going to have to go down there and look for Merryman herself. Entering a strip joint alone was not a pleasing prospect. If Teddy lived closer, she would have asked him to go along. But he wasn't closer. And this wasn't the first time she'd needed him to back her up. So she did what she usually did, which was to call the NOPD vehicle-impoundment station to see if Bubba Oustellette, Grandma O's grandson, would go with her. He answered in his usual chipper style.

"Impoundment—Bubba. Ah'll help you if Ah can."

"Glad to hear that, Bubba. It's Kit Franklyn."

"Hey, Doc Franklyn. What can Ah do you for? Hope Ah don' have your car over here."

"You don't. I need a different kind of favor."

"Jus' between you an' me, Ah'd rather do a favor for you than mos' anybody Ah know. Seems like we always do somethin' more interestin' than anything Ah'd do on my own. Where we goin'?"

"To a strip joint on Bourbon." There was a long pause. "Bubba, you there?"

"Ah'm here. Ah was jus' thinkin' what Gramma O'd do to me if she foun' out Ah went to a place like dat."

"I won't tell her."

"She seem to fin' out things with nobody tellin' her."

"If you'd rather not . . ."

"Doc Franklyn, if a man don' help a friend when he's asked, he ain't any kinda man. Ah'll take my chances with Gramma O. We gonna need da gun?"

He was referring to the large pistol he'd carried concealed in his coveralls on past excursions they'd made together. "I'm not expecting any trouble. I just didn't want to go into a place like that by myself."

"When we goin'?"

"Tonight . . . around eight."

"Uh-oh."

"Bad time?"

"Ah'm supposed to rebuild Bobby Dupree's brakes tonight. You know Bobby?"

"No."

"You say dis joint is on Bourbon?"

"Yes. It's called Shirley's Place."

"Tell you what. Bobby lives over near Rampart, so he's not far from Bourbon. How about Ah take a break and walk over at eight. Den, after we're done, Ah'll go back to work."

"Great. See you at Shirley's."

After hanging up, she put one of the remaining copies of the article and one of the prints back in her bag. Then her thoughts turned to Nick Lawson, who most likely was out nosing around, trying to track down the Heartbeats, too. If she was able to find Kyle Ricks and Bill Pope, so could he. But she had mentioned Lawson's name and described him to both men. If he should show up asking questions, wouldn't they be leery and likely to say nothing? But maybe he wouldn't *show up*. He might call and pass himself off as someone else. It wasn't ethical, but that didn't mean he wouldn't do it.

She checked the number, then pulled the phone over and called St. Francis Hospital, where she learned that Ricks had gone home. She tried him there and got no answer. She *was* able to reach Pope, though, at the pet store.

"Mr. Pope, this is Kit Franklyn. We spoke earlier today about the Heartbeats. That's right. Do you remember me mentioning a man named Nick Lawson?"

Pope remembered.

"He's a newspaper reporter who may contact you asking about the Heartbeats, and I wanted to warn you that if you discuss the case with him, it can get you in trouble with the police. He may call you and use a different name. He might say he's a detective. To be safe, you should speak to no one else about the band."

Assured by Pope that he did not want any trouble, Kit hung up, pleased at the impediment she'd placed in Lawson's path but sorry that she hadn't also found Ricks.

A LITTLE BEFORE EIGHT, Kit parked in a lot near the river and hoofed it over to Bourbon Street, which, as usual, reminded her of a carnival midway, but with more flesh to sell.

"Hey, buddy, bring the little woman in for some education. Boys, you ain't seen women till you seen ours."

In the window of a place specializing in staged sex orgies, she saw some black-and-white photographs of a pile of naked bodies that resembled a drunken fraternity party more than an erotic encounter.

In front of her, a black kid wearing baggy Bermuda shorts with a crotch that nearly hung on the sidewalk stepped up to one of the few men in the crowd not wearing some kind of sneaker.

"Yo, mister. Bet a dollar I know where you got them shoes."

The way this was supposed to work was that the guy would say, "It's a bet," then the kid would say, "You got 'em on your feet."

In the long history of this silly scam, Kit doubted that any money had ever changed hands. In this case, it ended predictably with the mark saying, "Beat it, kid."

Bubba's timing was perfect and she saw him approaching from the opposite direction at a pace that brought them simultaneously to Shirley's door. As far as she was able to tell, Bubba never dressed any differently from the way he was now: brown work shoes, navy blue coveralls over a navy T-shirt, green baseball cap bearing a picture of an ocean wave showing its teeth and carrying a football. His coveralls were crisp and spotless, so he'd probably taken an extra set over to Bobby Dupree's.

"Hey, Doc Franklyn. We both get high marks for punctuality." He grinned, showing even white teeth through his bushy black beard. The coveralls were so loose, Kit couldn't tell if he'd brought the gun. "You ready to go in?"

"Might as well."

They moved toward the entrance and a seedy lout who had been leaning with one foot against the building stepped in her way. "Momma, you can dance for me anytime."

"I'll put it on my list," Kit said, trying to go around him, "right below 'cut wrists.'"

He moved to block her again. "They won't let your kid in," he said, looking at Bubba, "not even with the phony beard."

"Get lost," Kit said, trying once more to go around him.

He moved again to block her way, but Bubba reached into his coveralls and drew out a pistol with a long barrel that he placed on the guy's pants at the midpoint of his zipper. "We really enjoyed talkin' to you," Bubba said, looking at the guy. "But it's time now for you to leave, don' you think?"

The guy didn't say a word, but simply bolted for safety. Bubba put the gun away and held out his arm for Kit to proceed. They were met inside by a blonde in tiger-striped shorts and a matching halter. Her hair, which was showing about an inch of brown near her scalp, had been back-combed into a "do" resembling a stork's nest. She said something, but Kit couldn't hear her over the blaring sound of saxophones and rim shots. Responding to Kit's hand cupped at her ear, she tried again. "You want Shirley?"

"No," Kit yelled. "Is Phyllis Merryman working to-night?"

The girl shrugged. "You want a table or not?"

Kit nodded and followed the girl into the bar's dim interior. She led them to a tiny round table a few feet from the door.

"Two-drink minimum...each," the girl said, leaning close.

"Rum and Coke," Kit replied.

The girl looked at Bubba. "Root beer with a nice head on it," he said.

While the girl went to the bar, Kit got her first good look at the place. The music came from a jukebox on an elevated shag rug-covered stage that reached halfway into the room from the right wall. There seemed to be many more tables on the other side of the stage than where she and Bubba sat. For the very adventuresome, chairs were also arranged along a narrow step-down attached to the three sides of the stage. Spotlights on the ceiling bathed the dancer now performing in a sensual red glow.

Kit was disappointed to see that the dancer was not Phyllis Merryman. In fact, it was stretching a point to say she was a dancer. She was dressed in a black teddy, black heels, and black net stockings. Her act consisted of a few clumsy dance steps and some pelvic action delivered while she buffed her crotch with a black scarf. For comic relief, she would occasionally throw a moon and peek at the customers from between heavy thighs that tapered quickly to skinny calves.

Kit could see only a few vague shapes at the tables on the far side of the room. The crowd was equally sparse on her side: two young guys in civvies with boot-camp haircuts at a table in the corner, a guy with slicked-down hair and a pitted neck two tables in front of them, and an old English professor type in one of the chairs at the step-down. Nobody in raincoats.

As unattractive and graceless as the dancer was, she had her audience's rapt attention, Bubba included, proof that the way to a man's heart is not through his stomach. The waitress arrived with four drinks and put them on the table. "Eighteen bucks."

Bubba's hand went for his wallet, but Kit stopped him and put a twenty on the girl's tray.

Not finding the entertainment as riveting as the other customers did, Kit examined the place more thoroughly. The bar was against the wall to her left, so that customers walking by outside would see only that as they looked in. At the far end of the bar was something she had not noticed earlier, a long swing suspended from the ceiling. In the swing, on her stomach, was a nude girl, her buns reflected in an angled mirror above her. She was not visible from the doorway because she was behind a black shade. It was difficult to see her face, but Kit concluded finally that this was not Phyllis Merryman, either.

In the dim corner on the opposite side of the room, Kit could see another girl performing at one of the tables. She idly watched that part of the room until the dancer seemed to drop from sight. Not wanting to imagine what was going on, she turned her attention back to the stage, where the girl with the heavy thighs was down to her G-string.

The dancer bent over and wiggled her shoulders, but she had such small breasts, it was largely wasted motion. As the music ended, she threw one final moon for the road and left the stage by some steps along the back wall, covering herself with a short silk pajama top.

From the moment Kit had entered, she'd felt self-conscious and ill at ease, part of her discomfort coming from the music, which was too loud for human ears. In its absence, though, she felt worse, as though the shrubbery she'd been hiding behind had suddenly been snatched away. Bubba's face was very pink and there were beads of sweat on his forehead. He took a long swig of his drink, which not only didn't have a head on it but, Kit suspected, was most likely not even root beer.

Another girl made her way onstage. She put a coin in the jukebox and the awkward silence in the room was banished by a raunchy guitar. This one was a better dancer and had a better body, but she was not Phyllis Merryman.

About six feet from the end of the stage, toward the bar, there was a brass pole that ended at the top in a brass circle that made the whole thing resemble a coatrack. Where the first girl had largely ignored it, it was an integral part of this one's routine and she lavished it with attention, mostly with her legs.

Abruptly, the first girl appeared in front of Kit. She parted her pajama top and thrust out her leg, showing a ruff of folded money tucked into her garter. Based on what Kit had seen of her talents, she suspected the girl had salted the garter herself.

Firmly believing that mediocrity should not be rewarded and feeling very funny about putting money in another woman's underwear, she did both, mentally adding the two dollars to the twenty for the drinks and five for parking. Twenty-seven bucks and so far she hadn't even *seen* Phyllis Merryman.

The girl moved over to Bubba and showed him her leg. He fumbled in his wallet, took out a one, and hesitated, apparently afraid to tuck it into her garter. Anxious to finish her rounds, the girl snatched it from his fingers and moved to the next table.

Onstage, the girl had undone her bra and was holding it in place with one hand while she swung around the pole with the other. Kit had never put much stock in psychic phenomena, but she could actually feel the collective anticipation of the men present, whose numbers had been significantly augmented in the last minute or two.

Finally, after some more teasing, the girl threw the bra to the side. It was a bad move. For what appeared to be firm and high was actually loose and low. Still, Kit sensed no disappointment in the room. Apparently, if it was bare, it was good.

The music ended and the girl left the stage, covering herself as the first one had. Looking past two men being seated at the table in front of her, Kit saw the girl begin to work the tables on the other side of the room. Bubba got another dollar ready.

The customer base had expanded so fast, it seemed as though a bus had dropped off its load right outside. This increased activity made Kit feel much less self-conscious during the entertainment interlude. After a short wait, the next dancer took the stage and fed the jukebox. Dressed in a red teddy with red net stockings and red heels, she was blond and gorgeous, with perfect legs and the sinuous grace of a real dancer. The years had definitely been good to Phyllis Merryman.

For a few minutes, she danced without removing anything. Then she slowly took off the teddy. By now, the place was nearly full and every chair at the step-down was taken. She did a few more steps and turns, then slinked to the brass pole and rubbed on it. Before Kit realized what was happening, Phyllis was hanging upside down by her legs from the brass ring at the top of the pole. She'd gotten up there so gracefully, Kit felt like applauding. But since no one else did, she didn't, either.

In that position, Phyllis removed her bra, revealing modestly sized, firm breasts that would likely remain just as perky when they were right side up. Somehow, she got down without an awkward moment and stepped onto the two feet of table ringing the stage.

Suddenly, her feet were sliding in opposite directions along the narrow table and she dropped easily into a split that ended with her crotch on the Formica. Even the Romanian judge would have had to give her a ten.

She crossed her arms and caressed her back with her fingers, making eye contact with the men on each side. One guy got up the courage to tuck a bill under her G-string. This set off a rush of other dim bulbs with the same idea.

Kit was sure there was no way for Phyllis to get out of that position without breaking the mood, but she did—by rolling up onto the stage, where she crawled on her knees around to Kit's side of the room, tossing her hair to the beat. Then, as smoothly as she'd gotten up onto the brass ring, she was on her back, her splayed legs thrown over her head, her pelvis thrusting to the music. It seemed to Kit that the room was getting very warm.

Phyllis began to work just her pelvic muscles, producing a pulsing heartbeat in her crotch that fluttered the dollar bill that had appeared under that part of her G-string. This had a hypnotic effect on all the men along that side of the step-down and they sat as though they were lifelike castings, their eyes all focused on the same spot. Bubba looked as though he might not fall over if you pulled his chair out from under him. From a psychological point of view, Kit found this uniformity of response quite remarkable. It was also disgusting.

Phyllis's location left those on the other side of the room with nothing to look at it, save maybe the soles of her shoes if they stood up. Understanding this, she shifted back onto her knees after barely a minute and took herself directly in front of the English professor, rendering him and his colleagues deaf and dumb with the same exercise. A minute more for the far side of the room and she was back on her feet for a final twirl center stage that ended with her feet together, hands on her knees, head turned toward the bar, a kiss on her lips. She finished exactly on the last note with a backward kick of one foot, turning on the other so that she could head for the steps. Amid a lot of whistling and foot stomping, she collected her bra and teddy, covered herself with a top, and began to circulate, gathering the tips she much deserved.

Phyllis was replaced by the girl with the bad body. Kit imagined that this would clear the room, but it didn't, everyone apparently waiting for a visit from Phyllis. For some reason, she got to Kit's table before the previous dancer.

"You were very good," Kit said over the music. "Is there a place where we can talk?"

Phyllis took the card Kit offered, read it, and returned it. "When I finish circulating, I've got a table dance in the back. After that, we can go to my dressing room." She moved over to Bubba, took his cap off, and replaced it with the bill pointing backward. She plucked the two dollars he was holding from his fingers and moved on.

Since most of the crowd had seen Phyllis, the girl on-stage did not fare as well this time as before and there was a lot of disinterest. Occasionally, Kit would check the dark table where Phyllis was working to make sure she hadn't ducked out.

Finally, the music ended and Phyllis came out of the darkness and headed for a doorway with a rest-room sign over it in the rear, back by the end of the bar. She paused there and motioned for Kit with her head.

"Bubba, I'll be right back."

By calling it, "my dressing room," Phyllis had over-stated the case on two counts. Not only was it the *only* dressing room but it also doubled as the ladies' john. The ceiling had been lowered with lattice panels that, like all the walls and the two toilet stalls in the far corner, were painted black. Extending from the toilet stalls to the right corner was a bank of gray metal lockers with the name of the current occupant scrawled on a strip of white adhesive tape above each door. Near the floor, the paint on the lockers had bubbled and flaked as though they'd been splashed by a caustic chemical.

It was likely the depressing color as much as the absence of windows that made the air in the room seem as though it had already been inhaled and expelled hundreds of times. Kit tried to breathe as little of it as possible. On the wall opposite the door, there was a full-length mirror without some of its silver backing, so that when Kit looked at herself in it, half her face and one foot was missing. Beside the mirror, there was a poster for Virginia Slims—"You've come a long way, baby." Across the girl's face, someone had written, "Then why am I here?"

Next to the door, there were two dressing tables with mirrors ringed by bulbs. Phyllis sat in front of the one with the chair and began touching up her eyeliner, which, in the good light, was already greatly overdone, making her look like Betty Boop.

Aside from the toilet stalls and the chair Phyllis was in, the only other place to sit was an armchair whose cushion visibly remembered every butt that had ever been in it. But it was the stains on the arms that made Kit decide to stand.

"You're amazing," Kit said. "I don't see how you do some of that stuff in your act."

"Two hours a day in the gym, seven days a week is how," Phyllis said, touching at the corner of her eye with her little finger.

"That's a lot."

"Everything has a price. It's push-pull. You want something, you have to give up something."

Kit suspected that Phyllis was not talking about exercise as much she was recalling the price she'd paid for her drug habit. She seemed clean now, though.

"You work out?" Phyllis said, looking at Kit in the mirror.

"I walk my dog every day."

A faint smirk passed across Phyllis's lips. "You're gonna have to start doing more if you want to keep that body."

The door burst open and the dancer with the low-slung boobs charged in. "Jesus H. Christ," she said, shrugging out of her pajama top, "there's something wrong with that guy out there. Look at me."

The light glistened off her breasts, which were soaking wet. "He's got a tongue like a dog." She shivered and headed for one of the lockers, where she pulled out a towel and dried herself off.

"Do you mind?" Phyllis said. "We're trying to have a private talk."

"Well, excuse me all to hell. Jesus, it ain't like I got any other place to go. I mean, you ain't got exclusive rights here."

"The longer you stay, the less money you'll make," Phyllis said.

"Yeah, well, you're right about that—but understand, I ain't goin' because of you."

She put the towel back and slammed the locker shut, then pushed past Kit without a glance and went back into the bar. As the door closed behind her, Phyllis said, "Like I told you. There's a price for everything, and she's mine for working here. Speaking of which, I'm not making any money either, sitting on my duff. You want something more than to tell me how much you like my act?"

"I wanted to talk about this...." Kit took the picture of the band from her bag and gave it to Phyllis.

As she looked at it, she pressed her lips together and began shaking her head, giving the impression she was remembering the Heartbeats with regrets. Abruptly, she looked up.

"Why are we so stupid when we're young?" She turned the picture and pointed at Gene Ochs. "I bet this guy makes two or three hundred K a year now. And I could have had him. And how bad would it have been? Doctors are never home, everybody knows that. A little grappling two or three times a week, in return, a nice house, clothes, a car...." She shook her head. "Stupid."

"I don't think so...if you didn't love him."

Phyllis gave Kit a look of incredulity. "Love? You gotta be kidding. What are you—thirty, thirty-one?"

Kit nodded.

"Married?"

"No."

"Take my advice, kiddo. Forget love and go for security. Men don't want love, anyway. They'll just use it against you."

"I don't believe that."

Now Phyllis *really* looked disgusted. "Where do you come from? No, don't answer that. Tell me this . . . what do you think of what I do for a living?"

"I'm not here to judge you."

"Oh bullshit. You've been judging me from the second I first talked to you. You think I didn't see that look in your eyes when Shauna came in here. You're judging all of us. But you're too dishonest to admit it. So don't give me any crap about honesty."

Kit felt her face color. "I'm sorry. . . ."

"About what? Being dishonest? You're not getting the point. Everybody's dishonest. So don't worry about it . . . use it, make it work for you." She handed the picture back. "I still don't know why you're here."

Kit explained, then said, "And I was hoping you might be able to tell me what the connection is."

"Aside from occasionally kicking myself for telling Ochs to take a hike, I haven't thought about the band in years. And I sure don't know anything about those murders. Now, I gotta get back to work."

"Sure, thanks for talking to me."

As Kit turned to go, Phyllis said, "How'd you find me?"

"Bill Pope told me you worked here."

"Yeah, I saw him in the pit a couple weeks ago, but he left before I started to circulate. What's he doing now?"

"Operates a pet shop on the West Bank."

"Pet shop." She considered this a moment and said, "Good thing I didn't hook up with *him*. I'll take that card now—in case I think of anything."

Kit gave her the card, then left the room, mulling over Phyllis Merryman's cynical views. Marrying a man just for the comfort he could provide was nothing more than legalized prostitution.

From a remote part of her brain, a small voice that sounded a lot like Phyllis Merryman said, What about

Teddy? You're sleeping with him and you're not sure you love him.

"That's different," Kit muttered.

Bullshit, the little Merryman said.

Back in the bar, she found Bubba in one of the chairs ringing the stage. When she crooked her finger at him, he jumped up and followed her out.

On the sidewalk, she turned his cap forward, saying, "Thanks for going in there with me. I appreciate it. How was the root beer?"

His brow furrowed and he looked into the gutter in thought. "Ah can't remember. An' dey say da legs are da first to go."

"I think legs had something to do with it all right."

"Now Doc, it ain't right for you to ride me. Ah only came 'cause you asked me."

"That's true. I apologize."

"Think you might wanna come back tomorrow night?"

Bubba grinned and Kit pulled his cap down so the bill covered his eyes. Putting it right, he said, "Someday you can tell me what we were doin'. But right now, if you don' need me anymore, Ah'm goin' back to work."

"That was all I wanted. Thanks."

He waved and headed back the way he'd come. Kit set off in the opposite direction.

A block from Shirley's Place, Kit saw, across Bourbon, the Amazing Living Statue, with a larger crowd around him than the last time she'd encountered him. She would have paid scant attention except that on the edge of the crowd was the little old lady who had stolen her purse in the library. Next to her, there was a pear-shaped guy in blue Bermudas eating a Lucky Dog and watching the living statue do nothing. On his hip was one of those ugly kangaroo pouches, which, in addition to his personal effects, contained the old lady's hand.

Kit crossed the street and sidled up to the old lady on the side opposite the guy with the hot dog. Carefully, she slipped her fingers around the twisted paper handles of the grocery bag the old lady was carrying, then leaned over and said, "I see we're being naughty again."

The old lady took a split-second look in Kit's direction and then she was gone, dodging through the crowded street like a human pinball. She'd made an admirable escape, but Kit now had the grocery bag, which she soon discovered, contained half a dozen wallets.

The guy eating the hot dog wandered off and Kit let him go, believing that she'd prevented him from losing anything. What to do now with all the wallets? Since there wasn't a cop in sight, she decided to take the wallets to the Vieux Carré police station a few blocks away on Royal.

She walked down to the corner, crossed the street, and turned toward Royal. In the middle of the block, she felt a sharp tug on the grocery bag, which would have torn it from her hand had her fingers not become tangled in the handles. Before she could turn to see what was happening, she was spun around and thrown against a brick wall by a man with high cheekbones and yellowish reptilian eyes.

He showed her his left fist, one finger of which wore a ring mounted with a bulky diamond. "Gimme the sack, honey, or I'm gonna damage you bad."

He was still pulling on the bag, so that she couldn't let go. "I can't. You're—"

Seeing his hand draw back, she brought her knee up, aiming at his crotch, but he turned, so the blow merely grazed the front of his pants. His nostrils flared and anger flamed in his eyes. As his hand arced toward her face, she wished for Bubba and his pistol.

FOURTEEN

KIT PRESSED the back of her head against the wall behind her, knowing even as she did that it would not save her face. A scant tick before the diamond crashed into her cheek, a blur came from her left, striking her assailant and altering the course of his fist so that it barely missed her nose as he was spun on one foot and driven against the wall himself. With an economy of movement that almost made the fight seem choreographed, the man who had come to her aid twisted her assailant's arm at the wrist with both hands, driving him to his knees, howling. Then the one standing delivered a vicious kick to the other one's arm, producing a sharp crack like a bat hitting a home run. This brought a horrible shriek from the injured man's mouth and he was allowed to roll into a ball, clutching his arm.

"You bastard. It's busted. You busted my goddamn arm."

The whole thing had lasted only a few seconds and they'd been moving fast, mostly with her rescuer's back to Kit. But she'd known immediately who it was.

"You all right?" Nick Lawson said, turning to her.

"I think so."

"Hey, Nick, what's this all about?" a loud voice said.

Finally, a cop, one Kit didn't recognize.

Lawson pointed at the mewling body on the pavement. "Tommy, that guy attacked my friend."

"He was after this," Kit said, holding out the grocery bag. "It's full of stolen wallets."

The cop's brow knitted. "How'd you come by them?"

"I took them from an old lady picking pockets on Bourbon Street. I think that's her accomplice."

The cop turned the guy on the pavement over so he could get a better look.

"I'm Dr. Franklyn. I work for the medical examiner and the police."

"I can vouch for her," Lawson said.

Though grateful for Lawson's intervention, Kit bristled at his presumption that she needed a reference.

"Where's the old lady?" the cop asked.

"Who knows?" Kit said. "When I caught her with her hand in somebody's kangaroo pouch, she took off."

"You mind comin' around to the station and giving us a statement? Won't take but a few minutes."

"Of course," Kit said. She looked at Lawson, who appeared a bit wild-eyed.

"Lead on," he said.

The cop got the guy up and handcuffed him, ignoring his screams of protest about his broken arm. After they'd given their statements and were back on the street, Lawson let out a whoop and clapped his hands together. "What a rush." He whooped again.

Unexpectedly, Kit's knees got a case of the wobbles.

"Whoa," Lawson said, steadying her. "I think you need to sit down." He guided her half a block down the street to a dimly lighted piano bar where, as soon as they found a table, a waitress in a short black skirt, pleated blouse, and a black bow tie appeared for their order.

"Rum and Coke," Kit said. "Heavy on the rum."

The waitress accepted Lawson's order of iced tea with no change in her pleasant expression. Kit, however, found it surprising. "You don't drink?"

"Dulls the senses," Lawson said. "And you never know when you're going to want to be sharp."

"That's right, you're a..." She hesitated, searching for a phrase that wouldn't offend. "You like to take risks."

Lawson cocked his head and his eyes narrowed. "How'd you know that?"

"Someone I was talking to mentioned it in passing."

"Terry Yardley, maybe?"

"I don't divulge my sources."

"Good for you. It's true. I once heard it said that life without risk is a twilight existence. I believe that. Be honest—didn't you get just the tiniest rush out of what happened out on the street?"

"Are you kidding?"

"Don't answer out of habit. Think about it. The possibility of serious injury, rescue at the last minute, most people have to experience that at the movies or in books. You got to live it."

"I'll take the movie version anytime. Did you have to break his arm?"

"We weren't dancing out there. That guy was serious. You get in a street fight with scum, you have to put them down for good. People like that survive by exploiting charity and timidity."

The waitress arrived with their order and Lawson paid her, including a tip, which, considering the run-down place he lived in, seemed to Kit too generous. Kit hadn't touched her drinks at Shirley's, but she took a long pull at this one and quickly felt the fiber returning to her legs.

"What were you thinking when you got involved with those pickpockets?" Lawson asked.

"Like I told the cops, the old lady tried to steal my purse in the library the other day. When I saw her again, doing the same thing, I couldn't help myself."

He nodded. "I can respect that, even if it did almost get you hurt. You should have kept that little guy with the gun around a while longer."

"How'd you know about him?"

Lawson looked at her oddly over the rim of his iced tea, then lowered the glass. "I didn't exactly just happen by. I was following you."

Kit straightened in her chair. "Why?"

"Because Kyle Ricks didn't tell me anything interesting and Bill Pope wouldn't talk to me at all. I didn't know what to do next. So I thought I'd see what you'd come up with. Is Merryman working at Shirley's?"

"What makes you think that picture has anything to do with the killer we're after?"

He shot her a disappointed look. "C'mon, Kit . . . Ricks told me what you and he discussed."

"How'd you get Ricks to talk to you?"

"Why shouldn't he? Did you tell him not to?"

"Actually, I didn't."

"Wouldn't have mattered if you had, because he somehow got the idea when I called that I was your superior, checking on your conversation with him."

"And Pope didn't get that idea?"

He shrugged. "So, is Merryman working at Shirley's?"

She considered lying about Merryman, but all Lawson had to do was hang out at Shirley's a while and he'd see her. Like he said, he was a clever guy. "She's working there as a dancer."

"Big change for an EKG tech."

"She had some drug trouble at the hospital where she worked and got canned. Apparently, she's had trouble getting a job at another hospital, so she took up stripping."

"Now that wasn't so hard, was it? You gave me something and now I'm going to give you something."

"What's that?"

"The right to tell me if I can use any of this."

"I wish you wouldn't. I think the band is the key to the killer's identity and I'd prefer that stay under wraps for now."

"All right...providing you keep me posted. And I promise that whatever you want off the record stays off the record until you say otherwise. Okay?"

"Okay."

"Now, since I always like to know who I'm working with, let's talk about you. Where'd you grow up?"

"I don't think that's—"

"Humor me, please."

Kit twirled the plastic stick around the ice in her drink, setting up a tiny whirlpool. "It was an obscure little town in New York State where they think Camp Fire Girls is preparation for life in the real world."

"Doesn't sound so bad."

Even though Kit had been with Broussard for over a year and had seen in that time nearly every kind of human depravity, Phyllis Merryman had spotted her for what she still was, a small-town WASP who didn't have a prayer of becoming the streetwise liberal she wanted to be. Still smarting from Merryman's discovery of that, Kit said, "It's just that I can't seem to shed what that town did to me. Sometimes I'm so parochial I can't stand myself."

"Supportive parents that got along well?"

"Sure, the whole bit."

"Mother a good cook?"

"It sounds crazy, but I can't recall. Maybe that means she wasn't. But then, food has never been very important to me."

"Doesn't sound like you get much use out of your kitchen."

"I not only have no ability there; I have no guilt about it. Grocery shopping is something I do when I'm out of toilet paper."

"When somebody says they have no guilt about something, does that mean they really do?"

"Usually, unless it's me."

Lawson smiled, not the wise-guy grin she'd seen in the past but a genuine smile with no hidden agenda lurking in the corners. Then his expression turned wistful.

"I wouldn't have minded parents like yours. Mine paid more attention to the dog than they did to me. I took off right after my high school graduation and I'm not sure they've noticed yet that I'm gone."

"You haven't done so badly for yourself."

"I suppose. If I had any ambition, though, I probably wouldn't still be in the cop shop. But I can't imagine doing anything else. That's where the action is." He moved his glass on the table in a figure eight. "Knew that's what I wanted from the time I was an intern. I'd get to a scene and see a guy lying there all bloody and wonder what had happened...how he'd gotten in such a mess. Was it his fault, or was he minding his own business and trouble found him? From there, it was a short hop to the one responsible. What brings someone to take a life? What makes a killer? You know what I mean?"

"I've spent a few hours trying to puzzle that one out myself. Murder in the heat of passion, I understand. Murder motivated by greed, jealousy, or a desire for revenge, I still have some questions about. But the predator...the serial killer...there's the ultimate challenge. Take this guy we're after now; he seems to be totally without conscience."

"I used to think this country invented serial killers, but then there was that one recently in Russia, the Rostov Ripper."

"My guess is, they've always had them. Only now, they're willing to admit it."

Lawson took another sip of his iced tea. "You figure every culture has them?"

"I'd hate to think so," Kit replied, "because that'd suggest it's genetic, that there's a certain number born every year, like hemophiliacs."

"Scary thought, but maybe not so wrong. That guy in Omaha in the early eighties who killed those two little boys said that when he was only six, he fantasized about killing and eating the baby-sitter. In a way, a genetic cause could prove useful. I mean, maybe they could find a marker...."

"Then what, screen all new babies?"

"Sure, why not?"

"What happens when they find one with the marker?"

Lawson thought about this a moment, then said, "Well, you'd never get a baby-sitter for him."

Despite the subject of the conversation, both smiled. Sitting there, all comfortable and safe with her belly warmed by the rum, Kit began to see what a charmer Lawson could be.

"Now a *very* personal question," he said. Getting no protest, he continued. "Are you seeing anyone?"

"Yes."

"Is it serious?"

"We don't date others."

Lawson raised one hand. "Okay, I accept that...for now. But things change. When they do, will you keep me in mind?"

Kit shook her head. He might have saved her, but she wasn't going to turn her personal life inside out for his inspection. "First, there's no chance in the wind. Second, you're not my type. I prefer men who aren't likely to come up missing someday because they were killed performing some fool stunt."

"I'd tell you I could change, but that'd be a lie. So I guess you'll have to."

"Don't count on it. Now, as pleasant as this has been, I'm going home."

Lawson had parked in the same lot, so they walked there together. In the rearview mirror, she saw him watch her drive away. It had indeed been a nice talk and she'd changed her opinion of him for the better. But that didn't mean she felt guilty for failing to mention the killer's forensic connection. Nor was she sorry she omitted her belief that when she and Phyllis Merryman were talking about the Heartbeats, Merryman had definitely held something back.

FIFTEEN

THE NEXT MORNING, out of ideas with her part of the investigation stalled, Kit headed for the Hyatt.

Just inside the main entrance, she saw a "48 Hours" TV crew tagging along after a small man in a blue suit, their camera trained on his feet. She did not recognize the object of their attention but was pretty sure it wasn't James Starrs, the head of the team that on Friday would be discussing the results of their exhumation of Huey Long's assassin. There would certainly be a lot of media coverage for that.

She wondered if someday at these meetings there might be a session on the killer she was chasing. Maybe...but only if he was caught. And right now, she wasn't being much help.

She went up the escalator to the Regency Foyer and scanned the milling attendees, hoping to see Broussard. But he was not there, most likely being in the Pathology session, where at 10:15 he'd be giving his paper. She walked to the hospitality table.

"Any crises?"

"Everything's running smoothly, dear," Mrs. Gervais said, so loudly that she could be heard far down the foyer.

"Can't tell you how much I appreciate you doing this," Kit said. "I know it isn't much fun sitting here all day."

"Don't be silly—I'm enjoying myself," Edna said. "Now I think I have a customer."

While Edna helped the attendee decide what he should do with his spare time, Kit went looking for Burgundy Rooms A-D. Ahead of her, two men going in opposite directions hailed each other.

"Poisoning anybody?" the one going her way said.

"Rigging the tests and denying it all," the other one replied.

Burgundy A-D was a series of small rooms on the fourth floor. Properly anticipating a good crowd, the organizers had pulled the partitions, making one large room. Kit found a seat on the right about six rows from the front, where five men were seated behind a draped table on a raised platform.

For the next forty minutes, she tried to concentrate on a succession of speakers discussing psychological autopsies conducted in the wake of the USS *Iowa* incident, where one of the crew was suspected of committing suicide by causing a gun turret to explode. Ordinarily, she would have listened intently, but her mind was too full of the week's events for that to be possible.

When the last speaker finished, a voice rose from the back. "I don't know why they called in psychiatrists in the first place. If they really wanted to know what happened, they should have come to a forensic pathologist. Face it, you boys are out of your depth here."

Kit looked back and saw that this came from a mustached man standing by the side door. His comment caused a thin old man in a brown suit to leave his chair a few rows behind Kit and charge to the front of the room, where he grabbed a microphone off the speaker's table. "You . . . you . . . pathologists are good when it comes to *cause* of death," he said in a foreign accent wavering with emotion. "But you are not so good at determining *mode*. I'd rather have a poor psychiatrist on a suicide case than a good pathologist."

This caused a great stir in the audience. Wearing a self-satisfied smile, the old man put the mike back and steered a course toward his seat. He was intercepted by a silver-haired man on the aisle who grabbed the old man's arm. "How many suicide scenes have you attended?"

"None," the old man said.

"That's what I thought," the other guy said, letting the old man go.

The room prickled with animosity. At this point, the moderator of the session leaned into his mike and said, "I can't tell you how good it is to see psychiatrists arguing with someone else for a change."

This caused a good deal of laughter and the session broke up on a congenial note. But Kit was not laughing. Psychiatrists and psychologists, she had expected at this session, but not pathologists.

The evidence Broussard had uncovered suggested that the killer might be a pathologist. She studied the silver-haired man, who was shaking hands with a colleague, then she glanced back for another look at the aggressive fellow by the door, who was now making notes in a tiny spiral pad. Both were normal in appearance, both well dressed. Neither seemed likely to cause alarm if they approached you on the street late at night.

She examined the faces of the men talking with the speakers, briefly fitting each of them into the malleable picture she had of the killer. Finally, she left by the front entrance and went back downstairs, keenly aware that if the killer had not been in the Burgundy Room, he might well be in the session she was about to join.

BROUSSARD LOWERED the laser pointer and began his summary, satisfied on two counts. Not only had his delivery been okay but he'd kept Franks from getting to his slides.

He had been feeling a shade better since figuring out what the three hairs meant, but there was still a lingering emptiness inside him. A part of him wanted to give in to that emptiness and follow the beckoning darkness. But he could not . . . not now . . . not when a murderous colleague with a colossal ego was still free to roam the city.

The chairman of the session called for questions from the huge audience and Jason Harvey rose from his seat near the back and made his way to a microphone on the aisle.

"Dr. Broussard, it strikes me that these cases you describe are not at all common."

There was a buzz in the room at this amazing statement.

"Which is perhaps why I described them as 'atypical' in my title," Broussard said pleasantly.

"It also strikes me that we should not be dwelling at these gatherings on the unlikely, but, rather should be concentrating on patterns that we'll be seeing in the great majority of cases we encounter. To do otherwise is merely to indulge in esoterica."

Harvey returned to his seat. His position was ridiculous. Believing that this was so self-evident as not to need reiteration, Broussard simply said, "I'm sure we'll all give your observation careful consideration, Dr. Harvey."

There were no more questions and the session took its midmorning break.

"What a jerk," Kit said as Broussard joined her in the foyer. "You let him off too easy."

"There's no virtue in engagin' in a battle of wits with an unarmed man," Broussard said, reaching in his pants pocket for a lemon ball, which he slipped into his mouth. He offered her the customary two wrapped in gold cellophane and she accepted. "You get anywhere with that singer you were gonna talk to?"

"Yes and no," she replied, putting the candies in her bag. "There's something there, but she won't come clean . . . and we're running out of time."

Kit was surprised to see Nick Lawson come out of the ballroom. His head was slightly bent so he could hear what the shorter man beside him was saying. Noticing her, he waved. She waved back and Broussard turned to see who might be joining them.

"You wavin' to Nick Lawson?"

"Yes."

"Thought you didn't like him."

"He did me a big favor. Last night when I was down in the Quarter to find that girl we were talking about, I got mixed up with a pickpocket."

"You lose your money?"

"Just the opposite. I ended up with six wallets that didn't belong to me."

"How many wallets the other pickpocket end up with?"

"Very funny. Anyway, while I was taking them to the police station, the pickpocket's partner tried to take them back by force. But Nick stopped him."

"You were together?"

"No. He was following me, trying to find the singer I talked to."

"So he knows about the article?"

"He was in the photo lab when my contact at the paper arranged to have prints of the band's picture made for me."

"He gonna write about it?"

"I don't think so. He said he wouldn't."

"You know who that is with him?"

"Who?"

"An anthropologist on Phillip's list."

"You're saying Lawson probably knows that we think the killer's at the meeting?"

"Hard to believe otherwise."

"I think I could get him not to write about it."

"Doesn't much matter. I'm sure it's all over the place by now."

"Interesting exchange you had in there with Harvey," Hugh Greenwood said, coming up to them. "The man needs a keeper. But you did well not to rise to the bait. Very mature."

"Believe me, the bait was temptin'."

"Andy..."

It was Zin Fanelli, looking sheepish and worried. "What Harvey said the other day about me saying you were never good with knife wounds... I swear to God, I never..."

Broussard put a hand on Fanelli's shoulder. "It's all right, Zin. I didn't take it seriously."

The contrition in Fanelli's face evaporated. "Great. I'm really glad to hear that. Thanks." He backed away, practically bowing. "Thanks a lot."

"What's with Fanelli?" Leo Fleming said, joining the group. "He was actin' like a Chinese houseboy."

"Apologizin' for somethin' he didn't do," Broussard said.

"Low self-esteem, probably," Fleming observed. "Guess you've already discussed Harvey's perceptive comment."

"Hard not to," Greenwood said.

"Anybody else hungry?" Broussard asked. "They've got a great bread pudding here."

"I wouldn't mind some coffee," Fleming said.

Kit had been hoping to get some time alone with Broussard to pick his brain about Phyllis Merryman. Now, that wouldn't be possible. Reluctantly, she followed the others to the restaurant in the atrium.

When they were seated and had placed their orders, Greenwood said, "I heard the police are grilling some of our colleagues about those murders. You thinking he's one of us?"

Broussard glanced knowingly at Kit and said, "Looks that way."

Greenwood smiled, or at least tried to, his scars pulling his lips into odd directions. "I like that, I really do.... Helluva' interesting twist. Why don't I ever get anything that unusual? Sort of puts you on the spot, though, doesn't it, Andy? Usually you're up against uninformed fools. But now... this is different. If he gets away, tongues will wag."

Broussard did not respond, his attention diverted by the approach of Phil Gatlin.

"Three down and a crowd to go," Gatlin said. "My ten-thirty rescheduled at the last minute, so I've got some time to kill."

"Pull up a chair," Broussard said. "You know Leo, but I don't believe you've met Hugh Greenwood."

As Gatlin took Greenwood's outstretched hand, he stared at Greenwood's name tag, his brow furrowed. He released Greenwood's hand and reached in his pocket for his little black book, which he consulted. Then, looking at Greenwood, he said, "I wonder if we could talk for a few minutes."

"Sure," Greenwood said. "Join us."

"You might prefer we do this in private."

"That sounds serious."

"Murder is always serious."

"Of course it is. If I can help, it'd be my pleasure."

"We can go..."

"I've got coffee and a sweet roll coming," Greenwood said. "So why don't we talk right here."

"Your call," Gatlin said, pulling a chair over from an adjoining table. "Dr. Greenwood, as I'm sure you know, we've had a series of murders over the last five days, all committed by the same person. The last occurred early yesterday morning down by the river. After the body was discovered, we had men stopping all pedestrians in the vicinity. My records indicate that you were one of those we stopped. Mind telling me what you were doing out at such an hour?"

"I don't sleep well when I travel," Greenwood said. "And after all, this *is* a town known for its nightlife."

"When did you get here?"

"Left Indie at seven-thirty P.M. Sunday, arrived at nine-thirty."

"Would you mind if we went to your room and had a look at your plane ticket?"

"Can't it wait until after I've eaten?"

"I don't have much time."

Greenwood pushed his chair back and stood up. Looking at Broussard, he said, "Have the waitress hold the order, will you?"

When they were out of earshot, Fleming said, "I know he's an odd duck, but I don't think he's *that* odd."

"Who do you know that *is* that odd?" Broussard asked.

"Good point."

"Remember that comment he made the other night while we were all walking to the Quarter for dinner?" Kit asked. "How he said in hand-to-hand combat with a knife, when you strike the lethal blow, it makes you want to howl...."

"But these are murders," Broussard said. "Except for the last one, the victims were unarmed. It's not the same thing."

"If you get away without being caught, wouldn't that give you the same feeling?"

Broussard shrugged. "Hard to say."

Over Broussard's shoulder, Kit saw a small man with thinning hair and a tie that stopped far too short of his belt coming their way. He was carrying a circular black slide tray.

"Dr. Broussard, glad I found you. You forgot your slides."

Broussard thanked him and put the tray on the table. Before the conversation could resume, he looked into the central circular opening of the tray and removed a folded piece of paper with a rubber band around it.

"What's that?" Fleming asked.

"A note with my name on it."

Broussard took off the rubber band and put it on the table along with a loose slip of paper bearing his name in

Courier typeface. As he unfolded the note, three large dried insects fell out of it onto the white tablecloth. Kit leaned over for a better look. They were a kind she'd never seen before, multiple legs on the front, smooth behind. "What are they?" she asked.

Broussard turned one over with his knife. "Eyelids," he said.

Kit's stomach pitched and yawed.

"I want to talk to that projectionist," Broussard said, coaxing the eyelids back onto the paper with his knife. He hastily refolded the paper with the eyelids inside and put it in his shirt pocket along with the slip of paper and the rubber band. He grabbed his slide carrier, got up, and headed for the ballroom.

Feeling a little better now that the eyelids were out of sight, Kit looked at Fleming and he looked back, both of them unsure of what to do. Then they both got up to follow Broussard, Fleming nearly knocking the waitress's tray from her hand as she arrived with their food.

"Darlin', somethin' has come up and we may not get back," he said. "Just figure the bill, give yourself twenty percent, and leave it with the cashier. I'll sign it later. I'm in eight-oh-two." He showed her his Hyatt key card and hurried to catch up with Kit and Broussard.

They found the projectionist fiddling with the slide carriers for the next round of talks, lining them up in order on some shelves under the projector stand, where he'd pasted temporary labels bearing the speakers' names on each carrier. He looked up at Broussard's approach.

"When you brought my slides to me, there was a folded piece of paper with my name on it in here," Broussard said, putting his fingers in the round opening. "Did you see who put it there?"

"Sure didn't. I put the tray on that shelf and racked up the next talk. Then my boss came by and we talked some about my work schedule. So I wasn't paying any attention. The other speakers picked up their slides and I noticed yours were still there. I didn't know if you were coming back, so I thought I'd better see if I could find you. To be honest, I didn't even notice the note."

"Okay, thanks."

Broussard herded Kit and Fleming back into the lobby, where they saw Phil Gatlin emerging from the elevators. Broussard called his name and he came their way.

"You all sure ate fast," he said.

Broussard explained what had happened and showed Gatlin the eyelids and the slip of paper with his name on it.

"Put 'em away," Gatlin said. "You didn't have to show me. I'd have taken your word for it. This guy's really enjoying himself, isn't he? Who's the projectionist? He in forensics?"

"Hotel employee," Broussard said. He went on to relate what the projectionist had said.

Gatlin gestured to the ballroom. "How many were in there during your talk?"

"Seven or eight hundred."

"That figures." Gatlin ran his big mitt down his face in exasperation, fuzzing his heavy eyebrows. "Was one of 'em Hugh Greenwood?"

"He was there," Broussard said. "But it could have been anybody."

Gatlin held out his hand. "Gimme the packet and what came with it. I'll have somebody drop it by the lab and see if they can come up with anything, or I could just throw it all in the river. Probably be the same either way. Basically, he's gonna win this one, but we did learn one thing. He's definitely here at the meeting."

"I already told you that," Broussard said.

"God forbid I should need proof," Gatlin said, crossing himself to ensure that his remark wouldn't be used against him someday by a heavenly prosecutor. Unhappily, he put the objects from Broussard into the outside pocket of his jacket, excused himself, and walked toward the phones at the far end of the lobby.

"He's usually not that contrary," Broussard explained to Fleming. "This case is just gettin' under his skin. Mine, too, for that matter."

"How is that guy Gatlin as a detective?" Hugh Greenwood said, joining the group.

"First-rate," Broussard replied.

"I'm not so sure. He seemed too satisfied with my plane ticket."

"What do you mean?" Fleming asked.

"He was trying to find out if I was in town when the first murder took place. But how does he know I don't have another ticket bought under a phony name? I could have come in earlier on that ticket and simply torn off the Indie—New Orleans leg on the one I showed him. I might not have even been on that plane."

At the phones, Gatlin pulled out a directory and looked up the number of Northwest Airlines.

SIXTEEN

"WHY'D EVERYBODY LEAVE the restaurant?" Greenwood asked.

Kit waited for Broussard to take this one, since she didn't want to blab something he wanted kept quiet. Of course, if Greenwood was the killer, they couldn't tell him anything he didn't already know, except maybe that his little prank had been found. As it turned out, Kit didn't get to see how Broussard would have answered, because Charlie Franks interrupted.

Charlie had missed the morning session because he had work to do at the morgue. From the look on his face, something was wrong. "We got trouble," he said, ignoring everyone but Broussard.

Taking the hint, Fleming and Greenwood said they'd see Broussard later. Still hoping to get a few minutes alone with him, Kit remained.

When it was safe to talk, Franks said, "McCasland has really screwed up this time—the incision for removal of the skullcap. Instead of going through the hairline, he made it just above the eyebrows."

Broussard groaned.

"What are we gonna do?" Franks said. "The family's gonna be mad as hell."

"How could he make such a mistake?" Broussard asked.

"Said he just wasn't thinking."

"No kiddin'. You chew him out?"

"Left him with pieces missing. But I saved a little for you."

"Good. I'd like a turn...." Broussard rubbed his beard hard in irritation. "I can probably fix it with some subcutaneous stitches and wax."

"You need me for anything? If not, I'm gonna stick around here a while."

"I can handle it. See you both later."

Disappointed, Kit watched Broussard move off toward the escalator.

"I almost forgot," Franks said, reaching into his shirt pocket. "Margaret said if I ran into you to give you this."

He handed Kit a pink message slip.

On it were three words—"Call Phyllis Merryman"—and a number.

As HE WAS ABOUT TO step on the escalator, Broussard was intercepted by Phil Gatlin. "What do you think about Greenwood being near the scene of the last murder?" he asked.

"Hard to know what to think."

"Like he said, his airline ticket was for a flight that arrived late Sunday, which would mean he wasn't even in town for the first murder. I checked with Northwest and they said he was on that flight."

"Based on what?"

"The ticket they take as you board. The records are based on that. So he didn't just tear off the ticket and throw it away. But who's to say he didn't make an earlier round-trip as well, using a different name? That way, he could have committed the first murder, gone home, then returned on the flight I checked. Here now legitimately, he could have done the other two."

"It's not possible," Broussard said.

"You two good friends?"

"I wouldn't go that far with it. Why?"

"Seems to me that there's a competitive element in this....
Whoever's doing it is trying to show you up."

"I'll have to make sure, then, that he doesn't succeed."

"Well you better hurry, because I'm sucking wind."

"I WAS TOLD YOU CALLED," Kit said into the pay phone.

"I've got something for you," Phyllis Merryman replied. "If you want it, meet me at the cosmetics section of
the Walgreen's on Canal in twenty minutes."

Twenty minutes was barely enough time. Kit walked
through the doors of Walgreen's two minutes late, but convinced that she hadn't inadvertently brought Nick Lawson
along. The place was bustling with lunch-hour business and
it was another minute before she made it to the cosmetics
section, where she found Phyllis Merryman at the lipsticks.

She was wearing a tight suit with padded shoulders, a skirt
that cut her at midthigh, and spike heels that would cause
any man's eyes to linger on her long legs. The suit was a
black houndstooth check that, minus the red buttons on the
sleeve, reminded Kit of the interference on her TV whenever the neighborhood ham radio operator transmitted. She
was carrying a red purse and a large manila envelope.

She turned at Kit's approach and pointed at one of the
phony lipsticks on display. "You like this color with this
outfit?"

Preferring lip gloss, Kit pointed at another color. "I think
it's a little too red. This one is better. You're very dressy today."

"Someone's taking me to lunch and then the art museum," she replied, obviously proud of herself. Then,
somewhat less confidently, she added, "You don't think I'm
overdressed for a museum?"

"No. You're fine."

Merryman wrinkled her nose. "Well, this is what I'm wearing, and if the museum crowd doesn't like it, they can take a flying leap."

"You said you had something for me."

"Excuse me, ladies, could I get in there?"

It was a clerk with a box of lipsticks to put up. They moved down a little and Merryman held out the manila envelope.

"What's this?" Kit said, taking it.

"I have no idea." Responding to Kit's puzzled expression, Merryman explained. "Couple weeks ago, a guy stops me on the street.... I never saw him before, but he knows me...asks if I want to make two hundred bucks. I figure he wants to get cozy, but he says no. What I have to do is keep this envelope and give it to anybody who comes around asking about the Heartbeats. I get a hundred on the front end and a hundred after it's delivered. I ask him how he's gonna know when I deliver it and he says he'll know. So I agree."

"What did this guy look like?"

"Short, heavyset, thin mustache."

"Why didn't you mention this when we talked yesterday?"

"I been thinking ever since I agreed to do this...I don't know what's in there; maybe it's something illegal that'll get me in trouble. What could be so important and be as flat as that, plans for a nuclear reactor maybe—who knows? Anyway, I wanted time to see if you were really who you said you were. Jesus, how much longer you gonna stand there without opening it? If I could have figured out how to get inside without tearing it, I'd have sneaked a look before this."

Kit tore the flap open and removed a single sheet of paper folded once in the middle. Printed on both sides were hundreds of cartoon figures. On one side, the figures were shirtless and hooded, a gathering of medieval executioners maybe, engaging in a variety of athletic contests, many of which involved rocks. On the back, where the figures looked more Oriental, they were waging war with pikes and spears. In the upper-left corner, there was a scroll whose surface was not smooth like the rest of the page but was raw and rough, as though it had been stripped off with adhesive tape.

"What is it?" Merryman asked.

"I don't know," Kit replied.

"You got some weird friends," Merryman said. "I gotta go." She went back to the lipsticks, picked one up, and came back down the aisle. "I'm going with my first choice," she said, holding it up. "See you around."

Kit stood for a moment staring at one side of the page, then turned it over. There was no doubt that the Heartbeats *had* been a clue and that she was on the right track. But what now? There was no message, no hint as to what this meant.

Executioners on one side and a battle on the other. The killer was certainly acting as an executioner and they *were* in a battle with him. But that couldn't be all there was to it. She needed help. Broussard? Maybe eventually. Not yet. Give it some more thought first.

One edge of the page was uneven as though it had been cut from a book, a comic book maybe—not a regular one; it was too big for that. Possibly an underground comic.

THE DAILY PLANET was on one end of a row of small one-story buildings constructed in the forties. It was painted gray except for the wall facing the parking lot. Here, there was a huge mural depicting Superman in midflight, carrying an adoring Lois Lane, her arms looped around his neck. This Superman's vulnerability was not limited to Kryptonite, for since the wall had been painted, some of the brick had flaked away, leaving the caped one with an ugly chest wound.

Kit parked next to an old Chevy with a broken taillight and a lopsided bumper, leaving plenty of room for its owner to open his door without hitting her car. Picking the manila envelope off the seat next to her, she locked up and went inside.

It hadn't taken much renovation for the Daily Planet to open. There was a cash register on a glass display case to the left, but the rest of the place was nothing but long folding tables loaded with cardboard boxes, each just wide enough to hold a column of comics individually packaged in plastic. Thumbing through the stock were two kids who should have been in school, the owners no doubt of the two bicycles locked to the rack out front.

She expected the clerk to be an overage skateboarder with a bad complexion. Instead, she found a middle-aged man quite normal in appearance, neatly dressed in a pale green madras shirt and pleated slacks the color of a well-ripened avocado. He was studying a piece of paper through the bifocal part of Clark Kent glasses. Across the counter, a fellow in his late thirties, wearing scuffed loafers and a wilted brown suit, was working on his nails with a folding tool attached to his key chain. On the counter beside him was a cardboard box sealed with duct tape.

This tableau lasted another few seconds, then the clerk looked up. "Hundred and fifty for the lot."

The other guy's eyebrows lifted in disbelief. "A hundred and fifty? C'mon, they're all early seventies and in mint condition. They never even been read. There's fifteen copies of Shazam number one in there. Those alone gotta be worth what you're offerin' for all of it. Christ, they got the original Captain Marvel artist to come out of retirement to do that issue."

"Sorry, hundred and fifty's the best I can do. Take it or leave it."

"Stuff that," the guy said, grabbing his box and making for the door.

The clerk watched him until he was out on the sidewalk, then turned to Kit. "See it all the time. People hear that old comics are worth a fortune, so they figure they'll make a little investment. They go out, buy up a bunch of new comics, put 'em in the attic, and twenty years later are ready to harvest the profits. What they don't think of is that if *they* had the idea, so did a thousand others. I could lay my hands on a hundred copies of Shazam number one practically by snapping my fingers. Only comics worth much are the ones that came out before anybody thought they'd be valuable. If mom had only known, she'd never have thrown junior's collection away. But that's why they're valuable. Love those moms. You looking to buy or sell?"

"I might be a buyer," Kit said, opening the manila folder and taking out the page of cartoons. She unfolded it and put it on the counter. "Do you know what this came from?"

He leaned over and studied the page briefly, then examined the other side, finally saying, "Don't think it's from a comic book, least not one I ever saw. Maybe a child's book."

BEATON BOOKS HAD OPENED barely a year earlier but had quickly become one of the area's best bookstores. Not only was it the biggest but it offered cappuccino at a reasonable price and had a reading area with big soft chairs.

Business was never slow at Beaton's, but today, at least, it wasn't packed like it usually was on weekends. Kit walked past the cashier, who had a small line vying for her attention, and went to the special-order section, which was manned by a thin young man whose neck cleared the collar

of his white shirt by a half inch all around. She did not remember seeing him there before.

"Did you need something?" he said.

Kit produced the page of cartoons and explained why
she'd come.

The clerk looked at the page briefly and his face shifted
to an expression that suggested he'd rather be in the back
opening boxes. Instead of simply admitting he couldn't help,
he made a big production out of it. "Lady, we got fifty
thousand books here," he said, waving one arm theatri-
cally. "Gimme a title and I can tell you if we have it, how
many we have, how many we've sold in the last two weeks,
the last two months, and since it first arrived. Gimme an
author and I can do the same thing.... But I don't think
anybody could look at one page of a book and tell you—"

"Maybe I can help," an older woman said, coming from
the curtained doorway behind the clerk.

Kit was encouraged to see that she wore her hair in a bun,
like Terry Yardley at the *Picayune*. It had been Kit's experience that women who wore their hair this way were usually very knowledgeable about their jobs. It was a peculiar
association that called for further study. "I was hoping I
might be able to find the book this page was taken from."

The woman picked up the page, looked at it, and smiled.
"It's over here," she said, coming from behind the counter.

Kit glanced at the skinny clerk to see if he was properly
humbled, but he was mesmerized by a girl in a short skirt
browsing at a nearby table of paperbacks.

Kit followed the woman into the children's section, where
she went to a display of oversized books and pulled one
from the shelf. She thumbed through it, then held it open so
Kit could see. "That's the page right there. And—" her
finger hovered over the page, drawing irregular patterns in
the air "—somewhere in there is Waldo."

"Waldo?" Kit echoed.

The woman fixed Kit with an expression of patronizing kindness. "You don't know Waldo? My goodness." She turned to the inside front cover, where there was a line of cartoon figures across both pages. "This is Waldo." She pointed at a figure carrying a cane and wearing a Santa Claus hat and a red-and-white-striped shirt. "I'm surprised you haven't heard of him. It's one of the best-selling children's series ever. The idea is to find Waldo among all the other figures on the page. This one is *The Great Waldo Search*. It's actually the third in the series." She pointed at a book on the shelf. "First, there was *Find Waldo*." Her finger moved to the right. "Then there was *Find Waldo Now*. In the first book, the scenes aren't all that crowded and it's easy to find him. Then with each succeeding book, it gets harder...more figures in each scene, figures that resemble Waldo more. In this one—" she turned to the back page and showed her five hundred Waldos "—you have to find the Waldo with only one shoe. If you have kids, it'll keep them busy for hours. It's become a real craze."

She closed the book and put it back on the shelf. "There's even this now...."

She picked up a transparent cylinder filled with liquid that contained a mass of glittering objects. She turned it end for end and the glittery stuff sank slowly in the thick liquid. "Somewhere in there is Waldo," she said. "It's astounding to me that you haven't heard of him."

Despite the help she was getting, Kit was growing weary of the woman's amazement at her lack of kiddie lore.

"Why, at the supermarket the other day, I even saw a 'Find Waldo' spaghetti."

SEVENTEEN

KIT WAS hugely disappointed. To have merely uncovered a bit of confirming information after all she'd gone through left her limp and disgusted. She sat dumbly behind the wheel, her limbs unwilling to move.

Find Waldo...

Clearly this was related to the fact that the killer was attending the Forensic meeting. Find Waldo in an obfuscating crowd of people in the same profession. Broussard had already given them that.

She reviewed her contributions to the case and found them meager indeed. Why was she always merely cleaning up after Broussard? Why couldn't she just once have a major influence on the direction of an investigation? Second fiddle was getting hard to play.

She couldn't sit in Beaton's parking lot all day, so she started the car and vaguely aimed it for downtown. Checking her watch, she found it was 1:10. She considered stopping somewhere for lunch but had no appetite.

As much as she regretted having to report to Broussard with so little, it had to be done. Thinking he might still be at the office, she began her search there. But Jolanda said that he'd just gone back to the Hyatt. Since he always seemed to be surrounded by an entourage at the hotel, she hurried to catch him en route.

When Kit stepped onto LaSalle, she saw Broussard's familiar shape a block away. She caught up with him a few steps beyond the Perdido intersection.

"You gettin' as tired of this walk as I am?" he said.

They would be at the hotel in a few minutes, so Kit launched directly into her report. "Our killer *was* the one that marked that newspaper article."

Broussard stopped walking and looked at her with interest.

"Remember, I was going to talk to the girl in the picture? Well, a few weeks ago someone gave her an envelope to pass along to anyone who came to her inquiring about the Heartbeats. This is what was in the envelope."

She opened it and gave Broussard the page of cartoons. "It's from a children's book called *The Great Waldo Search*. The point is to find Waldo, a little man in a Santa Claus hat and a red-and-white-striped shirt."

"That him?" Broussard said, ignoring the hundreds of figures on the page and pointing at Waldo, half-hidden by a gang of executioners.

"Yes," Kit said, impressed at how easily he'd found him.

He turned the page over and looked at the other crowded scene for barely a second and found Waldo again. "Too easy," he said, handing the page back.

"And redundant," Kit replied. "All that work for another clue that he's at the Forensic meeting."

They walked for another half a block, with Broussard deep in thought, Kit letting his wheels turn. Finally, he said, "What'd the guy look like who gave Merryman the envelope?"

Kit's outlook brightened. In her disappointment at the Waldo clue, she'd forgotten a potentially valuable piece of information.

"Short, heavyset, thin mustache."

Broussard remained in thought the rest of the way to the Hyatt. As they entered the Regency Foyer, they encountered an excited Leo Fleming.

"Andy, Kit, I was just talking to Brookie and he said something that could be important. That article Kit found—

the band—one of the members was an EKG tech, one a lab tech, one a cardiology resident, and the other a respiratory therapist. Wouldn't they make a good Harvey team?"

Kit stiffened. Harvey team was what some hospitals called the emergency unit that handled cardiac arrests. "Jason Harvey," she said breathlessly, her heart tripping.

"It makes sense, Andy," Fleming said. "He hates our guts. So he's doin' this to embarrass you on your own turf."

"We need to find Gatlin," Kit said, looking at Broussard.

"He's in the Waikiki Room," Broussard said, moving off toward the Regency Conference Center.

On the way, they passed Jason Harvey, who was talking to another man. Broussard and Fleming ignored him, but out of the corner of her eye, Kit saw Harvey watching them.

There were two cops in uniform outside the hall leading to the Hawaiian rooms. They nodded at Broussard when he passed and went back to their conversation. In the Waikiki Room, Broussard found Gatlin sitting on a metal chair at a folding table, a small pile of manila folders at one hand, a pitcher of water and a glass at the other. Opposite him, looking very uncomfortable, was a young anthropologist Broussard had met the day before.

"Sorry to butt in, Phillip, but could I have a word with you in private?"

Gatlin excused himself and left the anthropologist fidgeting and playing with his tie.

"What's up?" Gatlin said, closing the door behind him as he stepped into the hall.

Broussard took him out to where Kit and Fleming were waiting and related the information that had come their way. When Broussard finished, Gatlin said, "He was in town early enough. In fact, he was the one I interviewed before the guy in there now. Got on a high horse and gave me a lot of lip." He looked at Kit. "Could you find Phyllis Merry-man?"

Kit shrugged. "I suppose tonight, we could—"

"Not tonight . . . now."

"Why?"

"What Andy just told me doesn't amount to spit. I need her to identify Harvey as the guy who gave her the envelope."

"I never got her address," Kit said. "I met her at the bar where she dances. And she wouldn't be there now because . . ." *The art museum.* "She said she was going to the art museum after lunch."

"Stay right here," Gatlin said. "In a few minutes, we're going for a ride." He went down the hall, stuck his head into the Waikiki Room, and told the anthropologist he could go. After a short conversation with detective Woodsy Newsom, conducting interviews in the Maui Room next door, and another with detective Art Liberal in the Kulima Room, he headed for the Hyatt lobby, motioning for Kit to come along. Fleming looked at his watch.

"There's a paper I want to hear in the Anthro session," he said. "So I'm gonna leave you all to carry on alone. Good luck with that ID. *I* sure wouldn't lose any sleep if it turned out to be Harvey."

Fleming went up the steps to the mall, and Kit and Broussard hurried after Gatlin. His car was parked at the hotel's front entrance, under the huge portico. Before going to it, he said to Kit, "It's gonna be a few minutes before we leave. So you might want to wait in here."

"How about I catch a ride with you back to my office?" Broussard said. "There's somethin' I need to do."

Gatlin went to his car and, through the lobby window, Kit saw him pick up his cellular phone. Ten minutes later, a car pulled up beside Gatlin's Pontiac and Gatlin got out to meet its occupant. They talked briefly and the guy handed Gatlin some papers, which Gatlin examined, then folded and put in his jacket pocket.

He motioned for Kit and Broussard and they went outside. The guy who gave Gatlin the papers came in by a different door. Since Broussard was going only a short way, he sat in back, leaving the front for Kit.

"Who was that guy?" she said, buckling up.

"Dick Kimmel," Gatlin replied. "He's gonna finish my interviews for me."

"So you don't have a lot of faith in what we're doing?"

"Should I?"

"Andy does."

Gatlin looked in the mirror as he pulled onto Poydras. "That right?"

"Keep your eye on the road," Broussard groused. "I haven't got time to be in a car wreck."

They let Broussard out at the corner of LaSalle and Tulane, promised to keep him informed, then set out for the museum.

"How does Andy seem to you?" Kit said as Gatlin wheeled the Pontiac left onto Tulane.

"Opinionated, stubborn, obtuse. The usual. Why?"

"He seems down to me . . . distracted. Like going back to his office. He just came from there. It's not like him to be so disorganized."

"I wouldn't worry about it. He's wired different from the rest of us. It takes some getting used to. I've known him for nearly thirty years and I still don't understand him. Whatever it is, he'll handle it."

"I guess. Was the lab able to tell us anything about the packet with the eyelids?"

"Nothing that helps me."

"What's going to happen if we find Merryman?"

"Kimmel brought me a fax of Harvey's driver's license. I'll show her that and some others and we'll see what she says."

"Wouldn't a lineup be better?"

"If she actually saw one of the murders, yeah. But what have we got—somebody handed her an envelope with a page of cartoons in it. We'll need a lot more than that to convict him . . . if, in fact, he did it. Right now, he has no reason to be nervous. Sure, we questioned him, but we're talking to a lot of people. We put him in a lineup, he'll know we think it's him. I don't want to tell him that."

THE MUSEUM LAY at the end of a long oak-lined avenue divided by a wide, weedy median. It was columned and stepped in tiny lines inspired by the ancient Greeks, but out front it was bound to the present by a sculpture of flying scalpel blades sitting in a reflecting pool full of leaf litter.

Kit had been with Broussard long enough to know that investigations sometimes take perverse turns that help the wrong side. Today, that was not the case, for as she and Gatlin went up the steps of the museum, the door opened and Phyllis Merryman came out on the arm of a beefy male with a short haircut and a well-trimmed mustache. He was wearing gray pants with a knife-sharp crease and a gray-and-white sport coat of rough linen. His shirt was open at the neck and the sun flashed off a thin gold chain at his throat. Merryman did not look happy to see them.

"Phyllis, I need your help," Kit said.

Reading cop all over Gatlin, Merryman looked at her companion. "Kenny, would you mind if I talked to these people alone? It's some family business and kind of private."

Kenny patted Merryman's arm. "Sure, Phyll, no problem."

Respecting her wish to keep Kenny in the dark about who
they were, Kit waited until he was out of range, then introduced Gatlin.

"It's possible that the man who gave you the envelope is
the murderer we're after," he said. "But we can't do anything about it without an identification from you. I'd like
to show you some pictures to see if he's among them."

"I already did my part by passing along the envelope,"
Merryman said.

"We're not asking for much," Gatlin said, "and it'll only
take a minute. Surely you want to see this man put away
before he kills again. And there's every indication he will."

Merryman looked anxiously past Gatlin to where Kenny
waited in the car. "That guy I'm with ... he builds shopping malls and he likes me," she said. Her eyes shifted to
Kit. "He's not really my type, but I'm not making the same
mistake I did with Gene Ochs. I'm not letting this one get
away. And I don't want him thinking I'm mixed up in this."

"All you'll be doing is looking at some pictures," Gatlin
said. "The way we're standing, he won't even see what's
happening."

Merryman glanced again in Kenny's direction. "Okay,
let's get it over with."

Gatlin produced the sheaf of papers he'd been given by
the detective at the Hyatt. He unfolded them and handed
them to Merryman. She barely looked at the first one and
said, "Boy, are these crappy!"

"Just do your best."

Clearly impatient to be gone, she hurried through the
stack, giving each picture no more than a second or two.
Then she paused, cocked her head, and bit her red lip in
thought. She checked the last two pictures, flipped back to
the one she'd stalled on, and shifted it to the top.

"That looks like him," she said, giving the pile to Gatlin. "Now, can I get on with my life?"

Gatlin glanced at the picture she'd chosen, then gave the stack back to her. "I'd like you to write what you said at the bottom of the page...exactly those words—'That looks like him'—and then add, 'the man who gave me the envelope,' and sign it."

With a disgusted look, Phyllis took the pictures and the pen Gatlin offered. "You're determined to drag me into this, aren't you? I got nothing to write on."

Gatlin produced the leather jacket for his badge and slipped it under the last page in the stack. Phyllis scribbled her statement, signed it, and gave everything back.

"Is there anything else I can do for you?"

Gatlin put his badge and the pages in the inside pocket of his jacket and produced his little black book. "I'll need your address and a phone number where you can be reached."

The scowl on Merryman's pretty face deepened. Reluctantly, she gave Gatlin the requested information.

"Now, you need to take a vacation for a couple of days," Gatlin said.

"What do you mean?"

"We don't know what this guy's plans are. Could be you're on his list. To be safe, take a trip with Kenny. When you get there, give me a call and let me know where you are." He took out a card and gave it to her.

Merryman stared helplessly at the card for a couple of seconds, said, "Damn," and put it in her purse. Then she hurried down the steps to join Kenny.

"She picked Harvey, right?" Kit asked.

"Yeah, but I'm not crazy about her choice of words. 'That looks like him' isn't as good as 'That's definitely him,' but she's right, they are crappy pictures. Let's go."

In the car, Kit took a breath to ask another question, but Gatlin held up a cautioning finger and reached for the car phone. He punched in a number and after a brief wait said, "Hey, Cap, Slick here. What are my chances of getting two

teams tonight for a watch-and-see? Yeah, that's the case....
I think so. Great. I'll spell it out later. Anybody free now?
Switch me over, will you.... Sweet, this is Slick. Cap says
you can't figure out what to do today, so I thought I'd help
you earn your keep. Don't thank me. I need to know if one
Jason Harvey has a car out from any of the local rentals.
H-A-R-V-E-Y, like the rabbit. What rabbit? Jesus, Sweet.
Who's President in your world, Coolidge?... Soon as pos-
sible, buddy. I'll buy you a beer someday."

He broke the connection with his finger and entered another number. "Andy, this is Phillip. You gonna be there a
while? I want to run something by you. Good. About fifteen minutes."

Gatlin backed up, shifted into drive, and pulled into the
street.

"You really think he's after Merryman?" Kit asked.

"Dunno. Better to be careful."

"What happens now?"

"I'm not sure. We'll hash it over when we see Andy."

Broussard was at his desk, rocked back in his chair, hands
folded over his belly, a lemon ball in each cheek. On the long
table against the wall to his right, the Mr. Coffee gurgled
and chugged.

"Glad to see you're not overdoing things," Gatlin said.

"Sometimes you accomplish the most by sitting still,"
Broussard replied. "Coffee's ready. Want some?"

"About two fingers. Can I use your phone?"

Broussard went to the coffee maker, filled a guest mug
half full, and put it by the phone. Kit declined when he
pointed the pot at her. He inspected the interior of his huge
cup with the dancing crayfish on it, then filled it to the brim
and took it back to his chair.

"Thanks, Sweet," Gatlin said, hanging up the phone.

"That the little woman?" Broussard asked, taking a swig
of his coffee.

Gatlin picked up the mug Broussard had set out for him and looked at Kit. ''Someday we're gonna find him dead in his chair with one of those lemon balls stuck in his windpipe.''

Gatlin sampled his coffee, then sat on the edge of the long table that held Broussard's microscopes. ''Here's the deal.''

Kit moved to the vinyl sofa and sat down, pushing the stack of journals on the cushion next to her back in place when they threatened to topple into her lap.

''The woman who gave Doc that envelope made a reasonable good ID of Harvey as the guy who gave it to her.''

Broussard rocked back in his chair with his coffee.

''Add that to what we've already put together and I think we've got probable cause to get a search warrant for him and his room. There's no record of him renting a car in the city, so we don't have to worry about searching that. But we search his room and come up empty, we're through. Right now, he has no reason to be concerned. He knows we've interviewed a lot of people besides him. But we exercise our warrant, and he'll know he's a suspect.''

''Why not just go up to his room and search it while he's out?'' Kit asked.

Gatlin shook his head. ''We need to search him personally at the same time. Even if we did just do his room, we'd have to leave a copy of the warrant. No—we serve the warrant, we've tipped him.''

''What's the warrant gonna say you're lookin' for?'' Broussard asked. ''We already got the weapon.''

''That's kind of a problem,'' Gatlin said. ''But if we've figured it right, he's going to do at least one more. And these guys are creatures of habit, right, Doc?''

Kit nodded.

''Fleming said that the knife is a Wal-Mart cheapie. Chances are he's got another one just like the first. There should also be at least one more Scrabble letter and what's left of that newspaper he's been leaving. We get real lucky, we might even find pieces of morgue pad and a scalpel.''

"Sounds iffy," Broussard said.

"Which is why I've lined up a tail for him tonight. He goes again, we'll be there. Meanwhile, I'm going to get a search warrant and have it in my pocket. If he stays clean tonight, I'll use the warrant. We're running out of time. He leaves for home tomorrow at six P.M. We either get him in the next twenty-four hours or we never get him.''

"So let's get him," Kit said, feeling much less like a second fiddle. "Is there any way we can keep up with what's happening?"

"I could get you a radio and give you the channel we'll be communicating on.''

"Can we listen from the hotel?"

"Sure, you can sit in Andy's room and hear everything.''

Kit looked at Broussard. "Is that all right?"

"Could be interestin'.''

"I'd like to make sure we're on him when he leaves the hotel for dinner," Gatlin said, going to the sink in the corner and rinsing out his cup. "'Cause he may not come back.''

"There's a wine-and-cheese reception tonight from six to eight," Broussard said. "He'll probably attend that and go to dinner from there.''

"Where's he likely to be this afternoon?"

"If I'm not mistaken, he's got the four o'clock paper in the Path/Bio session.''

"Think I'll pin his tail on there.''

"I'm expectin' a call sometime around eight," Broussard said. "So I was plannin' on stayin' close to the phone tonight. But I can't make it on a few cheese squares and a glass of wine." He looked at Kit. "How about we go to Gramma O's for some dinner at five. It's an uncivilized time to eat, but these are special circumstances.''

"Fine with me."

Kit was too excited to work in her office or go back and listen to papers at the meeting. She needed to get out and do something that didn't require much thought or concentration. With two hours to kill and remembering Phyllis Merryman's comment about walking the dog not being enough of a workout, she strolled over to Maison Blanche on Canal. There, she bought two Liz Claiborne jogging suits, a purchase that made her feel so healthy and responsible, she was able to stop thinking about when she would actually begin exercising. On the way home to change for the reception, she made a detour past the upholsterer to pick up her recovered footstool.

EIGHTEEN

THE PARTITION between ballrooms D and E had been slid back, but there was still not much room for maneuvering. Broussard was in line with Kit's ticket for a free glass of wine, leaving her to scan the immense crowd for familiar faces. It was the first outing for her ivory bouclé suit with onyx-and-gold buttons, and judging from the attention she was getting, it was working.

Having felt too dressed up for Grandma O's, she'd removed her pearl-and-gold earrings at the restaurant and had put them in her vanilla velvet purse. She was about to retrieve them when two men came toward her.

"Kit, how nice to see you. Since we haven't run into each other until now, I can only conclude that you've been truant."

It was D. C. Burrows, the psychiatrist who had been the instructor in the Criminal Psych workshop she'd attended at Johns Hopkins last year. He was a brilliant man but too free with his hands around women. He was as heavy as she'd remembered and still wore a Vandyke beard. His hair was also as long and curly as before, but he'd shaved off his sideburns, which made his hair now look like a furry hat.

"This is my friend, Dr. Carlyle," Burrows said. "Whatever you think of me, you'll think of him." His companion was tall and thin, with a prominent Adam's apple. As if to compensate for Burrows's lack of sideburns, Carlyle's ran all the way to the angle of his jaw, where they terminated in a little jog, like the end of a hockey stick. Kit barely heard the conversation from that point on because, between the two men, she saw Jason Harvey staring in her direction.

Finding her so preoccupied, the two men soon moved on, and when they did, Harvey detached himself from the group he was with and came toward her.

Her mouth went dry and she considered fleeing into the crowd, but before she could act, he was standing in front of her.

"Dr. Franklyn, I'm Jason Harvey."

Forcing herself to act naturally, Kit took his outstretched hand, hoping he wouldn't notice how cold hers had become.

"I understand you do double duty here," he said, "suicide investigator for the medical examiner and psychological profiler for the police."

Usually when a man's eyes made Kit feel uncomfortable, it was because they seemed to be undressing her. But Harvey's cold gray stare went far deeper and she could feel him inside her brain, probing, searching. Until this moment, the chase had been largely an abstract exercise. Even when they'd begun to suspect it might be Harvey, there had been a distance between her and the reality of it all, mostly because she and Harvey had never met. She had seen him every day this week, often a mere few feet away, but she had always been with friends and he had never spoken to her. It was the difference between watching the tiger comfortably from the other side of the bars and being in the same cage with him.

"I expect you've been a great help in the search for the killer of those three people this week," Harvey said.

Kit felt like a small bird being stalked. What was he after?

"Monster, that's what he is," Harvey said, "an animal in human form."

And now he'd begun describing himself, toying with her, enjoying the game. . . . *Monster* was too complimentary a word.

"Are you close to an arrest?" he said bluntly, keeping any urgency out of his voice. But his eyes gave him away. He wanted the answer to this question far more than he let on.

She wanted to tell him exactly how close they were, so she could watch his confidence crumble and see fear grow in his eyes. Instead, she lied. "He's given us very little to work with and what we've got doesn't make much sense."

His eyes shifted a little from side to side, as though trying to find a knothole in the fence she'd erected. He said nothing in reply, letting the silence run on until it became palpable.

As much as he disgusted her, she had to admit it was an excellent response, one that might well make a liar back and fill. But she held her ground, meeting his eyes with her own, ignoring the silence.

After a short standoff, he said, "I've been considering adding a suicide investigator to my own staff. And I think you and I would get along well. There would, of course, be a joint appointment with the police. Would you be interested at, say, twice what you're making now?"

This was quite an unexpected turn of the conversation and through her surprise Kit wondered what its purpose was. She decided it was merely misdirection to get the subject off murder and onto safer ground now that he'd found out how they were progressing.

"I'm quite happy where I am," Kit said. "But I appreciate the offer."

Harvey reached into the side pocket of his jacket and produced a card. When she made no move to take it from him, he reached out, lifted her hand, and pressed it into her palm. "If you change your mind, give me a call." Then he moved off.

Kit wanted to fling the card away from her, but, more than that, she didn't want to arouse his suspicion. Her hand tingled from his touch—the touch of a madman.

She turned and nearly ran from the room. Outside it, she hurried across the foyer and down a short hall to the ladies' room. There, her investigative instincts prompted her to examine the card front and back briefly before throwing it in the bin for used towels. She turned on the water, intending to rid herself of the feel of his skin.

But she hesitated. She had touched the tiger. And under the revulsion, she felt excitement. Surprised by this emotion, she looked at herself in the mirror, wondering where it had come from. Annoyed that he had given her pleasure, she filled her palm with soap and rubbed her hands viciously under the faucet.

When she had cleaned him away, she dried her hands, put on her earrings, and returned to the reception, finding comfort in the belief that Harvey would likely remain free only a few more hours.

She looked for Broussard and saw him still in line, now only three away from being served.

"Hello, Kit."

She turned, to see Nick Lawson, in a suit and tie that made his ponytail look even more ridiculous. He leveled his index finger at her.

"You owe me an apology."

"For what?"

"For not telling me that you believed the killer was attending this convention. And after you agreed to keep me posted."

"Old habits die hard."

"I'll give you a chance to make it up to me. If the killer keeps to his pattern, he'll go again tonight. But I get the distinct feeling something's in the works. How about letting me in on it?"

This was bad news. If there was one thing they didn't need right now, it was Nick Lawson poking around.

"You're right," Kit said.

"About what . . . something going to happen?"

"And for being upset at me. After all, we did have an agreement." She looked around and stepped closer. Sensing that he was about to learn something juicy, Lawson turned an ear toward her so he wouldn't miss a word.

"First, promise me you won't get in the way," she said.

"I promise."

"There's a trap set for the killer at the Praline Connection in the Faubourg Marigny. I don't know exactly when it'll be sprung, but it's there." In principle, Kit disliked lying. In practice, it was sometimes necessary, and the two she'd told in the last five minutes didn't even nudge her conscience. Phyllis Merryman would be proud.

"Who's the killer?" Lawson said.

"We'll know after the trap is sprung."

"What's the setup?"

"Gatlin wouldn't tell me."

He leaned back and looked at her skeptically. "Is all this true?"

Even though she was lying, Kit became angered that he would question her integrity. "Accept it or not, makes no difference to me."

He studied her face a few seconds more, during which she tried to look truthful. Finally, he said, "I believe you."

Carefully fashioning an expression of concern, she said, "I hope you're not going over there."

"No, but I'll probably spend the night hanging around the central lockup waiting for them to bring him in. Thanks for the tip."

"Just don't make me regret I gave it to you."

As he made for the door, Kit congratulated herself on that last touch.

"We could use another couple of bartenders," Broussard said, appearing with a plastic cup of red wine in one hand, white in the other. "I'd complain, but it's my fault."

He offered her the white wine. "Sorry about the cup; that's not my fault. What'd Harvey want?"

"He asked me if we were close to an arrest."

"What'd you say?"

"I wanted to scare the pants off him, but instead, I played dumb."

"He believe you?"

"He's a hard read, but I think so. And get this, he offered me a job."

"First thing he ever did that showed any intelligence."

Kit's mouth opened in surprise. "Why...could that have been a compliment?"

The skin above Broussard's beard grew pink. He rarely put his feelings for people into words, expecting those he was fond of to read his mind. On those odd occasions when he slipped up, Kit always pressed to see how far he'd go.

"Nice turnout," he said, looking away.

One of his less adroit escapes, Kit thought, raising her cup to her lips.

Hugh Greenwood emerged from the crowd and came over, a plate of assorted cheeses in one hand, a cup of wine in the other. "Care for some?" he said, holding the plate up for Kit.

Not wanting to have cheese stuck in her teeth for the rest of the night, Kit declined.

"You might as well take it," Greenwood said. "I can't figure out how to get any."

"Put the plate on top of your wine," Kit suggested.

"And maybe I could twirl a couple of hoops from my left ankle at the same time."

Still, he took her suggestion and popped a square of cheddar into his mouth. Then he took the plate off his cup and washed the cheese down with some wine. He gestured to the crowd with his plate. "Care to guess what the major topic of conversation is out there?" He waited briefly and then, when no answer was forthcoming, said, "They're wondering if this killer can pull off another one. Some even have money riding on it."

"That's bizarre," Kit said.

Greenwood shrugged. "You get right down to it, we're a bizarre group of people. Before I laid out any money, thought I'd see if you had any tips for me."

The temptation to crow over the plans unfolding was almost as strong now as when Kit had spoken to Harvey. But she said nothing.

"Gamblin' is a vice," Broussard said. "My tip is...don't do it."

Greenwood looked at them suspiciously. "Do I sense that you're not being entirely open with me?"

"No two people ever said anything to each other without both of 'em holding back somethin'," Broussard said. "There anything *you'd* like to tell us?"

Greenwood's face twisted into a parody of a smile. "The best defense is a good offense, eh, Andy? Have it your way. It's your town and you're the one under the spotlight. You probably *should* be careful." He looked over the crowd. "I don't know about you two, but I'm having a good time." Then he wandered off.

"Strange man," Kit said. "I get the feeling he wants to be friendly, but he keeps people at arm's length with gibes like that remark about twirling a hoop and with obtuse little exchanges like you just had with him."

"He's sort of an acquired taste."

A heavy hand fell on Broussard's shoulder. "Thought you might be too busy to make it," Leo Fleming said. "Kit, you look as cool as ice cream and just as tasty." He glanced at Broussard and then at Crandall Brooks, who was with him. "Either of you two tell my wife I said that, and I'm a dead man."

Fleming's manner suddenly shifted from jocular to diffident. "Sorry Brookie...about mentioning my wife. I wasn't—"

"Leo, you're overdoing it," Brooks said. "Lighten up."

Fleming accepted Brooks's rebuke with apparent relief.

"How'd your paper go this afternoon?" Broussard said to Fleming. "Sorry I couldn't be there to ask you a hard question."

"One of my damn slides was in upside down. I must have checked 'em four times before comin' and one was upside down. I dunno...I just dunno how that kind of thing can happen."

"You didn't leave 'em anywhere around Charlie Franks, did you?" Broussard asked.

"Leo, it was a picture of a saw," Brooks said. "Who knows when a saw is upside down?"

"If that's true, how come you know which one I'm talkin' about?"

"Leo, it doesn't matter," Brooks said firmly. "Andy, you made any plans for dinner?"

"Already ate."

"So early?"

"I need to stay by the phone tonight, so I'm headin' for my room after this."

"How about you, Kit? Want to come with Leo and me?"

"I've eaten, too. But thanks for the invitation."

"Andy, Leo told me he mentioned the Harvey team to you. Anything come of that?"

"Let's just say wheels are turnin'."

AT 7:45, Harvey left the reception alone. Seeing him go, a slim, dark-complexioned man wearing a meeting ID that identified him as Victor Ochoa, a forensic serologist from Phoenix, tossed his plastic cup in the trash and moved in the same direction, well aware that there were half a dozen stairs that Harvey could duck down and be gone if he didn't hustle.

Harvey bypassed the corridors that would have taken him to those obscure passageways and stepped onto the down escalator behind the Mint Julep lounge. From the top of the moving walkway a few moments later, Ochoa saw Harvey leave the escalator and turn right. Not wanting him to get too far ahead, Ochoa doubled his rate of descent by adding his own speed to that of the moving steps.

At the plaza mall, Harvey turned left and Ochoa raised his hand to his mouth, simultaneously pressing the TALK button on the radio in his pocket. "Ochoa to code six. Subject is wearing a gray suit and appears to be heading for the Loyola exit."

To the rear of the parking lot near the Loyola exit, in a black van with heavily tinted windows and CRESCENT CITY PEST CONTROL lettered on the side, Phil Gatlin unfolded a map of the downtown area and spread it out on the van's fold-down table. Across Loyola, in a parking lot on the corner, the driver of an unmarked car containing three occupants waited for instructions.

Gatlin picked up his radio and pressed the TALK button. "Six leader to Ochoa. Is subject carrying anything?"

"Negative. Both hands are free."

"Nuts," Gatlin muttered.

From the driver's seat of the van, Jack Green said, "What's wrong?" Because of a florid complexion that made him too noticeable in a crowd, Green was rarely used as a foot soldier, but was usually assigned to drive either the van or a pace car.

"The pages of newspaper this guy's been leaving on the bodies have only been folded twice and he couldn't conceal a page that large on his clothes, which may mean he's not going to do one tonight."

"Maybe he's got a stash somewhere."

"It's also too early. The others were done after midnight."

"He might be thinking to pull a fast one in a dark corner before we're expecting it."

"There he is."

They watched Harvey walk past the parking lot driveway, losing him when he passed behind the jasmine-covered lattice panels lining the lot. Aware that the plantings in the neutral ground on Loyola would prevent a clear view of Harvey from the waiting car, Gatlin raised the radio to his lips. "Six leader to Larizzo. Dutch, he's heading for Poydras. You can get a look now if you go down Loyola. But keep moving and don't make it obvious."

"Larizzo to six leader. Leaving now...." Larizzo pulled onto Loyola and nudged the gas.

"This is a short guy, right?" Howie Turgeon said from the back seat.

"Yeah, Slick estimated him at about five ten," Larizzo replied. "Okay, there he is."

"Gonna be hell to keep up with him in the Quarter if it's crowded."

"We could ask him to carry a flag on a stick for you."

"Constructive, real constructive," Turgeon said. "You ain't gonna be the one gets his ass reamed if we lose him. All you gotta do is drive the car."

Nobody liked this duty, least of all Frank Fortier, the detective in the seat beside Larizzo. But he wasn't going to cry about it like Turgeon.

Faces front, they passed Harvey and continued on through the Poydras intersection.

A minute later, Gatlin heard, "Ochoa to code six. Subject has crossed Poydras and turned toward the river."

Gatlin picked up his radio. "Six leader to Ochoa. Victor, if he turns toward Canal before Baronne, stay with him until we can get someone else in position. Six leader to Larizzo. Dutch, let Frank out on the Canal side of Baronne, just shy of Poydras.''

When Kit and Broussard had seen Harvey leave the reception and get on the escalator, they'd immediately gone to Broussard's room, where they now sat at the round table by the window, Kit listening attentively to the radio traffic, Broussard mostly reading his book.

There were many things about Broussard that Kit did not understand: his almost mystical ability to assimilate facts, his fondness for working in the kitchen, his apparent choice to live without sex—although that was one she didn't like to dwell on—and now his ability to read a book calmly in the midst of all this. . . . But then, he'd been in forensics from almost the day she'd been born. Thirty years probably would take the edge off.

"Ochoa to code six. Subject has turned onto South Rampart.''

"Six leader to Ochoa. Stay with him. Dutch, where are you?''

"Larizzo to code six . . . Gravier and Baronne.''

"Six leader to Larizzo. Let Frank out there.''

The radio was silent for several minutes then: "Ochoa to code six. Subject has turned onto Gravier.''

In Broussard's room, he closed his book and listened, his chubby thumb marking his place.

"What the hell's Harvey doing?'' Gatlin muttered in the van. "Six leader to Ochoa. Victor, don't follow him down Gravier or he's likely to make you. Stay on Rampart to Canal. We'll take him for a while.''

Without waiting for instructions, Green started the van and headed for Gravier, where, in less than two minutes, he pulled to the curb just short of the intersection with South Rampart. "Is that him?'' he said, pointing.

Gatlin checked through his binoculars. "Yeah.''

It was tricky, this shadowing of someone through nearly empty city streets. "Uh-oh." He put his radio to his lips. "Leader to code six. Subject has turned onto O'Keefe. We're with him." He lowered his radio. "Not too fast, Jack."

Green took the van leisurely to O'Keefe. "Good thing most stores over here are closed," he said. "Nothin' hardly for him to duck into. You want to go onto O'Keefe?"

"Yeah, but hang back so we can see what he's gonna do at Common."

When they turned the corner, Harvey was in the middle of the block. They parked at the curb and stayed there until he crossed Common. They then proceeded to the corner. "Six leader to Ochoa. Subject has entered University Place. Pick him up on Canal. If he stays on your side, cross over and walk him to Baronne. If he crosses Canal, stay on your side and let me know if he goes down Burgundy or turns on Canal. Dutch, take him down University. We're gonna peel off. Frank get yourself to Canal."

Shortly, another message came in. "Ochoa to code six. Subject has crossed Canal and is turning toward the river."

"Six leader to Ochoa. Walk him to Frank, then get lost."

Gatlin considered their position. Once they hit the Quarter and the crowds, the chances of Harvey noticing he was being tailed would be much more remote. Of course it was possible they'd lose him in all the action. At least they'd managed to get this far without using Turgeon. That gave him a fresh face in reserve.

At Baronne, Ochoa and Fortier's paths crossed. Without looking at him, Ochoa muttered, "He's all yours," and kept walking.

Across Canal, Fortier saw Harvey turn down Dauphine. For the next few minutes, Fortier kept about half a block between himself and Harvey, who crossed to the right sidewalk at Iberville and continued down Dauphine. At the next intersection, Harvey turned right and disappeared onto Bienville, heading toward Bourbon.

This was the weakest moment in a tail. You couldn't stand next to the guy at every intersection. So if he went around the corner, you always had a fifteen- to twenty-second blind spot.

Generally, this didn't create a problem. You'd turn the corner and find him. Occasionally, though, he'd go into a restaurant or shop and he'd be gone. In cases like that, it was usually best just to wait and eventually he'd come out and everything'd be fine. But it gave you a queasy feeling when you were waiting, not knowing if you'd blown it. And if he was in a restaurant, you'd have to wait a long time.

To make his blind spot as small as possible, Fortier picked up the pace. He rounded the corner and nearly collided with someone leaning against the wall. "Charge me or get off my ass," Harvey said.

NINETEEN

"FORTIER TO SIX LEADER."

"Six leader to Fortier. Yeah, Frank, what is it?"

"Sorry to say this, Phil, but I been made."

"In-damn-credible," Gatlin muttered. "Jack, we may have just lost the war." He hit the button on his radio. "Six leader to Fortier. Serve your warrant, Frank, and take him in for questioning. I'll be there shortly. Andy, Kit . . . don't go anywhere. I'm coming up."

"The Hyatt?" Green asked over his shoulder.

"Yeah, I'm gonna toss his room. Nothing turns up there, we've had it."

"You want me?"

"Not many places to hide things in a hotel room. You might as well pack it in."

THE ASSISTANT MANAGER of the hotel unlocked the door to Harvey's room, tapped the light switch, and stepped aside. "I still think we deserve to know what this is about," he said, the tiny muscle under his right eye twitching.

"Sometimes people get what they deserve and sometimes they don't," Gatlin said, still angry at Fortier's screwup. He pushed past the man and entered a small alcove with a bathroom on his right and a closet with sliding glass doors on his left, Kit close behind. Broussard was back in his room waiting for that phone call, which, to Kit's mind, couldn't be as important as this.

The assistant manager came in behind Kit.

Gatlin had already learned that Harvey had nothing in the hotel's safe. His first objective, therefore, was to get a look at the room safe to see if he was going to need hotel help in getting it open. Sitting as it did, in plain view from the doorway, he saw instantly that no safecracking would be required.

"We need anything else, we'll let you know," Gatlin said, looking over Kit's shoulder. Obviously put out, the assistant manager left, grumbling.

Gatlin went into the main part of the room and pushed the door of the safe fully open with his foot. "Bad sign," he said, stepping back and looking inside to be sure it was empty. "Best place in the room to put something you don't want anybody to know about."

"Maybe not," Kit said. "It's the first place *you* looked."

Gatlin examined her through narrowed eyes and said, "Want to help?"

Ignoring the faint suspicion he was about to tell her to keep quiet and stay out of the way, she said, "Sure."

"Ordinarily, there are rules to a search. If you're looking for something the size of a bread box, you can't look in a shoe box, 'cause you can't get a bread box in a shoe box."

"Sounds like the law was made to protect criminals rather than put them away," Kit said.

"Too damn many liberals in the country," Gatlin growled. "But you want to see a liberal turn mean, show him one of *his* relatives on a morgue table. Anyway, one of the things we're looking for is Scrabble letters. Since they're small, we can look anywhere. How about you go through whatever's in the closet."

While Kit frisked Harvey's suits, Gatlin went to Harvey's Forensic Academy tote bag, which was on the bed, and dumped out the contents. It contained the thick black book of abstracts Gatlin had seen everyone carrying around, as well as a thin yellow pamphlet listing the times and places of all the talks. He also found a small loose-leaf notebook, which he thumbed through, a couple of Bic pens, and an unopened roll of Rolaids.

The foul-up with the tail had brought back his indigestion, so when he was putting everything back in the bag, he helped himself to a couple of the Rolaids. He tossed Harvey's one suitcase onto the bed and opened it.

The main compartment was empty, but he found three Band-Aids and another roll of Rolaids in a side pocket. A compartment on the other side yielded a small umbrella and an adapter for 220 electrical outlets.

"Nothing in his suits," Kit said.

Gatlin gestured vaguely to the low-slung bureau of pale oak and black Formica. "Check those drawers."

He went into the bathroom and rummaged through Harvey's leather toiletry bag, felt inside the Kleenex dispenser, then took the lid off the commode and peered in.

"I wouldn't have thought to look there," Kit said.

"It's why I get the big money," Gatlin replied. "His drawers clean?"

"Some are, some aren't."

Snorting a small chuckle, he put the lid back in place, then felt behind the commode as far as his fingers would reach. He took a quick look behind the shower curtain, then shook out all the towels and spread one on the floor so that part of it went under the Formica faceplate for the sink. He got down with his back on the towel and slid forward so he could look at the large hidden space under the sink.

"Anything?" Kit asked hopefully.

He made a negative grunt and his face reappeared, his color distinctly higher from his efforts. They returned to the main room, where he pulled out one of the bureau drawers and held it up so he could examine the underside. "See if he's taped anything inside there."

Kit peered into the dim recess where the drawer fit. "Nothing."

They did the same for the other two drawers, then Gatlin moved the bureau away from the wall and checked on the back. "See if there's anything under the beds."

"Isn't that kind of obvious?"

"We once had a guy kill somebody in a hotel room and leave the corpse under the bed. It was two days before it was found and two different couples had occupied the room."

Gatlin examined the underside of the round table and two chairs by the window and looked behind the curtain. He went to the nightstand, opened the drawer, and flipped through the phone books and the Bible, tossing each onto the bed as he finished. He pulled the drawer all the way out and gave it the same treatment as those in the bureau, then tugged the nightstand away from the wall and looked on its back panel. He would have looked behind the headboards as well, but they wouldn't budge.

While Kit waited for further instructions, he put the nightstand back in order, then patted the pillows and began yanking the blankets and sheets off the bed near the window. Following his lead, Kit did the same with the other bed. After they both had worked their way down to bare mattress, Gatlin hoisted his off the springs.

"The maids are going to love this," Kit said.

"I don't really care," Gatlin replied, flopping the mattress more or less back in place. He moved to the other bed and did the same.

They both saw the brass key at the same time.

"Get that, will you?" Gatlin asked.

"Do I have to pick it up any special way?"

"Don't worry about it."

Kit got the key and Gatlin let the mattress drop.

The key had a square head and the number 251 inscribed on one side. The other side was blank. The Hyatt used plastic cards as keys.

Gatlin held out his hand and Kit put the key in his palm. He examined it briefly, then took it to the lamp on the bureau and perused it again in better light. Suddenly, Kit saw what the key could mean. "If we locate the room that key opens, we might find the things we're looking for."

Instead of being pleased at the find, Gatlin's perpetually unhappy expression darkened, if anything. "Law says we can't take the key. But that doesn't mean we have to leave empty-handed."

He put the key on the bureau, took out his wallet, and fished a business card from between his folding money. He laid the card facedown on the bureau and centered the key on it. With his pen, he traced the key's outline.

"You can't take the key, but that's legal?" Kit said.

"Justice is a fickle mistress," he said. "I read that somewhere. Wouldn't want you to think I was profound or anything."

Pocketing the card, he took the key back to the bed where he'd found it. He hoisted one corner of the mattress and tossed the key back onto the bedsprings. "Now, let's go over to the YMCA," he said, letting the mattress fall.

"How do you know that's where the key came from?" He opened his mouth to answer, but she raised a cautioning hand and said, "I know...that's why you get the big money."

"No, there was a *Y* scratched on the back."

"Could belong to the YWCA...."

Gatlin shrugged. "Could be neither one."

THE HOUSING DIVISION of the YMCA sits on St. Charles Avenue at the edge of Lee Circle. In the center of the circle, Robert E. Lee stands with his arms folded on a sixty-foot spire of Tennessee marble, apparently greatly offended at the Y's orange facade with horizontal black stripes. Gatlin parked out front and Kit followed him into a seedy lobby with a stained yellow YMCA banner on the wall behind a small U-shaped registration counter. The clerk at the counter had thinning hair, a pale oval face with a big nose, and closely spaced eyes that were partially closed by drooping lids.

Gatlin flashed his badge. "You got a room two-five-one?"

"Yeah...why?" the clerk asked in a neutral tone.

Gatlin put the tracing of the key on the counter. "Your keys shaped like that?"

The clerk bent down for a closer look and stayed that way for a long time.

Finally, Gatlin knocked on the counter with his fist. "Hey, buddy, you asleep?"

"Looks like ours," the clerk said, straightening up. He had a slow, uncertain cadence to his speech that seemed at odds with the importance of the situation.

"How about letting me see a dupe for two-five-one," Gatlin said.

Puzzle lines appeared above the clerk's thin eyebrows.

"Duplicate key," Gatlin said as though he thought the guy might be a lip-reader.

"I'll see if it's okay." The clerk left the enclosure and headed for the stairs to his left.

"It's police business," Gatlin reminded him. "So it's gonna be okay."

The clerk didn't acknowledge this, continuing up the stairs.

While they waited for his return, Gatlin busied himself studying the intricate compass design in the terrazzo floor, hands thrust unhappily in his pockets. Figuring that they might be there a while, Kit sat in one of the two plastic and vinyl chairs flanking a big plant that seemed to be growing too well for the available light. Over the next few minutes, several men came down the stairs and dispersed in various directions without so much as a glance their way. None of them looked like derelicts.

Finally, the clerk appeared on the stairs and Kit joined Gatlin at the counter.

His face a blank, the clerk moved behind the counter and began working on something under it. There was the sound of a drawer opening and the jingle of metal. He came up with the key.

Gatlin took it and placed it against the outline on the card. While Kit waited breathlessly at his side, he shifted the key around, then said, "We got a match." Then to the clerk, he said, "Who's got that room?"

Instead of turning to the cards in a rack on the wall behind him, the clerk stared at Gatlin without moving. Finally, after a long pause, he said, "Ain't no occupant. It's empty."

"How long's it been empty?"

"What-time is it?"

Gatlin checked his watch. "Nine-thirty."

The guy went into hibernation again and Kit half-expected Gatlin to grab him by the shirt front and shake him. Eventually, the guy said, "Nine and a half hours."

"Then there was somebody in it this morning?"

The clerk made a vague gesture with one hand. "Dunno when he was last in it. I ain't got time to keep up with that kind of stuff."

Kit had begun to think this clerk and the one she'd encountered at the toy store were related.

"Are you telling me he checked out at noon?"

"Didn't check out."

"Skipped without paying?"

The clerk shook his head. "Paid in advance for three days."

Gatlin pulled out the faxes he'd shown Phyllis Merryman and put them on the counter. "Is one of these the guy who rented the room?"

The clerk shifted slowly through the pile, then shook his head. "Ain't a one even close."

Exhaling forcibly and shaking his own head like he'd just come up from swimming across the YMCA pool underwater, Gatlin folded the faxes and put them back in his pocket. "That's all I want to know."

"So the key didn't belong to Harvey, after all," Kit said.

"Apparently not."

"You want to talk to the guy who rented the room?" the clerk said.

"I might," Gatlin replied, turning. "You know where he is?"

"No."

Gatlin seemed about to reach for the clerk's neck when the guy said, "But he might come back for the stuff he left in his room."

"What stuff is that?"

The clerk bent down and came up with an old briefcase that he put on the counter. He flipped the latches and turned it around. Inside was a folded newspaper, a Baggie full of Scrabble tiles, and two large serrated knives still in their cardboard and plastic wrappers.

HEART TRIPPING with excitement, Kit knocked on Broussard's door at the Hyatt. When he opened it, her story poured out.

"It *was* Harvey. We found a key under his mattress to a room at the YMCA and when—"

"Why don't you come and sit down," Broussard said, stepping away from the door.

She went in, still talking. "When we got to the Y, Gatlin showed the desk clerk a picture of Harvey, but the clerk said he wasn't the one who'd rented the room whose number was on the key." She pursued Broussard to his chair at the table by the window and sat opposite him.

"And at that point, we almost gave up, but as we were about to leave, the clerk said something about the last guy who rented the room leaving some belongings behind." Feeling too restricted by her chair, she got up. "He put this briefcase on the counter, opened it, and there they were—Scrabble tiles, the rest of the newspaper he's been leaving, and two more knives just like the one we found with the third body."

"Where's Phillip?"

"Went to the office to charge Harvey with the murders."

"He think it'll stick?"

Kit lost some of her enthusiasm. "He has doubts. He says it's all circumstantial, the big problem being that we can't tie Harvey directly to the briefcase. Even if we had his fingerprints on the key to the room at the Y, the key would likely be inadmissible evidence, since it wasn't listed on the search warrant. We would have been better off to see Harvey claim the briefcase, but since he realized he was being tailed, he wouldn't have done that. And he goes home tomorrow. Gatlin figured the best thing to do was take the briefcase and have the lab run the contents for prints. He seemed to think he was on safer legal ground with the briefcase than the key. He thought that the clerk saying it wasn't Harvey who rented the room hurts, though."

"He could have hired somebody to rent the room for him," Broussard suggested. "I take it the rent was paid in advance?"

"Yes."

"At the Y, a cash transaction wouldn't require any ID, not that it'll help the case much."

Since Gatlin was always pessimistic, Kit hadn't really given his concerns much weight. But Broussard was another matter.

"You think he'll beat it?"

"I think a good lawyer'll make mincemeat out of it."

"Then he just walks away?"

"That's how things work."

"But he's guilty."

"Not until it's proven in court."

"If he walks, I'm going to be very upset."

"I'm sure you'll have company."

"At least we've ended his game. He can't get at anyone else now. Whatever he was building up to, we've stopped him."

"You ought to go home now and get some sleep."

"I suppose."

"Starrs'll be givin' his results on the assassination of Huey Long tomorrow mornin'. Oughta be a good show."

"What time?"

"Eight-thirty—" he reached for his yellow pamphlet of presentation times and places "—in the Peach Tree Room."

"I don't know...maybe I'll see you there."

As KIT DROVE HOME, she reflected on how quickly things had changed. When they'd first found the briefcase at the Y, it had set every nerve tingling and she'd experienced a heady rush of exhilaration. And it wasn't just because she'd believed that Harvey was nailed. Much of it was because it wouldn't have happened without her help. And that should have earned her at least a word of acknowledgment from Broussard. But he'd said practically nothing, except to exceed even Gatlin's pessimism.

She turned off St. Charles onto her street, well aware that a self-assured personality wouldn't need outside approval for a job well done. But she *had* done well, damn it. It wasn't her fault that Harvey might walk.

She pulled into her driveway and cut off the engine. Instead of getting out, she thought about Harvey's offer of a job. What would she have said if it had been someone else offering... at twice her present salary? Would she have considered it? Probably not. She still had unfinished business here. Someday, she was going to get Broussard to cough up a direct, unambiguous compliment on her work.

She got out of the car and went up the porch steps. By the light of a streetlamp, she found the front-door lock with her key and went inside. With the days since Lucky's poisoning so full, she had often gone hours without thinking of him. But every evening, when she opened the door to a silent house, her thoughts had gone to the little varmint. Tonight, coming in so late, the gap his absence had left in her life loomed even larger. She took solace, though, in what she'd found out when she'd stopped at the animal hospital on the way home from the upholsterer. She could pick him up tomorrow.

She locked the front door, took off her shoes, and carried them into the bedroom, where she undressed and put on a long nightie and robe that Teddy had given her on her last birthday.

She looked at the digital clock on the nightstand: 10:30... not all *that* late. She went into the hall, picked up the phone, and entered Teddy's number.

"Hi, it's me," she said when he answered. "Did I wake you?"

"No. I just got in from a heavy date."

"Didn't know you liked overweight women."

"It's a relatively recent interest. Is Lucky home yet?"

"I'll pick him up tomorrow."

"Terrific. How you doing with those murders?"

"Solved."

"No kidding."

"It was a medical examiner attending the Forensics meeting."

"What was his motive?"

The question caught Kit by surprise, for this was something she had not discussed with either Gatlin or Broussard since their first inkling it was Harvey. Thinking about it now, she saw that Fleming's comment in Broussard's office was right on the mark. "Broussard and this guy clashed in court once and since then they've really disliked each other. They even had a couple of run-ins at the meeting. It looks like Harvey—that's the guy who did it—was playing a sick chess game with Broussard, trying to embarrass him. You were right about the numbers on the Scrabble tiles. That was the key to it.... You're still coming over on Saturday, aren't you?"

"Sure."

"That part is pretty complex, so I'll wait and explain more when I see you. The short version is that Harvey was leaving clues to his identity that he didn't think we were clever enough to get. But he was wrong."

"There has to be more to it than that. You don't kill people as part of a game."

"Not if you're sane. Anyway, thanks for the help on the letters. It was a major factor in figuring it out."

"I exist but to serve."

"Oh really. We'll have to discuss that Saturday night."

Since the poisoning of Lucky and the discovery of the first body, Kit's life had been out of kilter. Now, with Harvey in custody, Lucky's return imminent, and Teddy's voice fresh in her mind, she felt herself inching toward normality.

Still too edgy to be sleepy, she went into the kitchen and made herself a cup of hot chocolate in the microwave. She would have preferred to make it with milk rather than water, but when you won't shop, there are penalties.

She took her cup to the big chair in front of the TV, sat down, and threw her legs over the arm. In thinking about the steps leading to Harvey's arrest, she remembered Grandma O's role. True, her comment about the Scrabble number being a date was not intuitive, but sort of an accident; it was still extremely important. And unlike some people she could name, she wasn't one to ignore a person's contribution. Maybe she'd buy Grandma O some of that gardenia perfume she liked so much.

Tired of thinking, she picked up the remote and clicked on the TV. Not interested enough to check the schedule, she channel-surfed, pausing on a forties musical with all the girls dressed as bananas. If any film needed colorizing, this one did. Still, the images were intriguing enough that she watched the routine all the way through. Then she moved on, stopping a couple of channels later to watch a few minutes of *Citizen Kane*. Maybe it was because she'd never seen it from the beginning, but she couldn't get into it any more this time than any of the other times she'd tried.

Sleepy now, she turned off the set and shuffled to the kitchen, where she rinsed her cup and put it in the dishwasher. From there, she went to the bathroom and brushed her teeth. Coming out of the bathroom into the bedroom, she detoured past the light switch by the door, flicked it off, and headed for bed, guided by the old night-light with a cloudy shade on the far wall. Well before she reached her pillow, her big toe smacked against something hard. Holding her breath, she prepared herself for the pain.

Ahhh. It was worse than she expected. Though the puny night-light allowed her to see nothing of the floor between the bed and the near wall, she knew what it was without even turning on the light—the damn footstool. In its absence, she must have unconsciously adopted a new, more direct course to her bed from the light switch. Now that it was back from the upholsterer, she'd blundered into it.

Ahhh, but that hurt. She hobbled the last few feet and dropped into bed. This had been *some* kind of day.

The pain gradually subsided to where it could no longer stave off the drowsiness that had sent her to bed, and she lapsed into a deep sleep.

Two hours later, Kit's eyes flicked open and she sat up quickly at the sound of the doorbell. Fully awake now, she got up, pulled on her robe, and headed into the hall, a remnant of pain in her toe reminding her to avoid the footstool.

When she switched on the porch light, she saw two shapes through the sheers at the glass in the front door. Pulling a corner of the curtain aside, she peeked out at two uniformed cops.

Her first thought was that something had happened with Harvey. She turned the latch and opened the door, confronting a wall of blue. One cop was blond and had huge shoulders. The other, though more normal in size, still looked like he could take care of himself. They smelled like leather and when they shifted the least bit, they squeaked like leather.

"Sorry to bother you, miss," the blond one said. "We—"

"Are you from Lieutenant Gatlin?"

"No, ma'am. Dispatcher sent us. We got a report that there was some kind of trouble here."

Remembering how the cops had gone to the house across the street a few months ago when she'd called them to report a screaming row in the backyard of the house behind her, Kit said, "Are you sure you've got the right address? There's no trouble here. I was asleep when you rang."

"Would you step out on the porch, please?" the blond one said.

"Why?"

"Please, ma'am. We'll explain in a minute."

The cops moved back and, reluctantly, Kit went out onto the porch, which felt cool and gritty on her bare feet. While she pulled her robe tighter around her, the big cop went inside and looked behind the door. From the sound of his footsteps, she concluded that he went over to the threshold of the living room. Then he came back outside.

"Just wanted to be sure nobody was making you say things were okay when they weren't," he said. "Guess it was a mix-up. It happens. Hope we didn't disturb you too much."

"Not at all. Thanks for checking."

"Our pleasure. Good night."

Back inside with the door shut and locked, Kit rubbed the grit from her feet on the hall carpet and hurried back to bed. Had she not been who she was, a visit like she'd just had might have caused lingering excitement. But since she worked with cops all the time, the event was of no particular consequence and she was soon as lost in sleep as before they'd showed up.

Twenty minutes later, she woke to the sound of the footstool stuttering across the floor.

TWENTY

PEOPLE OFTEN CLAIM to have experienced fear when they have merely lived through a moment or two of discomfort. Bone-chilling, marrow-withering fear is truly known to only a few. As she lay on her side, her eyes barely open, in the one place above all others that should be safe, Kit joined their numbers. She could sense a presence, unseen because it was in the shadowy recess formed by the end of the hall closet, unheard because of her heart drumming in her ears. But it was there...in her home...in her bedroom.

Her instincts called for a scream. But a scream would simply fly off into the darkness, heard only by one who would not help her. By a force of will she was not aware she possessed, she suppressed the scream and evaluated her situation.

Chances are this was a simple burglary. That's all...a burglary. The worst thing she could do was confront him. Better to feign sleep and let him take what he wished.

She fought to keep her breathing full and slow, but her lungs seemed shrunken and hard. Her mind began to chase her heart. What if robbery wasn't his goal? What if he wanted...

Her eyes left the shadows across the room and flicked to the drawer of the nightstand. Inside, there was Mace—but if she tried to get it, he'd know she was awake.

Useless...the damn stuff was useless if you didn't carry it in your hand wherever you went.

The pounding in her ears grew louder. Moving...he was moving toward her.

In the faint glow of the night-light, there was a glint of steel.

A knife . . . God, he has a knife. . . .

The scream she had been hoarding erupted from her throat, bringing him to her in a rush. Distantly, she heard a crash and the tinkle of broken glass.

He came like a living shadow, faintly visible. The knife went up over his head and he lunged.

She rolled away from the attack and went off the far side of the bed, knocking the nightstand over and bringing the lamp down on top of her.

Caught.

She was tangled in the sheet, which held her legs like the wrappings on a mummy. Kicking to get free, she felt the floor vibrate and was faintly aware of thudding steps. The bed surged toward her, the springs groaning.

The damn sheet—she couldn't get free of it. She rolled a few feet farther toward the wall and this loosened the hold on her legs. The bedsprings wailed again, followed by another huge crash.

She stripped away the imprisoning sheet and struggled to her feet as a dark mass flew past the foot of the bed and slammed into the wall. There was a grunt of pain.

The shape went to the floor and Kit darted for the bed, kicking the lamp with the same toe she'd banged earlier. But this time, her surging adrenaline washed away the hurt. She hit the bed in a roll that carried her across it and onto her feet again. Nearly falling over the footstool, she scrambled to the door and darted into the hall, where she clawed at the light switch and grabbed for the phone.

Even 911 seemed like too many numbers.

Damn it—no dial tone.

She dropped the receiver and started for the front door, noticing for the first time that it stood wide open, its glass lying in shards on the floor.

"Kit."

She was being called from the bedroom.

"Kit, help me."

Warily, she moved toward the bedroom.

"Kit."

That voice.... Moving now with more courage, she went into the bedroom and switched on the light.

There on the floor was Broussard. Straddling him was a figure dressed in black and wearing a black ski mask. The knife was inches from Broussard's throat, the prowler pushing it forward with both hands, slowly overcoming the counterforce Broussard was applying at the prowler's wrists.

Mace... now she could get the Mace—but there wasn't time.

She bolted for the footstool. Clutching it to her bosom, she threw herself at the prowler, hitting him from the side. As he fell, he turned so that she ended up on his chest, the stool between them, their faces almost touching. From the corner of her eye, she saw the serrated blade still in his hand—and his arm... free to move... free to reach her. In the frozen instant as he turned the knife in his hand, she saw that the blade was tinged with blood.

She rolled away from the knife and thumped to the floor on her back, knocking the breath out of her. The prowler threw off the footstool and it came her way, one leg headed for her face. She made a half roll toward the bed and the stool hit her on the shoulder. Expecting at any second to feel the knife passing into her, she turned onto her back and grabbed for the stool's skirt.

The prowler sat up and lunged toward her, swinging the knife in a looping overhand motion designed to clear the obstacle between them. A heartbeat before the blade reached her, she pulled the stool toward her. The prowler's wrist hit the lightly padded edge of the frame and the knife came free, clattering to the floor beside her.

Broussard grabbed the knife hand and twisted the prowler's arm behind his back. By the time Kit got to her feet, Broussard had one knee in the prowler's back and had both his arms pinned behind him.

She was safe.... They were both safe. She almost felt like howling.

"Something to tie his hands," Broussard said breathlessly.

Kit's mind windmilled. Rope...

Spotting her robe lying on the floor, she went to it and tore the sash free. She took the sash to Broussard and while he wrapped the prowler's hands, she examined herself for wounds. The blood on the knife did not appear to be hers.

"His ankles, too," Broussard muttered.

With what? Kit thought. She hurried to her closet and pawed through her clothes. She grabbed a belt and returned to the figure on the floor. Broussard was still working on his hands, so she did his ankles, wrapping the belt around them twice and fastening it as she would around her waist.

With the prowler's hands secured, Broussard looked at what she'd accomplished, then struggled to his feet. Kit saw to her horror a huge bloodstain spreading into the fabric of Broussard's shirt.

"You're hurt," she said, as though he didn't know it.

"It's okay... I'm..." He began to teeter and Kit rushed to him, intending to guide him to the bed. But his legs buckled and he tacked toward the wall by the door. It was like trying to hold up a falling building, and all she could do was go along with him.

He hit the wall with his back and slid to the floor. Forgetting the prowler, Kit rushed for the bathroom, grabbed a towel, and dashed back to his side.

Kneeling to get at the buttons on his shirt, she saw a gun lying against the baseboard, its barrel covered by a spray-deodorant can. Not important now....

As she unbuttoned Broussard's shirt, his eyes fluttered open. She slipped the folded towel under his T-shirt and placed it over the wound. "Can you hold it while I get help?"

Broussard's hand came up and he pressed it against the towel. Still barefoot, Kit hurried into the hall and picked her way past the glass on the floor. She flew down the porch steps and hesitated. Mrs. Bergeron was closest, but she was so arthritic, it would take her forever to answer the door—and she was a dog poisoner.

Across the front yard, she went, her speed pressing her nightgown against her in front, blades of grass slipping between her toes. She vaulted the short boxwood hedge lining the Caruso property and landed on a large hosta, crushing it. Even though the man who owned the house usually kept his car in the garage at night, its absence from the driveway gave her cause for concern, partly because he was out of town a lot, partly because she needed him so badly.

She rang the bell and pounded on the storm door until the porch light came on. The inner door inched open and a face appeared in the crack.

"Mr. Caruso. I'm Kit, from next door. There's a prowler in my house and I need the police and an ambulance. Please, call nine-one-one."

The door swung inward and a man wearing pajama bottoms but no top unlocked the storm door. The hand behind him trailed a baseball bat. "Come in. Are you hurt?"

"No, I'm fine. But a friend of mine has been injured and I've got to get back...."

He reached for her through the open door. "You shouldn't do that. He might still be there."

She stepped away from his grasp. "He is still there, but we've got him tied up. Please, just make the call."

"All right, I'll do it now. Don't worry. I'll get help."

He disappeared into the dark house and Kit turned to go, but then she had a terrible thought. If her phone wasn't working, maybe his wasn't either. She opened the storm door and leaned inside. "Is the phone working?"

"Yes," Caruso said from somewhere she couldn't see. "I've got them now."

Satisfied that there was nothing more she could accomplish here, she hurried home the way she'd come.

Afraid to look, she returned to the bedroom and found Broussard with his eyes wide open. For a moment, she thought he might be—but then he blinked.

"Help is on the way," she said. "You should lie down."

He held up his free hand in a weak restraining gesture. "I'm okay." His eyes went past her, to the prowler, and he said, "*Why*, Brookie... *Why*?"

Brookie? Kit's brow knitted in confusion. As she turned, the prowler got up on one elbow and then to a sitting position. "Get this mask off me and I'll tell you."

Kit edged over, removed the mask, and quickly stepped back.

"I did it because you took Susan," Brooks said angrily.

"I don't understand," Broussard said. "It was cancer...."

Brooks glared at Broussard, his lips curling down at the corners, his face so full of hate, he barely looked like the same man. "Before that... our life together."

"I'm not following you."

The fury in Brooks's face subsided. His eyes focused beyond the walls. "I would have done anything for that woman," he said. "But from the very first, she returned only a fraction of what I offered, keeping a part of herself from me... unreachable. I gave everything, but she held back, even denying me children." His voice took on a dreamy quality. "It's not a man's work that matters. It's children...the giving of life...passing on the genetic flame...two people merging their separate identities to create a new individual whose every breath is their breath, whose very existence could never have happened without one moment of utter surrender."

Kit found the word *surrender* an odd choice, almost as though Brooks would have viewed a child as a symbol of some sort of victory over his wife. She moved to the bed and sat down.

"Being Catholic and not disposed to the use of contraceptives, or at least that's what she said, she kept me away from her except for those few days when she believed there was no chance of her getting pregnant. So there were to be no children and I was to live my life out and die with no heirs. I used to go to bookstores and look at the children's books and imagine which ones I would buy if I had..."

The words caught in Brooks's throat. He closed his eyes and rocked his head back. Face to the ceiling, he rolled his head from side to side. Abruptly, his eyes popped open and he looked at Broussard, all the anger back. "Of course I don't expect a self-centered egotist like you to understand," he snapped. "And at first, that made it hard for me...to see where you could be hurt. Then I remembered Kit and how you spoke of her when Susan and I were here last year...the sound of your voice, your expression.... And I knew that was the way."

Broussard shook his head. "What did I have to do with Susan's decision not to give you children?"

As fascinated as Kit was with what was happening, she yearned for the sound of an ambulance, for Broussard was shockingly pale.

"Everything," Brooks shouted. "You had *everything* to do with it." He stared at his knees. When he spoke again, it

was Susan Brooks's husband, not Broussard's enemy. "There were to be no children and I would never possess Susan like I wished. But I still adored her and decided to take whatever she'd give, thinking that maybe she was simply incapable of more. But then—" his voice grew strident again "—when I was going through her papers after her death, I found the letters."

"I never wrote to her," Broussard said.

"Letters she had written to *you,*" Brooks snapped, "but didn't mail. Letters saying that she should never have left you and gone to New York for her residency, and that marrying me was a mistake. A divorce? Out of the question. Too hard on her devoutly Catholic, sickly mother. So she stayed with me and doled herself out a little at a time."

Brooks's expression turned even more malignant. "And then, on the bottom of the stack, I found the letter telling you about her abortion—*the abortion she never mentioned to me.* With all the restrictions she placed on me . . . a child, *our* child. And she found the idea so abhorrent, she ignored church doctrine and destroyed it. There's not even a grave to visit . . . flushed away like a dirty tissue. But I don't blame her. It was *you.* It's always been you. She wanted you and that poisoned her mind against me. And for that, I decided to hurt you the way I had been hurt."

"But the others you killed had nothing to do with me."

Brooks's face shifted into a satisfied smirk. "You're very much mistaken. Everything I did here was because of you. That means every death is on your head. Three people dead because of you . . . *dead.* Think how their friends and families are feeling. The pain . . . But if you had never existed, they'd still be alive." He was almost laughing now. "Oh the guilt you must feel. If you'd been smart enough, you could have stopped it after just one. That's why I gave you all the Scrabble tiles from the start. But you were too slow. You needed more help and more time. You were too *stupid.*"

Kit's mind was humming now, tearing at the logjam of facts that had accumulated since Saturday. This explained so much. Yet... "Suppose you *had* been able to pull this off," she said. "The only way you could get satisfaction would be by explaining the whole thing to Andy. And that would mean..."

Brooks looked at her as if she was retarded. "Do you think my life means anything to me now... without Susan? It ended when she died."

Broussard was no longer listening, but was years away... medical school... the first pathology exam.

"Name three organs that are radiosensitive," Susan asked. She was wearing white shorts and a man's white shirt, tied at the waist so her midriff showed. Her long, tan legs were crossed and her foot was bouncing, her heel out of her sandals. He was lying on his back, on the floor, thinking not of pathology but her clean, sharp smell and how you could see tiny blond hairs on her thighs when the sun was just right. It was no way to study, but he couldn't imagine doing it any other way.

"The clock's ticking," Susan said.

"Radiosensitive organs," he began. "Lymphoid, testes, ovary." He glanced at her for approval, knowing he was correct.

She looked back, one tawny eyebrow arching. "Testes, ovary," she repeated slowly, putting the book down. She got up and knelt beside his face. "I love it when you talk dirty." She bent to kiss him, her long hair forming a tent around their faces that trapped her scent inside.

The image wavered and grew fuzzy at the edges.

"My Susan," Brooks moaned. "My dear Susan." He closed his eyes and began to draw quick deep breaths, his lower lip trembling. Then he toppled over, hitting the floor with a thump, sobbing as though there was no one else in the room.

TWENTY-ONE

THE DAY AFTER the adventure in Kit's bedroom, the bruises had begun appearing. Today, they looked even worse, but fortunately, they were all hidden by her clothing. She knocked on the heavy green door and went in without being asked. Broussard was sitting up in bed with a bottle of clear liquid in a rack overhead, connected to his arm with transparent tubing. Phil Gatlin was sitting on a small vinyl sofa by the window; Leo Fleming was seated in a chair on the opposite side of the bed.

"How are you feeling?" she said.

"Well enough to leave," Broussard replied. "But I'm supposed to stay a few more days. Kit, I want to apologize...."

"For what?"

"For what happened...for nearly gettin' you killed."

"Nonsense. You had nothing to do with it, or the others. And if you persist in thinking so, you'll be giving Brooks exactly what he wants. Actually, his coming after me was a compliment."

Broussard's brow furrowed.

"He only did it because he believed you were...well, fond of me."

Fleming and Gatlin sat straighter in their seats, interested in what Broussard would say to this.

Falling back on the dodge he'd used at the reception, he looked away, but there was Gatlin. Above his beard, Broussard's cheeks grew pink and there was a trapped look in his eyes that made Kit think he might tear out his IV and run for it. She had him now, but since he wasn't well, it didn't seem fair.

"I brought you something," she said, setting the Forensic Academy tote bag she'd brought onto the bed. The look of relief in his eyes changed to pleasure as she put the glass bowl of lemon drops from his office on the nightstand.

"I'm sure this is forbidden, too," he said testily, thrusting his chubby hand into the bowl. He put a lemon drop in his mouth and folded his hands over his belly.

"Now I want some answers," Kit said. "How did you know it was Brooks?"

"I got a bone to pick with you about that myself," Gatlin said, getting up and moving to the foot of the bed. "Why'd you let me make an ass of myself with Harvey if you knew it wasn't him?"

"I didn't know for sure who it was until one A.M. Friday mornin'. That's when the phone call I was waitin' for came."

"Who was it?" Kit said.

"Gene Ochs, the cardiologist in the Heartbeats."

Kit shook her head. "I'm lost."

"When Brookie first arrived at the hotel, he gave me a picture taken of himself and Susan at a party celebratin' their twentieth anniversary. The drummer in the photo you got from the paper looked a lot like one of the faces in the background at Brookie's party."

Kit groaned. "Ochs was Waldo."

"I'm *still* lost," Fleming said.

"It was all a brilliant game of cat and mouse engineered around two photographs," Broussard said patiently. "Brookie gave me one of them the day the meetin' started. To get the other one, the picture of the Heartbeats, Kit had to solve the riddle of the Scrabble letters and the newspaper pages Brookie left on his victims. If she hadn't figured out that the clue was in the little score-keeping numbers and not the letters, we'd never have found the second picture in the paper."

"We can thank Grandma O and Teddy LaBiche for that," Kit said.

"So, now we had both pictures but had no idea they were related," Broussard continued. "I'd been lookin' at the picture of Brookie and Susan quite a bit over the last few days and had noticed that one of the faces in the background resembled Gene Ochs, the drummer in the Heartbeats. But I didn't think anything of it until that singer, Merryman, gave Kit the envelope containin' a page from a *Find Waldo* book."

"Which Merryman got from Brooks," Fleming said.

"Yeah, but most likely not directly from him."

Gatlin nodded knowingly.

"Coupled with the hairs Brookie also left on the victims to tell us the killer was a forensic colleague, I began to see the light. But I wasn't sure the drummer in the Heartbeats and the guy in the picture of Brookie and Susan were the same person. I wanted to believe they weren't, that Jason Harvey really *was* behind it all as it first appeared and that the Heartbeats were involved only because they constituted a Harvey team. But I had to check. So when Kit and Phillip went to find Merryman at the museum, I caught a ride with them back to my office and looked up the drummer, Ochs, in my specialty directories. He lives in Carmel, California, but when I called, his answerin' service said he was out of town until late that night. I left a message for him to call me no matter what time he got in. We were lucky he was conscientious enough to check his messages so late. When he reached me, I asked if he'd been at Brookie and Susan's twentieth anniversary party. He said he had, and that was all I needed."

"How did they know each other?" Kit asked.

"Ochs is the son of Brookie's sister. He was home visitin' her when the party was held. So he tagged along to pay his respects. She probably sent Brookie a copy of the article on the Heartbeats when it first appeared."

"I guess Brooks thought that since Ochs didn't live in the city, nobody would bother to quiz *him* about the band," Fleming said.

"That's the way I see it," Broussard said. "Anyway, it was a few minutes after I hung up before I realized the rest of it—that he was after Kit. Lookin' back, it was so obvious, I should have known.... He practically handed it to me the night we all went to Felix's. He made two mistakes that night, one on the way over and one comin' back."

"I was there," Kit said, "and I didn't notice anything."

"Remember when we were decidin' where to eat and Charlie suggested Tortorici's? Well, Brookie said they were closed. But they were open, because Hugh Greenwood said he'd eaten there Monday night. Of course, they *were* closed *Saturday* night. We saw that for ourselves when Leo and I ran into you and Teddy. So Brookie wasn't tellin' the truth when he told me Monday mornin' that he'd just arrived. The other mistake—and this one was huge—was when you and he were talkin' on the way back from dinner Tuesday night. I was right in front of you and I heard you talk about Lucky bein' poisoned. Brookie referred to Lucky as a *little* dog. When I mentioned your dog to him at lunch on Monday, he said he didn't know you had a dog. And in our conversation, I never said what kind of dog it was or how big it was. So how did he know it was little?"

Kit felt her jaw drop. "Jesus, *he* was the one who poisoned Lucky."

"So there'd be no barkin' when he came for you. After Lucky was gone, he probably returned while you were workin' and checked out the room arrangement, makin' plans for later."

Kit's thoughts went to the Mace in her nightstand and she knew that had she tried to use it, she would have found it empty. Then... "I remember now that the night we all went to Felix's, he maneuvered the conversation around to the vet I was using. I bet he called him to make sure Lucky wouldn't be home. And it almost worked, because you were about a minute too late. If he hadn't stumbled against the footstool in my bedroom, I might be dead."

"I'd say we both got your money's worth from the footstool," Broussard said.

"Why'd he kick the stool?" Fleming asked. "If he cased your house, he should have known it was there."

"Because it wasn't there when he was. Lucky had thrown up on it after being poisoned and it was away being recovered."

"Like I told you," Broussard said, "it's not the big thing that sends you over the cliff, but the untied shoelace. Too bad the shoelace works both ways. Did you get a visit from a police car a short while before everything happened?"

"Yes. Did you send it?"

"Soon as I realized what Brookie was up to, I tried to get hold of you, but there was no answer. I called nine-one-one and told them to get to your house right away. For all I knew, it was already too late."

"Brooks cut the phone line," Kit said. "They repaired it yesterday. Apparently when a line is cut like that, it still sounds like it's ringing to someone calling in."

"Well, it sure worried me," Broussard said. "Those cops were supposed to stay with you until I got there to explain and see that you stayed the night someplace safe. Obviously, things didn't go as planned. Fortunately, they didn't for Brookie, either."

Kit turned to Gatlin. "So Brooks was the one who put the key under Harvey's mattress."

"Yeah, we finally got him talking late yesterday," Gatlin said. "He told us he did it one night when he and Harvey and some others played bridge. After playing for a few hours, he suggested they go down to the bar for a drink. When they were all out in the hallway, he pretended to remember a call he had to make and asked Harvey if he could use his phone, knowing everybody'd stay in the hall to give him privacy. The whole Harvey ploy was just to keep us looking in the wrong direction."

"Clever of him to mention the Harvey team to Leo rather than come to us with it directly," Kit said.

Fleming's mouth drooped in disgust. "And like a sap, I came runnin' right to you."

Gatlin looked at Broussard. "Andy, Brooks said it was you who let him know we took the bait."

"When was that?"

"At the reception."

"I don't think so."

"You didn't say anything about wheels turning when he asked you about Harvey?"

"Well, I might have."

"He took that to mean he had us. So he went from you right to Harvey and told him to watch his step. He thought we'd search Harvey's room only as a last resort and that we'd probably tail him instead. But if he let that happen, Kit might have stayed up all night keeping tabs on what was happening. He had to make sure it was resolved early in the evening so Kit would go home and turn in. Given Harvey's personality, he figured Harvey'd confront us and force our hand."

"How'd he know for sure Harvey'd be at the meetin'?" Fleming asked.

"He hasn't missed one in twenty years," Broussard said.

"And Brooks saw his name on an advance copy of the program," Gatlin added.

"Who gave Phyllis Merryman that envelope?" Kit asked.

"An actor," Gatlin replied. "From one of the talent agencies in town. Brooks said that even with makeup the guy didn't look exactly like Harvey, but Merryman would have seen him only briefly a month earlier. He didn't think she'd remember how they differed. And the whole charade only had to hold up for a short while."

"I don't understand his choice of weapon," Fleming said. "A knife meant he had to find victims who were thinly dressed. And that'd be possible only if the weather was mild, which it has been this year. But I understand that sometimes it's a lot cooler here in February. If he planned this months ago—and it's obvious he did—why make the whole thing dependent on warm weather? What would he have done if it had turned chilly and people bundled up?"

"When he came after me, he also brought a gun," Kit said. Then to Gatlin, she added, "What was that deodorant can on it, a homemade silencer?"

"Yeah, packed with sheet rubber. Pretty neat job. The whole thing was light as a feather. He had another one with a silencer in his room. They were his backup. He took one with him each time he went out in case things went wrong. And if the weather turned . . ."

"Why not use a gun from the beginning?" Fleming asked. "Be a lot simpler."

"He wanted Doc to die by a knife," Gatlin said. "He believed that would have made Andy even more miserable. I don't know exactly what he meant. . . ."

"It's a rare woman who doesn't fear a knife more than a gun," Broussard said. "The night we all went to dinner, he got Kit to say that's how she felt. The whole conversation on that issue was for my benefit. 'Course I didn't realize the significance at the time. In usin' a knife on the other victims, he had us all thinkin' and talkin' knives, so it was a natural topic to bring up. If the weather'd turned, he'd have still gotten the job done. Not with the same continuity, but with the same results.''

''But if he'd used a gun, there wouldn't have been any white fibers,'' Fleming said. ''The fibers are what helped put you on to the fact he was a forensic expert. And he did want you to know that.''

''The fibers were redundant and most likely left by accident,'' Broussard said. ''The hairs were to be the clue he was in forensics.''

''We didn't locate any pieces of morgue pad in his room because he got rid of them right after that meeting where we discussed the fibers left on the first victim,'' Gatlin said. ''He didn't want you finding any of those fibers on *his* clothing.''

''Why do you suppose he left the knife on the third victim?'' Fleming asked.

''Not planned,'' Broussard said. ''And also redundant. Just somethin' he decided to do to thumb his nose at me. Like puttin' those eyelids in my slide tray.''

''I guess if he'd gone with his backup instead of knives in the briefcase at the Y, we'd have found one of the guns,'' Kit said.

''Give one up, keep one,'' Gatlin said. ''He thought of most everything. We also found a black wig and a phony mustache in his room.''

Kit's eyebrows lifted. ''So that *was* him the cop at the third murder saw crossing the street.''

''Tryin' to look like Harvey, I guess,'' Fleming said. ''Couldn't have been a very close resemblance, though, seein' how much taller he is.''

''He didn't have to look a lot like him,'' Gatlin said. ''Mostly, he just had not to look like himself; anybody else'd do. But while he was at it, why not take a crack at Harvey? Witnesses never agree on anything—black hair, black mustache. If two people had seen him, one probably would have said he was a dwarf. Found the scalpel he used on the eyelids, too. Had it rigged to a penlight."

"What was the point in takin' eyelids?" Fleming asked.

"More subterfuge," Kit said. "To make it look like something it wasn't."

Gatlin turned to Broussard. "Where'd he come by his expertise with a knife?"

"Not sure," Broussard said. "But he was an officer in the army reserves. Might have picked it up there."

"The time it must have taken to plan this," Kit mused.

"Brookie always was a planner," Broussard said. "Phillip... how is he?"

"Quiet...cooperative. Speaking of shoelaces, we took his away from him and his belt, too, so he couldn't harm himself."

Broussard looked at the sheets and shook his head. Then he turned to Kit. "By the way, sorry about your front door."

"You break it in anytime you feel it's necessary. Which reminds me, Lieutenant, how did Brooks get in my house twice?"

"Locks only keep out the casual trespasser. The serious ones just get delayed. He used an electronic pick gun. Probably took him only about ten seconds. Gives you the willies, doesn't it?"

"He's a man with a lot of talents," Kit said.

"Doesn't take any talent to use a pick gun. He waited until your heat pump came on to mask what little noise it makes. It's probably in your yard, somewhere near the back door. I been meaning to come by and look for it but haven't had the chance. Also been meaning to tell you to trim that big holly beside the house. That's where he went over the fence."

"Say, I really appreciate you all visitin' me," Broussard said, "but I'm feelin' kind of bushed."

"We'll get out, then, and let you rest," Kit replied.

"Leo, you goin' back today?" Broussard asked.

"Plane leaves in two hours."

"Thanks for comin' by and for your help. Glad you weren't the killer."

"Was there ever any doubt?"

"'Course not," Broussard said unconvincingly.

"We get anything Charlie can't handle, I'll have it wheeled up here so you can have a look," Gatlin said.

"Soon as you leave, I'm gonna have them hide me."

"Are you going straight home?" Gatlin asked Kit. "I thought I'd come by and look for that pick gun if it's okay."

"Sure. Come on."

Gatlin looked at Fleming. "You need a ride anywhere?"

"Back to the hotel would be nice."

"Oh, by the way," Fleming said to Broussard, "I saw Hugh Greenwood yesterday as he was checkin' out and he said to tell you to quit screwin' around and get back to work. I didn't know you two were so close."

"Good-bye, Leo."

When they were gone, Broussard's shoulders slumped and he let his chin drop to his chest. With all that was on his mind, he'd had to force himself to participate in the conversation.

He had prevailed. He had solved the puzzle and the killer was caught. His wound, though serious, would heal. But this time, there was no satisfaction, no warmth in his belly, only brass and the realization that he'd been responsible for the deaths of three people—and in the process had also lost one more friend.

And there was Susan. To know that he had been in her mind all those years as she had remained in his produced a yawning hole in his center. And now she was gone...and he was adrift with no anchor.

It was not good to get too close to people. In the end, they always leave you. How could he have forgotten the deaths of his parents so quickly and allowed Susan in? Then she had taken herself a thousand miles away, and now... truly gone. And the friends... gone... Brookie, gone. What illumination had been able to penetrate his clouds of despair during the chase had been growing steadily weaker. Now, suffocating night rolled in, blotting out hope.

But in the distance, there was light... tiny and as yet unseen. In time, possibly a long time, he would see that light and follow it to a new place. Not exactly like the old, but a place where he could live and work and perhaps even be content. But now, he just needed to be left alone.

Outside the hospital entrance, Gatlin and Fleming went one way and Kit went another. Now that she'd seen how well Broussard was doing, she was eager to get home to Lucky and, of course, Teddy, who had come in as usual early that morning and was now busy repairing the damage Broussard had done to the door and the jamb. There was a lesson for her, she thought, in what had happened to Susan Brooks. Susan had let Broussard go and been sorry the rest of her life. Then there was Phyllis Merryman. In waiting for something better, she had passed on Gene Ochs. And now she, too, was sorry. Kit didn't know exactly what she and Teddy had together, but whatever it was, it was pretty good, and maybe pretty good is all anybody could expect.

When she reached her car, there was a red two-seater with the top down, blocking it. The driver tilted his sunglasses onto his head at her approach.

"How did you find me?" she said.

"Your office said you'd come over here to see Broussard," Nick Lawson said. "How is he?"

"He'll be fine in a few days."

"You know how long I waited near the Praline Connection Thursday night?"

"You weren't supposed to go over there."

"Well, I did, and I sat there all night. You lied to me."

SELENA

GORDON RANDOLPH
WILLEY

A Colin Edwards Mystery

First Time in Paperback

BURIED SECRETS

Colin Edwards returns to St. Christopher's, the small town on Florida's Gulf Coast where the steamy, languid air evokes many memories, especially of his first love, Selena, still a beautiful, intriguing woman.

Colin is here at the urgent request of his cousin Charles, who is convinced that valuable Indian artifacts exist on family owned land now being sold for ten million dollars. He is also convinced there's a killer among them.

Charles's fears prove true when one of the four trustees is murdered. And as Colin becomes entwined in dark secrets of past and present, another victim is claimed. Two trustees remain, including Selena. But will she be the next to die? Or to kill?

"A fine debut."—*Kirkus Reviews*

Available in January at your favorite retail stores.

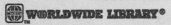
WORLDWIDE LIBRARY®

SELENA

First Time In Paperback

The Lost Keats
Terence Faherty

An Owen Keane Mystery

FROM KEATS TO A KILLER...

A man with more questions than answers, Owen Keane has one foot in the priesthood, the other in detective novels—a trait that finds him questioning his own vocation. So when a fellow seminarian disappears, Owen sees it as a chance to unravel a mystery, and perhaps his own inner struggles.

But it's not until he meets a descendant of the English poet John Keats that scattered clues fall into place. At the center is a missing sonnet, but from there things turn modern—with marijuana and murder adding to the mystery that becomes deadly as Owen gets closer to the truth...and to a killer with a message just for him.

"A near-faultless performance." —*Publishers Weekly*

Available in February at your favorite retail stores.

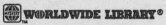 **WORLDWIDE LIBRARY®**

KEATS

DEATH PRONE

First Time in Paperback

Clare CURZON

A Thames Valley Mystery

MALICE AND AFORETHOUGHT

When ancient Hadrian Bascombe summons his heirs to announce he's bequeathing his vast fortune to just one of them, his malicious intent is to set them at each other's throats.

And it works. Superintendent Mike Yeadings and his Thames Valley coppers now have their hands full investigating this cultured family whose members are meeting untimely deaths.

Greed appears to be the primary motive, but in stripping away the various facades, secrets are revealed that turn the tables in bizarre ways. With a stubborn refusal to accept the usual, Yeadings follows an intuitive thread that ends in confrontation with an embittered killer.

"Smooth writing that never lets you down..."
—*Chicago Tribune*

Available in January at your favorite retail stores.

KINDNESS CAN KILL
JANIE BOLITHO

First Time In Paperback

An Inspector Ian Roper Mystery

NOT A PRETTY PICTURE

Stunningly beautiful, brazenly sexy, Julia Henderson was every man's fantasy and every wife's nightmare—until her brutal murder rocks the quiet English village of Rickenham Green.

Detective Chief Inspector Ian Roper and his team sort out the clues and conclude this was no illicit one-nighter gone insane. It was deliberate and emotional. Whoever killed Julia knew her well.

So twisted are the sins and secrets of some community members that two will confess to killing Julia. But it's the identity of her true killer that remains as shocking as it is inevitable.

"Taut, psychologically compelling..."   *—Publishers Weekly*

Available in February at your favorite retail stores.

 **WORLDWIDE LIBRARY**®

KINDNESS

A RECONSTRUCTED CORPSE

SIMON BRETT

A Charles Paris Mystery

First Time in Paperback

A STIFF ACT TO FOLLOW...

If playing a dead man could be called a role, Charles Paris has sunk to new lows when he agrees to play missing Martin Earnshaw on the true crime TV series "Public Enemies."

The show has all the hallmarks of a hit: a vulnerable, tearful wife, a sexy female detective and, best of all, dismembered limbs probably belonging to Earnshaw turning up each week just before airtime.

As viewers shudder gleefully and ratings soar, Paris discovers there's more to the whole production than meets the eye...and the climax is a killer.

"A perfect vacation read."   *—People*

Available in March at your favorite retail stores.

 **WORLDWIDE LIBRARY®**

CORPSE

PO 447
SC

STAND-IN FOR MURDER

First Time in Paperback

LYNN BRADLEY
A Cole January Mystery

STRANGE BEDFELLOWS

It all began when a very hung over Cole January stepped out of a warm bed and onto a stone-cold corpse—a beautiful blonde in a slinky number that would have done his male ego proud if she'd had a pulse.

She is identified as Molly Jones-Heitkamp. That is, until the real and remarkably alive Ms. Jones-Heitkamp asks January to find out who's trying to kill her. So who's the gorgeous stiff? And who's trying to frame Cole?

The answers take him to Houston's mayoralty race, as well as the dirty laundry of some prominent citizens. Cole begins to wish he'd stuck to insurance fraud, because murder was becoming bad for his health.

"Will please mystery lovers." —*Abilene Reporter-News*

Available in April at your favorite retail stores.